# THE GIFT

## Sam Martin

# THE GIFT

British Library Cataloguing-in-publication data
A catalogue record for this book is available from the British Library.
Copyright ©2000 by Sam Martin
Published by Rabbit Books, 6 Chaplin Grove, Crownhill,
Milton Keynes. Bucks. MK8 0DQ
Email: writers@beamish3.fsnet.co.uk

ISBN 1-902651-25-1

First Edition 2000

All rights reserved. No part of this book may be reproduced or stored in an information retrieval system other than short extracts for review purposes, without the express permission of the Publishers given in writing.

The author has asserted his/her right under the Copyright, Design and Patents Act 1988 to be identified as the author of this work.
All characters and events portrayed in this book are fictitious. Any Similarities to anyone living or dead is purely coincidental.

# FOREWORD

A brief history of Emanon

For over five hundred million years of geological history continents have moved over the earth's surface like flotsam floating on a pond. Land has appeared and disappeared, islands come and gone, mountains have been pushed upwards and then ground down to sand. Two hundred million years ago the north and south of Britain were parts of two separate continents, Avalonia and Caledonia. What is now the north of Ireland and Scotland were separated from England and the rest of present day western Europe by a huge ocean called Iapetus, which was as wide as the Atlantic but much older. Not until some fifty million years ago did the two continents clash in a gigantic Palaeozoic Act of Union which gave rise to the Scottish Highland and established the coasts of present day Europe. But these ancient geological events and earth movements resulted in another island being formed far out in the Atlantic on the very edge of the continental shelf itself. In the Middle Ages it was a mystical island and became known as Emanon.

Modern archaeological research has shown that Emanon had first become occupied by early Mesolithic settlers over nine thousand years ago, long before the land bridges with Scotland had been engulfed by the rise in sea level at the end of the ice ages. In spite of their isolation, these pre-Celtic peoples had flourished, but from around 1000BC had increasingly come under the subjection of the emerging Celtic civilisation that was spreading out from the heartland's of Europe. Protected for centuries from invasion by both the fierceness of the surrounding ocean and the ruggedness of its coastline, the Emanon civilisation had been untouched by the Roman conquest of Britain. But it did succumb to the teaching of St Patrick, whose mission, co-ordinated by the early British Christian Church, was soon to extend throughout the Celtic islands. By the beginning of the 1st millennium Emanon had well developed their art of defence and repulsed repeated invasions by the Vikings and Norman's and unlike Iceland and Ireland, had remained an independent nation. It's culture flourished and its, clergy, scholars and philosophers were highly respected throughout Europe. Protected again by the trouble that the English had had subduing the Irish, the Emanons were left unmolested for many centuries. However, in 1492, thing were to change drastically. Columbus discovered America. Until then, isolated, secure and self-sufficient on the western fringes of the then known world, Emanon, within a few years, became a springboard to the New World. Battles raged between England, France and Spain over it, but Emanon, itself, was never conquered. The prize across the Atlantic was too big to waste time on little Emanon and instead it became a valued and wealthy haven and port. Later, during the industrial revolution, diamonds were discovered in the volcanic core of a large isolated oceanic Rock that was well within their territorial waters and over the following centuries it became an affluent, modern and technologically sophisticated nation.

Now, read on...........

Chapter One

High in the mountainous region along the northern coast, young Tessa O'Malley was in the grip of severe birth pangs. She lay on a mattress in the back of an old van travelling along a rough mountain road heading for the small fishing hamlet of Dunfooey.

The headlights, reflecting from the torrential rain, reminded Frank, the driver, of flickering porcupine quills. He strained his eyes to watch the treacherous road. Ahead, a river had burst its banks and foaming water surged across the road blocking his way forward.

"We're stuck, Tessa," Frank spoke back to his cousin. "The bridge has gone. I should never have tried to get across the mountain during a night like this."

"Can't we get round another way? You must get me to the hospital." Tessa called back above the roar of the rain hammering on the metal roof.

"There's no chance. When the river is as high as this then all the roads through the mountains are flooded as well. We just got through the Pass in time. I'm afraid we're stuck here for the night."

Tessa moaned. "Please go on. I can't wait much longer."

Frank reached back and wiped away the sweat on her brow and gently smoothed her damp red hair. "You'll be all right, Tessa. I've delivered many a wee lamb over the years. You're in good hands."

"I'd no idea it would come so soon." Tessa said, her eyes full of fear and dread. "Oh, but the pains came on so quickly tonight that I had to call you."

"Now, don't you worry," Frank spoke back with a confident and considerate voice. "You and your baby are far too important for us to let anything happen to you. Sure, it'll be the first baby born in Emanon for the past six months." He looked out at the fierce spring storm that was tearing apart the bleak, dying land. How he and his family had fought for generations to make a living in the northern wilderness, the hard stony ground, the harsh storms and icy cold winters, the skinny herds of mountain sheep and goats that had been their main source of income. He had grown up to the spring chorus of bleating lambs and hedgerows of chattering birds, the penetrating call of the newly arrived cuckoo in the thicket in the glen. But now all that had gone. The moors and the glens were silent, the long cold icy winter eating into the spring. It had been all so gradual. No one had noticed it happening until it was too late. Year by year their herds on the mountain pastures had become smaller and smaller. At first lambs and kids were found deformed and then weren't born at all. Babies had become fewer and fewer over the last decade. There had been more and more infertile couples, more frequent miscarriages and deformed babies born. Frank was a biologist and had studied for years the impact of environmental pollution on wild life, but even he had been surprised at the rapidly with which the infertility crisis had developed. He had worked abroad for a numbers of years in both America and Europe, but had been glad to return to his home in the north-west corner of Emanon where he was now warden of the nature reserve and was able to continue his research on the impact of the infertility disaster on the wild life of his small maritime country.

On his return he had been surprised to see how his little cousin, Tessa, had grown into a beautiful young woman. In their small isolated community he had been like an elder brother to her and had been shocked when he had learnt that she had become pregnant. She had kept her condition a secret, embarrassed, afraid, unbelieving. He had guessed who the father was, but it was his secret too, and he would watch out for him should he ever return to the village. But that she was pregnant at all seemed a miracle. There had been no births for nearly a year. Maybe the infertility plague was over. Their shocked family believed that Tessa's mysterious pregnancy was a good sign. The baby would be a new beginning.

Tessa dozed, but she could feel the baby move and struggle inside and her head was full of dreams and the agony of her recent loneliness. Why had he gone so soon? So soon, after that one time on the hay in the barn behind O'Flafferty's. Would he remember and come back and take her away from the poverty of the dying land to the rich heart of the world? But she had sinned. Oh, God! How she had sinned! It had all been so quick. It had been so good. She remembered the feel of his smooth face, his moist lips, the silky touch of his blond hair. It had been so natural, the gentle rhythm and growing heat of his touch, the angelic glow that had engulfed them as they rolled for that brief moment in the hay. His blue eyes, full of tears when he kissed her goodbye and his fingers running through her long red hair, as Frank's was now. He would write. He would be back. But in the morning, Mike someone, had gone. There had been no letters and next year would never come.

Like the angry blustering gale outside, the waves of pain surged through Tessa's body, casting aside her dreams and memories and lifting her being to the ultimate limits of endurance. Then at last as the storm eased and the dawn sun broke through the receding clouds, with the patient and gentle hands of Frank, the god-father, beautiful, perfect, little Sophie, was born.

Chapter Two

Harry Atkins clambered into his small boat and was stooped over the radio in the cramped cabin, listening for the voice of his controller back on the Rock, his oil-stained finger hovering over the transmission switch.

"HELLO! Harry speaking," he shouted into the microphone. "What's the matter? Over." He waited,

"I'm sorry, Harry," a sympathetic voice spoke from the console. "You must come back right away. There's an emergency back on home. It's about your wife. We have a cable link-up arranged for three o'clock. Come back right away. Over."

A cold shudder ran down Harry's back as he snapped the transmission switch on. "I'm on my way. Over and out," he said, his voice barely audible above the static.

He called to his workmate who was working on the construction of the dyke. "Ron," he shouted, "I have to go back. There's an emergency back home. Will you check my section."

"Sure, Harry. Glad to help. Hope the family's OK." Ron's big eyes smiled at him, recalling years of friendship and support that the harsh life demanded from all those who chose to work on the desolate and isolated rock.

Harry was always excited as he approached the Rock which he admired as a monument to Emanon's ingenuity, engineering skills and imagination. The massive rock that had stood alone, far out in the Atlantic, was now surrounded by a huge man made reef that he and many of his forefathers had helped to build with their sweat and effort. The Rock itself had long ago become the entrance to huge undersea diamond mine, that had provided Emanon with its wealth for the past century and more recently with the nearby oil and gas development with all its current energy requirements. The billions of tons of rubble from the excavations had been used to build a safe and sheltered harbour and huge reef that now at low tide was covered by green and brown seaweed and thousands of seals. Harry drove his amphibious craft directly at a concrete ramp and followed the winding road, gradually climbing the fifty feet from the water's edge to the cave-like entrance, whose huge steel weatherproof doors slid open on his arrival.

Harry changed out of his sea clothes and descended by lift into the depths of the complex to the main communications room.

"Ah, there you are," the radio officer said anxiously as Harry came into the room. "The call will be through in five minutes. You're just in time."

The message had been from his father. Harry read it a dozen times as he waited for the signal to enter the studio for instantaneous visual transmission.

"HARRY. SERIOUS ACCIDENT. GRETA UNWELL. MUST TALK. CONFIRM 3.00 pm. DAD."

From the moment the bleeper had sounded, Harry had known that it was the baby. It was too soon for it to be born even prematurely. He'd only been on the Rock for two months this trip. He hadn't seen Greta since he'd heard she was pregnant.

"OK, Harry," the officer called, "you're on now. Come over here."

Harry sat down in front of the TV screen and waited a few moments while the officer pressed buttons on his keyboard and the screen flashed into life. His father's face appeared.

"Hello, Harry. I've got bad news, I'm afraid. It's Greta."

Harry gripped the arms of the chair and his body tensed like a bow about to shoot an arrow across the universe. "What's happened?" he snapped in anxiety.

"I'm sorry, Harry. Greta had a car accident. It was a pile-up in fog. You know what it's like here in Southport at this time of year."

"Oh Lord," Harry said, tears in his eyes. "Is she ...?"

"No," his father countered, continuing, "she was very badly injured and has been on the life-support system for the past three days. But her head is .... ", he could not find the words. "Harry, she is never going to know anything again. The doctors give us no hope that she'll recover. They say she is comatosed."

"My God!" Harry froze to his seat, his hands shaking and sweat breaking out in beads on his forehead. He felt the cold steel of the priest in his hand and the crunch as it sank into the skull of an infant seal, that they often killed out on the surrounding rocks, when they wanted fresh meat. He looked down at his hands expecting to see blood, but saw only the uncontrollable shake of his large fists. The tender anxious, loving face of his father was on the screen, searching for him across the emptiness of space. "Oh, dad, what should we do? Is there no hope?" he asked, looking at the screen and leaning forward, seeking comfort.

"There's also the baby," his father said quietly. "It's only a foetus really. That's what they called it."

"Who calls it a foetus?" Harry snapped. The others in the studio also sensed something sinister and there was a sudden tenseness in the air.

"Harry, the doctors say it's very small and not really a baby yet. They say it will not survive, even if Greta is kept alive on the machine. They've asked if they can have permission to remove it and use it for medical research."

"What!" Harry's face was red and angry with spontaneous revulsion and disbelief. "They can't do that. That's wrong. That's our baby. My God, it's enough to have lost my Greta without murdering our unborn child. If they die, they'll die together and they will go to heaven together and that's what Greta would have wanted. No! No! Definitely No!"

Harry was now beside himself with righteous anger and was sitting forward on the edge of the seat searching out his father's eyes, seeking agreement, approval and support. Harry's family were simple folk, deeply committed Christians.

"But Harry," his father said quietly, "you know things have changed now. The birth rate is falling. The infertility."

"I wasn't infertile," interrupted Harry. "We made a baby. Now they want to kill it too."

"No, no, Harry. You mustn't say that. I'm sure the doctors don't want to kill your baby. They want to help. They say they may be able to make a large number of new babies from the cells of your unborn baby, provided they get them at an early enough stage. That's why they need the foetus."

"That's disgusting," Harry wept, his large curly red hair and bearded face sunk on his hands, his back curled like a foetus. "How can you talk like that?"

"Listen, Harry, I have a doctor here who would like to speak to you. Will you talk to him? He operated for hours on Greta and nearly saved her life."

"But he didn't. Did he?" Harry snapped back. "Why didn't he save her? Did they decide that they wanted the baby instead? Did some message come through from the President that they needed the baby to save Emanon and so my Greta was left to die?"

"Now Harry, that's unreasonable," a new voice spoke from

the console. It was a man in a white coat and he had a stern face that looked both sad and hurt. "Greta was very badly injured. She'd broken arms, legs and ribs. Her lung was punctured. We operated on her for seven hours. It took time to assess the damage to her brain. Her skull was severely cracked and I can assure you that unfortunately the damage to her brain is irreparable. She was back in the intensive care ward and was stabilised on the life support system before we got the request about the foetus. You must believe me."

"Oh Lord, I'm sorry," Harry murmured, embarrassed at having to speak to this stranger, to the doctor who had tried to save his wife's life. He felt ashamed by his unjustified outburst. "Doctor, you know I'm very upset. I'm sure you did all you could."

"Look, Harry," the doctor continued, "all we need is your permission to remove the foetus and to stop the life support system. Scientists will take a small amount of tissue from your daughter, her body will be returned for burial along with your wife's. The funeral will be delayed until your return. You must realise how important this will be for all of Emanon. Your Greta was one of the last to conceive by normal methods. We had all hoped that her pregnancy was a sign of recovery of fertility, but it could just be the last one. You know as well as I do that men have not been producing normal numbers of fertile sperm for many years and now during the past ten or so years women have stopped producing viable eggs and we cannot even get surrogate mothers. Now Doctors have had success by using foetal tissue and by taking just a few very special cells from your baby daughter, which can be made to replicate in culture and then we will be able to produce thousand of cloned babies. Other countries are using this approach and if we don't soon get suitable foetal tissue we will lose the genes of Emanons for ever. I'm sure you want to try and help, Harry. It is your duty. The future of our race is in your hands."

Harry closed his eyes and held his head in his large hands. He loved to be away on the Rock, away from the hassle of life on the mainland, the crowds, the noise - except for Greta - all for Greta and their baby. A knot gathered in the pit of his stomach and he retched. He held it back for a second, the blood draining from his face, his body going cold and his limbs uncontrollably trembling. And then it began to grow, tearing his gut and chest apart as it rose like a great pregnant ball, choking in his throat. His body seemed to turn inside out as he staggered from the room on the arm of the attendant.

Later that evening, Harry braced against the strong gale as he stood on the balcony of his small apartment in the accommodation unit. A sudden winter storm had blown up, delaying his return home. The black curling clouds were sharpened by the forked lightning as huge waves crashed on the cliffs below him. His red curly beard was moist with tears that flooded down his cheeks in uncontrolled spasms of anguish. Why had it to be Greta? Would their baby live even if the doctors took it away from her? Should he agree to their request and donate the baby to the cloning programme? They would probably take it anyway, without his consent. They say there's going to be a new Law. There are so few babies born now, their child was going to be very special. If only he was at home. If only he could see Greta, just once more. He moved inside to the warmth and comfort of his small room and lay alone with his memories of Greta and their unfulfilled hopes and plans for their unborn child and stared unbelieving into the darkness, sleep refusing to conquer the ferment of his mind, his mood flitting between rage and sorrow.

Chapter Three

Michael Rand noticed with interest a red alert indicating that a baby had been born in an isolated mountainous region in north Emanon. That's near Dunfooey, he thought and recalled his holiday last year. But that's strange, we'd never heard of a pregnancy up there! He continued to cast his eye over the computer screen looking for information or reports that would indicate a possible source of early foetal tissue. The latest information about any newly pregnant women and the occasional unreported births was sent to the National Institute of Emanon Genetics from all parts of the island. He was anxious that his recent discoveries on the development of embryos in vitro could be exploited. He had been lucky. He had been part of the team that had eventually solved the cell regeneration problem. However, in Emanon, their work had been consistently frustrated by the strong social ethic that had prohibited the sacrifice of the unborn or the use of human embryos or foetal tissue for research purposes. But now, suddenly, surgical teams across Emanon were constantly on the outlook for likely miscarriages and were anxiously awaiting the introduction of the new Cloning Law that would allow them to deal with the tragedy of the infertility crisis.

"Is there anything new?" The quiet voice from behind him made him glance round from the screen. He looked up at the tall, slim figure in a white coat, who had just entered the laboratory.

"Good morning, Karen," he greeted and returned her smile. He was conscious of her hand resting gently on his shoulder as she looked past him at the screen. He felt that they had developed a closeness during the short period since he had joined her staff at the Institute. She was quite different from what he'd thought, when he'd first heard that he was to join the team under the famous Dr Karen Rowlands.

"There's a bit of good news," he added. "There's been one baby born. In a van, believe it or not. Stuck in the middle of nowhere, away up in Dunfooey. Her pregnancy had never even been reported. God knows who the father is. But this report shows that the child is doing well. It's a little girl."

"Lucky thing," Karen murmured. "Look, that woman, Greta Atkins, in the hospital in Southport. She's still on life-support. Let's see." Karen reached across the keyboard and highlighted the report.

"We should get ready for that one," Karen said with an unexpected degree of confidence. "That girl is too weak. Look!" She flicked through the information sheet. "But her husband, Harry, has not given permission yet. He's still on the Rock and won't get back for days if the weather doesn't break."

"Damn," Michael hissed. "We can't wait that long. I'll get in touch with the hospital and see what the situation is. Maybe they can keep her alive for a few more days until we get the Cloning Law passed. Let's hope President Neilson agrees with us at the conference tomorrow so that we can go ahead without the permission of this chap on the Rock."

"Don't forget, he's the father," Karen said, concerned as she slipped quietly out of the room. Michael was already talking via the computer link with the doctor in Southport.

Chapter Four

Karen looked out the window as the helijet banked to the right and crossed the ridge of the escarpment and started its descent to Konburg with the great Lough Rana stretching away to the east and west.

"Oh, look!" she said, making room and encouraging her neighbour to see the view from the small window. "I've never seen the Palace like this before. Isn't it fantastic?"

"Wonderful view," Professor Bernard Langwood said, his sturdy frame struggling against the seat belt as he bent over her towards the window. Karen strained back, making room for her aged friend and mentor. The plane swung away from the cliffs revealing the shimmering Lough Rana stretching away to the east while the morning sun was glinting from the tall buildings of Emanon's capital city and reflecting from the long golden painted suspension bridge that linked the city to the southern suburbs and the great winding autoroute to Southport. Below them, the Presidential Palace stood out white against the steep green wooded hillside.

"Are you ready, now?" Karen remarked as they prepared for landing and the Professor gathered together the notes he had been reading and fussing over during their short flight from the Institute to the Palace.

"Oh, I hate these meetings ... all politics ... much rather be talking real science to scientists ... there's no point in talking to the Bishops." Bernard continued to fumble with his papers, stuffing them into his briefcase in a nervous, haphazard fashion. "But it has to be done," he added, resignedly. "You know, Karen, really, I'm so tired fighting this. It's a brick wall of history. What would I do without your support? You've all been great." He touched her gently on the hand in a fatherly fashion.

"Good luck, Professor. You're the one that will swing this if anyone can. But do emphasise the possibility of an anti-infertility drug. People are more able to accept that than the cloning and I'm sure we just need more time."

"Yes, yes, dear," he said, still fussing with his papers. "I'll leave that aspect for you to deal with this afternoon. But, I'm afraid old Longfellow will be a handful this morning," he added in a quiet whisper, looking round, hoping no one had overheard and recalling the numerous arguments and debates that he had had with the Church leader over a life time of controversy.

They gathered their items and prepared to disembark as the helijet settled on the landing pad.

"That was a nice flight," Michael spoke over to Karen as the delegates strolled through the Terrace towards the Palace. "These machines are improving every year."

"Wonderful," Karen replied. "Poor Bernard - he's so nervous at this stage - fussed with his notes all the way over."

"Let's hope he doesn't mess it up," Michael murmured, momentarily returning the sullen gaze of the huge stone statutes of the ancient Kings which lined the Terrace. "He should have let you do it. It's too much of a strain for him now."

The delegates became quiet as they approached the Palace and ascended the grand marble steps to the main entrance. Private thoughts took over. Karen touched her hair and moistened her lips, straightened and pulled her red jacket down at the waist over her neat black shirt. Would she meet the President? Perhaps Mrs Neilson, the first lady? "Good luck, everybody. Here we go," she laughed. As she led the group of geneticists to the top of the steps, her eyes sparkled in response to the general murmur of appreciation of her contribution to the development of the new cloning programme.

Bernard noticed the shadow of a frown cross Michael Rand's face. He had hoped young Mike and Karen would get along. He had trained them both. He saw how they could complement each other's work. Together they must succeed.

They entered the huge palatial reception hall, with its richly painted domed ceiling depicting the long history of Emanon. Since dawn a continuous stream of cars had been wending their way up the twisting road to the Palace and the persistent roar of the helijets echoed over the ridges above as they delivered the Mayors from the distant provinces. It was an impressive gathering. The Archbishop and his cortege of bishops and attendants had already arrived. Their colourful silk robes, studded with sparkling jewels contrasted markedly with the modern neat suits of the politicians and scientists.

Karen mingled with the crowd, sipping a cold coffee as she chatted with colleagues and other participants. Then the bell was ringing and the participants began to move unremittingly towards the doors of the conference hall.

By 11 o'clock, everyone was seated. Karen was on the left of the semicircular front row beside Bernard. Michael was a few rows behind and she smiled to him as they took their seats. She sensed that his eyes held a shadow of disappointment. He would have liked to have been in the front row, giving the specialist lecture in the afternoon instead of her, but he was still young, his time would come. Suddenly, the buzz of excited conversation, the rustle of papers and feet were drowned by the peal of applause as President Neilson entered from the right of the platform and walked across to the central podium. He was a tall man, straight for his age, his silver grey hair brushed back from his high forehead and his lightly tanned skin glistening in the bright spotlight. As he reached the podium he stood for a moment, his hands folded in front of him. It was his eyes that captured the attention of his audience. They seemed to look directly at everyone in the hall, directly into their minds. His frank open gaze, taking in every corner of the hall, brought silence and respect from his people.

Abruptly, the palace organist launched into the anthem, "Emanon for Ever" and the audience stood and sang with gusto as the stirring chords filled the air.

President Neilson was popular and was in his fourth term of office. He had been in residence in the Palace for nearly thirty years and had ruled Emanon with a gentle yet strong and firm hand. By the end of the century he had brought Emanon to be a modern nation, yet proudly retaining its ancient culture, language and traditions. Now in the moment of crisis, all this was forgotten and disaster loomed.

"Friends," the President started simply, as the dying notes of the organ echoed from the high corners of the great hall. "You all know that we have today a crisis that Emanon has never before had to face. But it is not the first time that we have head to fight for our survival and freedom. From the dawn of time, and throughout history we have fought for our children and for our culture and heritage. In the past we resisted the Viking and Norman invasions and have stood proudly on our own, as a independent nation, isolated but strong, always avoiding the turmoil that has raged for centuries across our continental neighbours. But now, we are having no more babies. What we have done to deserve this, God only knows. My friends, we are faced with extinction of all the things we hold so precious, unless we can find a cure for infertility. We had all hoped and prayed, that the problem would go away, that the cause would be found and a cure produced.

"Of course you will all remember how the first signs of population decrease were welcomed. We said it would solve, in a natural way, the bulging population that our new technologies had allowed Emanon to support. It was God's way.

"But no. The years have slipped by and the situation is worsening. Some scientists tell us that it is the result of pollution, from our over use of drugs, some blame the use of GM food. But we do know that there has been excessive production of industrial waste that has polluted our water sources with oestrogen-like products which may well have resulted in the consistent increase in the incidents of deformed births and a severe reduction in sperm count. Now new births have practically stopped. Worse still, for some unknown reason, women no longer produce viable eggs and hence cloning or reproductive methods that depend upon in vitro fertilisation and surrogate mothers no longer work. Even the agricultural industry is in serious jeopardy as there are similar problems with animals. As you know we now are having to depend on seal meat to supplement our diet. How indeed we must thank all those men and women who work on the Rock and supply us not only with energy, but now also with precious food.

"What we must now decide on is a strategy for the survival of Emanon. Unfortunately, it appears that our infertility has been passed on to the second generation. Even our few teenagers are now found to be infertile.

A ripple of concern and sighs of disgust went round the Council. When silence had returned, the President continued.

"As you know, the few animals we see in the fields or in our farm factories today are not born in the normal way. Today, our farm animals are clones."

There was a hush in the hall and the President held the silence for an extra moment and then added in a deeper voice. "Today we must decide if the genetic engineering technology that has been successful with animals can now be applied to ourselves."

There was a moment of silence while the implications sank in and then, led by Archbishop Longfellow, the representatives and supporters of the Church were on their feet waving their conference papers at the President and shouting in unison, "No cloned Emanons! No cloned Emanons!" Shrill whistles were blown by groups of spectators who had crowded into the public galleries and were waving banners and flags of the Omega Corps.

The uproar continued for some minutes but President Neilson remained at the podium and regained control of the proceedings with the support of many of the other delegates.

"Let's not be hasty," he pleaded. "Listen to the experts and let them explain how they see the future and what the alternatives are."

"Agreed, agreed." There were calls from various parts of the hall.

"I now want to introduce the Director of the Institute of Genetics who is looking into the whole problem and searching for a cure to infertility. The Director is Professor Bernard Langwood and I am very pleased he is able to be with us today to tell us at first hand about the progress being made. Professor Langwood, please come forward."

"Good luck," Karen whispered, as the Professor rose stiffly from his seat. She watched anxiously as he made his slow progress to the podium.

Bernard was a short, overweight man and he wobbled forward rather than walked to the platform. A polite lingering round of applause followed his progress and he mounted the platform, one leg stiff, hesitating on the steps. His head was completely shaven and he wore dark rimmed spectacles with thick lenses through which he peered at the jumble of papers he had spread out on the podium. Professor Langwood was an experienced public speaker. He looked at the audience through his glasses, then over his glasses and then again consulted his notes and shuffled and ordered his papers. Eventually he looked up, searched out the President once again, and then removing his glasses, hesitatingly said, "President Neilson."

"Go on. Go on. Don't lose it!" Karen said to herself, praying silently, her white teeth biting into her lips.

Michael's brow was furrowed. "The old fool's messing it up!" he murmured to his neighbour who nodded, embarrassed. I should be doing it. It's my work, he thought to himself.

There was a further respectful silence as the Professor once again referred to his notes and then he seemed to become transformed. His glasses were folded away into his breast pocket and his hands and fingers became an integral part of the flow of his words as he talked. His voice, now confident and strong, carried clearly to every corner of the chamber. His words were simple and straightforward and he outlined the Institute's view of how to deal with the problem. Time was running out. Fewer and fewer babies were being born.

And then came the crunch. By long tradition and custom the constitution of Emanon has not allowed any interference with conception or the birth of babies. But the new reproductive technologies has given us a way forward. It had been successful in other countries, and now the whole of modern agriculture depended on it. Even in Emanon, except for fish and seal meat, all food was now from cloned farm animal. "Essential for this is the recently developed artificial placenta and the embryonic modules, invented, as many of you know, by my colleague and collaborator Dr Karen Rowlands, right here in Konburg." There was a spontaneous round of applause and the Professor carried the audience along by his enthusiasm and dedication and his obvious hope and trust in the future. He concluded by saying in a strong confident voice, "You must give us a Law so we can develop the clones of Emanon." He looked down at the celibate Fathers, in their long robes, the shadows of their ancient beliefs imprinted on their faces. "Now, listen to me," he challenged, looking directly down at the Archbishop who was sitting in the centre of the front row. "We must have this Law. We have no alternative. Give us this Law, President Neilson. Give us this Law for the sake of Emanon."

The Professor looked across at the President. "Thank you, Mr President," he said in a quiet voice. Putting his glasses back on, he gathered up his unread papers and unsteadily descended the steps from the platform. The organist struck up a few chords of music as the audience burst into restrained applause.

Karen watched him, her eyes moist, her heart pounding with admiration and relief. He had been wonderful to her throughout her student days, picked her out from among the other students and given her that special chance. He had given her encouragement to develop the artificial placenta when others laughed at the idea. He had faith in her and she had given him loyalty when the going was hard, during the long battle to build up the Institute in the early days, when the politicians and the Fathers had opposed the study of Emanon genetics. She knew her success had only been possible because of his great vision of the future. She stood and helped him into his seat, taking the bulging folder of notes that were drifting to the floor in his wake only to be collected by his associates in the front row. Karen kissed him on the cheek and the applause rang in her ears long after they had been seated and waited for the President to return to the podium.

"Mr President," a voice boomed out from the centre of the front row. Archbishop Longfellow was on his feet. He was a big man, towering above his audience in his flowing purple robes.

"Archbishop Longfellow," the President said, acknowledging the head of the Church. "I welcome you and the Fathers to the Palace. We know you represent the great Soul of Emanon. We know you have been struggling with this problem for many years. But, I hope you have come here today to tell us of a way to bring your people to a new understanding of the future. Please come forward."

Karen watched, her body suddenly tense as the majestic figure of the Archbishop strode powerfully to the platform, the hem of his great flowing robe brushing her ankle as he passed her. He glided up the steps to the platform in marked contrast to the Professor, to the thundering notes of "The Lord be Praised". The large jewels and gold and silver chains sparkling on his robes focused Karen's attention, pulling her irresistibly back to the past. He was a huge figure. His robes magnified his size and the gems in his tall mitre that he had placed on his head before rising from his seat, glinted in the sunlight that was shining through the stained glass windows. With a slight move of his head, the curtains of the numerous windows silently slid closed and a spotlight picked him out alone.

"That's clever," the Professor whispered in Karen's ear above the sound of the music that filled the hall.

"Too clever," she replied quietly, "someone's been bought."

There was a sudden hush in the darkened chamber. The Archbishop towered erect and still, waiting for the silence to grow deeper, allowing the minds of the audience to clear of the confusion, to adjust, to accept him as the route to their salvation. He raised his arms and gave the sign of the Holy Cross, and in a quiet voice that scarcely reached the back of the hall, he said, "Let us pray."

For Karen, time seemed to stand still. Her mind flashed back to her childhood, to the family, to the faith of her father and mother, her daily prayers, her priest, her confessions, her teenage vows. She was on the annual pilgrimage to the holy city of Tanark. She felt again, her young innocent body cold and wet, praying in the Holy River at the foot of the Great Falls of Shanna where the salt and the fresh water mixed.

"Oh God," the Archbishop spoke in a monotone, his words

being broadcast to the four corners of Emanon. "Oh Lord, Thou, who hast given us all things, now protect us from the evil forces that roam throughout the length and breadth of Emanon.

"Thou who hast so designed the world to shelter us from the evils and rages of the oceans, now lead us along the paths of truth and guide us through these hours of darkness into Thy arms of everlasting love.

"Do not, Oh Lord, forsake us in this hour of need. Thou who didst tell us in the ancient words in stone that Thou had made us in Thine image, forged us from Thy flesh, breathed into each of us at conception a fragment of Thy Love, of Thyself, Oh Lord, to succour and to grow, to nourish and protect from the dark evil forces that threaten Thee and all things Good.

"Oh Lord, we know our duty well, to tend your special creation that makes us different from the lower forms of life.

"Do not let us forget the job Thou hast given us to do. Oh Lord, we pray today for strength to fight the evil that stalks our beautiful and bounteous land and threatens to extinguish the flame of Love.

"Oh Lord, today, forgive us our sins and guide us forward to our promised land.

"With Thee for ever,

"Amen."

His voice seemed to hang in the air. The silence grew deep, broken only by the shuffle of people moving in their seats and a few embarrassed coughs. All eyes were still on the Archbishop.

"Mr President," Longfellow continued. "We are asked today to agree to sanctify the sacrifice of an unborn child. Of a number of unborn children. I am sure, Sir, for a good cause. But a cause, Sir, that is only a good cause in the eyes of those that believe that we are in control. That we are responsible for our own destiny. Are you, Sir, so confident that you are in control and responsible for the destiny of this world, of this universe, that you are willing to condemn the Soul of an unborn child to everlasting damnation? Do you know enough of the plans of God? Should you not let the Lord decide?"

"Nonsense!" Pent-up and enraged with frustration, Michael Rand was suddenly on his feet. "Nonsense!" he shouted again, his words ringing around the darkened galleries. For a moment the spotlight picked him out and Karen caught a glimpse of the demonic glare in his eyes reflecting the light and as he settled back into his seat she saw him grin, satisfied and elated by the attention that his spontaneous exhibition had received.

The chamber was silent. There was not a breath. The large figure of the Archbishop hovered like a bird gathering chickens under its wings for protection, his face red and sweating and passionate in the spotlight.

"Mr President, Sir," he continued, after wiping his brow with a purple silk handkerchief, which he carefully tucked back into his sleeve. He was perfectly controlled and well rehearsed. "In spite of the crude confidence of the young scientist, does he know the Lord's plan for Emanon? As we all know and believe, once before God came down and intervened in the ways of man and gave us his son, Jesus Christ. Will he not come to our salvation again. Where is your faith? Does centuries of praying and believing mean nothing to you. This crisis is a test of our love and trust in the Lord. Is our young friend," he pointed directly at Michael, his eyes blazing down at him from the podium. "Is he so sure that the Lord has forsaken us that he is willing to turn humans into animals? Surely, without that sacred divine love between a father and a mother at the moment of conception how can the Soul of the infant be created? Has he forgotten the sanctity of the family unit, the sole basis of our society, the sole reason for our existence? How does he know that the Lord's plan is not to have a smaller population, so that we can survive forever on this small fragile piece of land that He has given us? Your factory babies, Sir, with due respect to the Professor and his young friends, will be without Souls.

"Mr President, Sir, I believe, and the Council of the Church requests, that the few fertile people who are scattered across Emanon today should be brought together. They are the Lord's chosen few. They should be brought together and their children brought up in the Faith. Bring the chosen ones together and let them bear the fruits of the Lord."

The Archbishop raised his arms again, bowed his head and said in his monotone voice, "May the Lord be with you all, Amen." He wrapped his robe around him and with his head bowed in silent prayer, descended from the podium and walked back to his seat with slow deliberate steps. Many in the audience prayed with him.

Chapter Five

Harry watched from his window on the left of the cabin as the helijet hung momentarily above the Rock as its great blue dome closed over, making the pad both ocean and storm proof. He noticed that the new harbour extension was nearly complete and a number of Tall Ships were being load with freight, preparing for another delivery of processed fish and seal meat that was now essential for survival in the major cities throughout Emanon.
    Harry's mind had been in torment as he had just received, before leaving his apartment, the fatal message about his wife, Greta, and their baby daughter.
    He had been told very briefly that immediately following the announcement of the new Cloning Laws, the previous day, a team of surgeons and paramedicals supported by the National Guards had gone to Southport General Hospital. Although personally devastating for Harry, the news of the Emanon Cloning Laws came as no surprise. For months the rumour had been rife that a new strategy was necessary to maintain the population. It had been argued in the newspapers, on radio and television, in the churches as well as in the council chambers of all the Provinces and in bars and clubs throughout Emanon. Indeed the television channels had been saturated with discussion of the crisis and how different countries were dealing with the situation for many months. In Emanon it had been generally assumed that the long planned Cloning Conference would provide the solution, that the President would make a major statement that the crisis was at last under control. But the conference had been divided. The Fathers led by Archbishop Longfellow had stormed out leaving in conference in disarray. Eventually the President had declared a State of Emergency so that the new Cloning Law could be enforced without further delay.
    Harry stared at the TV screen and watched a rerun of the recent Presidential address. "... all of you know that I have the greatest love for God and a firm belief in the fundamental Christian laws of our Church. But I believe that we as a nation and a society have transgressed those laws, once too often. The Lord has taught us a lesson, but has also shown us a way forward. Through our scientists he has shown us a way to ensure the survival of Emanon. So today we

must grasp this opportunity and move forward in hope and faith, knowing that the Lord is watching over us. Resist those who would prefer to stand and watch the ageing world perish for ever...." The President played the Archbishop at his own game, Harry thought to himself. Few people would challenge that plea from the past. Perhaps it was why he felt so attached to the Rock. He was back in the cradle of the world and he thought of his lost child, a daughter, they said, that was to be part of the great experiment. Perhaps, he should feel honoured, but his heart ached and he switched channels - he'd had enough of the President for one day.

The following News Bulletin showed pictures of how cloning experiments were done with animals and he saw briefly a small animal being dissected. His heart thumped faster and he slammed off the TV. The ocean below was a sparkling silver, reflecting the morning sun and the sky a crisp clear blue after the storm that had delayed his return to mainland. The coastline was rugged and he could see the white breakers crashing on the rocky forelands. Harry glanced at his watch. It would only be a few minutes now before they reached Southport. Below the valleys were green and rich, speckled with small villages. Highland chalets were scattered among the forests and rivers that wound down steep gorges and waterfalls sparkled in the distance. They were flying low now, just a few hundred feet above the high spires of the great cathedral that was the pride and jewel of the capital city of the southern province.

"Fasten your seat belts, please. We're preparing to land," the hostess announced.

Harry adjusted his belt and continued to look out the window looking for his favourite landmarks where he had spent many happy days as a boy. Then, he saw the tall tower of the hospital block and the agony of his recent loss and thoughts of Greta returned.

His father and mother met him at Arrivals. His mother wept. Greta had been like a second daughter to her and the exciting news of the baby had meant so much to them all. But the baby had been taken and Greta was near the end.

The traffic into the city centre was heavy and it took some time to make their way across to the hospital where Greta was on the life support unit. Harry stayed with her alone for a short while and then after speaking to a doctor for a few minutes, signed the consenting documents. He held her hand as the machines were switched off and thought that she gave a slight quiver. He waited until her hands grew cold.

Harry was silent and dazed during the short journey to his parents' apartment and he spent some time standing alone at his favourite window looking out at the river and the small marina that was packed with boats. As a youth he had been an expert yachtsman and had sailed in the Tall Ships that had won many international prizes for Emanon.

"By the way, Harry," his father said gently, "there are two letters for you. They're official. One arrived yesterday and the other this morning by special delivery."

Harry glanced from the window to the small table where the two grey envelopes lay, neatly placed apart by a thoughtful, anxious parent. They were headed by bold black letters - OFFICIAL PALACE BUSINESS. Harry lifted them both, turned them over and considered which to open first. Cautiously he lifted the paperknife and slit down the second letter that said - BY SPECIAL DELIVERY. He left it down and slit open the other envelope and put it also back down on the table. The smooth silver dagger in his hand suddenly felt like a scalpel and he turned it over, confused, and it slipped from his hand and dropped on the floor with a slight clatter that broke the tense silence.

"Take them as they come, son," his father prompted from across the room, his mother clinging anxiously to his arm.

"OK. Here goes." He lifted the first envelope and slid out the folded sheet of stiff paper, opened it and read in silence. His mother noticed his hand shake and she pressed her husband's arm. Harry finished reading the letter without saying a word and passed it over to his father.

"They want me to go away to some Fertility Clinic," he murmured blankly, as he pulled out the second letter. He frowned and then his eyes opened wide. A flush came to his cheeks even above the light brown of his skin.

"God! This is from the President himself," he gasped. His parents moved over to his side.

"Dear Mr Atkins," it said in clear handwriting. "You will already have received an official letter from my office concerning our request for you to attend the new Fertility Clinic in Konburg. I must personally apologise that this letter was sent to you at the time of your private tragedy, the details of which I have only learnt about this moment.

"I am sure you will understand the tremendous urgency that exists in completing the experiments of the cloning project. I wish to thank you for the great sacrifice you and your family have made for the future of Emanon.

"Please ignore therefore the urgent request to come immediately to Konburg. When your mourning is over, I know you will realise how important it is for you, as one of the few fertile men left in the world, to participate fully in our new programme organised at the Fertility Clinic.

"Also, within a few weeks we will know how well the cloning experiment on your daughter is progressing and I have instructed the staff involved to keep you fully informed. Needless to say, if successful, you will have a daughter from the clone, if that is what you wish.

"Once again, on behalf of all the people of Emanon, please accept our thanks for the great sacrifice that you have had to make."
It was signed with a flourish of the Presidential signature.

"Now, isn't that very nice? He's a real gentleman," his father said. "I always knew Neilson was a good President. It's those scientists that forced him to make the new Law."

"It's not so bad, dear," his mother said, holding the letter from the President proudly in her hand. "Imagine us getting a letter from the President. We'll have to frame this..." Her words were cut off by a sharp snap from Harry, whose fist was clenched around the small paperknife that he'd picked up unconsciously from the floor.

"Bastard!" he cried, plunging the paper-knife through the official letter into the polished wood of the table. "Murderer! He ordered the slaughter of our baby. And Mother," he screeched, uncontrollably. "They cut it up into bits - I saw it on the telly on the plane - they butchered it even before it was born."

"Now, now, dear, it will be all right," his mother consoled him. "At the hospital they told us that her remains would be returned for the funeral."

"Only in bits!" Harry snapped. "He murdered her and then he sent me this." He walked around the room, clenching his fists and confused, his mind whirling with arguments that had gone on for the past year about cloning, the pros and the cons of the good and the evil of it. "Damn it, Mother! If we bury her and her Soul goes to heaven with Greta's what will happen to the clone children if they survive? Will they have no Souls?"

"Now, Harry," his mother said sternly, "you must calm down. We can't know all the answers. We must trust the Palace authorities. The Masters will do the right thing. Believe that the Lord will look after things."

"No, Anna," his father said, abruptly. He was a more devout follower of the Church than his wife. "Harry is right. The Fathers didn't agree to this new Law. There'll be strong opposition. When I told my friends in the Omega Corps, they rushed immediately to demonstrate at the hospital. The Masters can't ignore the Holy Fathers. Just wait, you'll see. It's not settled yet. It's good honest, natural fertility we want. Not clones. That's why I think the Archbishop's idea of grouping fertile people in a fertility clinic is a good idea, Harry. You should go. The Omega Corps support it."

## Chapter Six

Tessa was nursing baby Sophie in the warmth of her father's farmhouse kitchen. Her eyes were full of tears and she frequently dabbed her wet cheeks with a white handkerchief. A crumpled letter was lying at her feet on the floor. An envelope with an official Palace stamp that had been torn open in haste was burning brightly on the peat fire. Sophie suckled contentedly, and Tessa held her firmly against her breast.

Tessa's eyes turned from watching the flames consume the envelope across the room to the large window that gave a panoramic view of the rugged countryside falling away down to the sea and the wide sandy beach where she had played as a child. Black threatening clouds were rolling in from the west bringing yet another late spring storm. Below the house, her father was herding in a few stray sheep. Jip, the dog, was old and ran lamely. She recalled her childhood, when the land stretching down to the bay had been home for hundreds of sheep. She had often saved an orphan lamb and nursed it in the same big chair looking over the blue sea and the fresh spring green land. Perhaps next spring the lambs would come back, like her baby had come and things would get better. But now this!

"Tessa, dear," her mother said from across the fire as she threw on another piece of turf. There was a sudden chill in the air as the thick clouds blocked out the sun and cast a shadow over the house. "We knew it would come. We'll just have to accept it. It might not be for very long. You'll be back by the summer."

"I don't think so, Mother. Things must have got really bad for the President to agree to something like this." Tessa's eyes had dried and there was anger in them now rather than sadness. "They can't force people to do things. I won't," she added adamantly.

"But look at your father," her mother said, quietly, gazing out the window at her husband as he painfully made his way up the hill. "He's worn out. We've only a dozen sheep left, just one a month. There's none of them pregnant and there'll be no lambs at all this spring. You know we can't afford to buy those factory lambs and our wild mountain sheep and goats don't even breed any more. What are we going to do? He's too old to start going out in the boats. Fish and seal meat are too dear for us to buy if the farm isn't producing anything."

"But I should be here to help," Tessa replied. "I've got my job in the hotel and ..."

"And we know what that got you!" Her mother was immediately sorry she'd spoken. She rose and took the baby from her daughter's arms. "Oh, what a lovely child," she mused. "Sophie is going to grow up to be beautiful like her mother." She rocked the infant and was pleased to feel the sturdy plumpness of her healthy granddaughter. "Oh, how I'm going to miss you, my dear. But you'll come back. Won't you?" She rubbed her nose on Sophie's and tears came to her eyes. "Perhaps your Mammy will find your Daddy when she's in the big city and then you'll all come back."

"Mother, you're such a dreamer. Really, I don't think it will be like that at all. But at least I will be able to send you money and father can take it easy and not kill himself working so hard for next to nothing."

"It's come then," her father said as he entered the room in his stocking soles, having left his muddy boots at the back door. "What's it say?" He bent down stiffly and picked up the crumpled letter and smoothed it out, taking his spectacles from the mantelpiece above the fire.

"So, they're coming for you in the morning. My God, they're not wasting any time, are they?" he said gruffly. He was a mountain man, a man of few words but of a deep faith and he stood for a moment with his head bowed and murmured a prayer. "Oh Lord, forgive us our sins. But, please Lord, stand by and look over this little one in her hour of need. Protect her from all things evil and bring us all together again, in Thy will, in Thy Love."

"Amen," his wife said, who had whispered every word in quiet unison with her husband.

By morning the storm had passed. The sky was blue and the distant ocean white with the crested waves that flung themselves against the rocky forelands and rolled with splendid plumes up the long silver strand. Above, white frost and the morning mist still clung to the high ridges.

The birth of Sophie had brought hope to the small community at Dunfooey. Was she a sign of a new beginning? There was whispered talk that she was a holy child, that a miracle had happened and that little Sophie would grow up to save the world. That their little town would become famous. Tessa was revered. Gifts and presents for the child had been brought from far and near. Father Sean had said nothing, but his eyes were aglow. But a sad gloom descended on the village when the news came that Tessa and her baby were to be taken a new institute in the big city across the mountains. The next morning Cousin Frank drove them to Dunfooey and friends and neighbours from all over the region came to the Station to see them off. There were good wishes and tears were shed as the small crowd gathered in the early morning on the platform waiting the arrival of the special coach.

Frank took Tessa's hand and kissed her on the cheek. "I'll miss you, Tessa. You know that."

"I know, Frank. You're a dear." Tessa looked in his keen brown eyes and put her hand on the wild ginger beard that covered most of his face. "You've been a great friend, Frank. You really have."

"I know," Frank said sadly, holding her hands for a moment longer. "Good luck, Tessa. We'll all be thinking about you." He helped her up into the coach and she joined the special State Nurse who had been sent to escort her and Sophie to Konburg.

Tessa sat silently, holding her baby, her eyes staring ahead, oblivious to the beautiful scenery and soaring mountains around them, her soul torn between her past and her future.

Chapter Seven

"It's coming," Michael grinned over the desk at Karen as he dropped the phone back on the receiver with a satisfying crunch. Things had moved quickly after the collapse of conference at the Palace and the President's declaration of a State of Emergency. By midnight Karen's team had gathered in the Institute awaiting developments following the implementation of the new Cloning Laws.

"Did they say what it was?" Karen asked, a slight furrow deepening in her forehead as she reached for the phone and dialled their secretary.

"It's a girl," Michael replied as the phone rang in the outer office.

"Hello, Jane. It's Dr Rowlands here. Will you put out a general alert to all of team A? I want the lab ready by 1.00 am."

"Yes, Dr Rowlands. The staff have decided to stay in the Institute overnight. So they're all here already. Is there anything else?" the secretary asked with interest.

"It's a girl," Karen mentioned and then rapidly added. "Who is on mobile duty this evening?"

"It's Malcolm."

"Good," Karen replied. "Tell him he must be at the airport for 12.30 and meet the special flight from Southport. That's all, Jane. Thanks." She replaced the receiver quietly, looking up at Michael. "Well, it's started."

Michael was shaking his head and looking intently at the paper on his desk. There was a graph of survival rates based on experiments he had done with pigs and a variety of other farm animals.

"You know, Karen, I think this one may be too old. As a percentage of the normal gestation period for the species, this one is old. If only the Law had come in earlier."

"You heard what the President said," Karen said with deep concern in her voice. "It's terrible that the Palace has had to split with the Holy Fathers over this. If only we had more time. I'm sure that we could find an anti fertility drug if given the time."

"But Karen," Michael snapped, "you've been saying that for years. There is no more time left to spend on longterm research for a drug that maybe doesn't exist. Just now, we have to concentrate on something that we know will work. You can get back to your fertility work after we get a few clones started."

"I know, I know," Karen replied quietly and bit her lower lip in annoyance. She felt her authority and control slipping away, but she accepted that Michael was right. The Palace had decided that cloning was to be their top priority. "I've kept hoping that we were on the right track for a cure, but there is always some factor missing. It's something very simple. It must be staring us in the face, but I just can't find it." Her eyes were moist with tears and she turned away to the other side of the room. "Still, I think it wrong that the parents weren't given the opportunity to agree."

"Look, Karen, I understand your feelings. We would all like to keep things as they were but it's too late. You know that the combination of your research on artificial placenta and mine on the regeneration of stem cells to make viable zygotes does make cloning from foetal tissue possible, without any need for viable eggs or surrogate mothers. At the present time there is no other way forward. You've seen that there are only a handful of pregnant women left in the whole of Emanon. Come on, dry your eyes. There," he reached her a handkerchief and she stretched over the desk, accepting his peace offering.

"Yes, Michael," she whispered. Of course, you're right. We'd better get ready." She hesitated a moment as their hands touched on the desktop.

Three research teams had been kept on call for the last three days and nights awaiting the report of the departure of the samples from Southport and as Karen and Michael took the elevator up to the fifth floor they were hoping that this was not just another false alarm.

Years ago Karen's research had shown that animal embryos could be obtained by in vitro gestation. By mixing live sperm and ova in a test tube she had shown that the fertilised eggs would develop into small embryos which could then be implanted onto artificial placentas and successfully brought to term in specially designed incubators or embryonic modules. Because of the gradual loss of fertility of farm animals, her methods had become widely used in the production of farm animals throughout Emanon and her embryonic modules were now in great demand from across the world as the infertility crisis reached a climax. Now Michael's more recent discoveries complemented Karen's earlier work. He had found a means of converting foetal stem cells into embryos without the need for live sperm or ova. Jointly, they had now succeeded in bringing the embryos derived from foetal stem cells to term in the embryonic modules. Jointly, their new technology was at the forefront in the world and Emanon should have been leading the way in the cloning revolution and the race to overcome the infertility crisis. But Emanon had delayed the use of their new technology and now lagged behind numerous other countries. Now at last there was a chance to catch up.

By 1.00 am team A was ready and the call had come through that Malcolm was on his way from the Airport with the foetus.

"I bet you he gets a puncture," an assistant said as they all waited nervously in the sterile lab.

"More likely he drops off to sleep dreaming about the air hostess he's been chatting up," someone else suggested.

"Well let's hope the Omega Corps don't get him," Liam Curran, a young microscopist said. "I just heard from my parents - they live in Southport - that they had a demonstration outside the Hospital early this morning. Apparently the father of the chap on Rock alerted the Corps about what was happening. But, they must have got the foetus out safely."

They chatted, but tension was growing and glances at the clock became more frequent. Sweat glistened on Michael's brow. Suddenly there was a shrill ring on the phone. Karen was closest and grabbed the receiver and held it tight to her ear, her hand shaking nervously. There was dead silence in the laboratory, accentuating the persistent hum of the refrigerators and the sterile air filtration system. "He's arrived safely. It's on its way up." Her eyes latched on to Michael's in a moment of mutual understanding and hope. Could they be the saviours of Emanon?

The team worked through the night, each group of specialists at their own part. Initially the surgical team took over and a preliminary dissection was made. Samples passed to the histologists and microscopists for screening. Michael and Karen supervised the screening operation and looked at anything that the assistants considered positive. They watched the bank of monitors that showed pictures of the tissue. Suddenly Liam shouted, "I've got it." Both Karen and Michael moved rapidly towards him. Karen was nearer but held back briefly to let Michael look first.

Michael slipped into the seat vacated by Liam and adjusted

the focus of the microscope. His hand was shaking slightly and there was a hushed silence. All heads now turned to watch the centre of the lab. The surgeons, at the far end, left the table, their gloved hands red and moist, their scalpels poised.

"What do you think, Karen?" Michael deferred, before he made any statement, although his eyes told her what he thought.

She looked down the microscope and made a minor adjustment to the focus. Michael's hand was resting on her shoulder as she straightened up and she pressed his hand with hers. "It's there. We've found them."

A cheer went up from around the lab and a stamping of feet and "Well done Liam," from his close colleagues.

The sudden noise of the mainly male staff made Karen feel enraged.

"Quiet!" Her voice shrilled across the laboratory, bringing a sharp silence. "Please remember this is not a game. Do have some respect. The mother is at death's door if not already dead and the father probably doesn't know yet that his daughter's been taken. Don't act like savages, when the future of Emanon lies in your hands."

"Sorry, Dr Rowlands," someone said humbly.

"Should we ask the Fathers to come and bless the cells," Liam said. "They say that baby clones may have no Souls."

"Nonsense," snapped Michael, "we have no time now. That can be dealt with later when the embryos are formed, if you want, but we must get on with the experiment. It's stupid raising this query now."

Karen glanced at Liam and smiled. "It's all right," her eyes told him without speaking. There was no need. They had been close colleagues and friends for a long time. The specially selected cells were placed in small plastic flasks containing a growth medium that would stimulate the cells to multiply. The first phase of cloning Harry's unborn daughter was well under way.

Exhausted by their long stretch in the tense atmosphere of the laboratory the staff gradually left. Karen and Michael showered and met in his office, refreshed but still excited and stimulated by the success of the experiment.

"Want a drink?" he asked as she came into the room. She was wearing a white dressing gown after her warm shower, and her long black hair, normally tied in a tight bun, was flowing over her shoulders.

"I could do with one. Thanks," she said accepting a liberal portion of brandy that Michael had poured her.

"Cheers. To the future of the clone girl," Michael said. Their arms entwined in a customary gesture and they drank a long slow mouthful of the strong spirit.

Karen felt the heat of the spirit and the touch of his arm against hers sent quivers of sensation throughout her body. He was so nice - that captivating face and those blue eyes that held hers in a vice-like grip. He was so young. She was his boss. Since Claude's suicide a year ago she'd had no one. Was Michael really attracted by her? She had been beautiful, but the years and the useless struggle with Claude had taken their toll. Yet over the past weeks there had been something. She had sensed it. How often their eyes had met, had lingered and followed and watched and waited for those private moments. Thoughts, that were pushed away, but came back again and again.

"To our future as well, Karen," Michael said in a whisper, half afraid to hear his thoughts spoken. They sipped their cognac, their eyes fixed over their glasses, afraid, yet excited by the new adventure that neither could resist.

Chapter Eight

Karen was in the lab early and had examined the culture flasks with Liam, before Michael and the others arrived.

"They look good," she said, glancing up from her microscope as Michael came in. "I think we should treat some of the cultures today and see if the blastulas will form. What do you think?"

Michael looked for a long time at a variety of flasks and selected a few. "Yes. Let's get a cell count done on these and if the concentration is right, I think we should go ahead."

Liam took the selected flasks into the neighbouring laboratory for analysis. Michael swung round in his swivel chair and looked into the warm depths of her dark brown eyes that were suddenly, once again, so full of life and sparkle.

"Last night," he hesitated. "Last night. It was very special."

"Yes. It was wonderful." Karen let her hand linger in his. "It was very special to me, too." Karen smiled down at him.

"I hadn't heard what had happened to your husband. It must have been terrible for you."

"You know, sometimes I just can't believe that Claude is still not with me. And then other times it seems all so long ago."

"I understand," Michael said, leaning back in his chair, and holding his hands around his knees, looking up at Karen.

"Well, you know it was difficult. When he realised that we'd both become infertile he lost interest in me. He was depressed and felt he'd lost his manhood. He drank himself to sleep every night. Then he started going to the club with his ex-teacher friends who had become redundant. He had been so keen on teaching. It had been his life. He loved the children and when the school closed down he was lost."

Liam came briefly to the door with the results of the test but his sensitive nature told him that Karen and Michael were needing to be alone and he quietly closed the door.

"I did love him once," Karen continued. "We'd been married nearly twelve years. We'd got together while we were students you know. It was great. Claude was so clever, bright, popular, often a bit wild but I enjoyed that. His career seemed secure. He loved the children and was deputy Head before he was thirty. He was excited about my research as well. We made a perfect couple, except that we'd no children. He'd always talked about a son. When he realised that he was sterile he seemed to lose heart. Then when the school amalgamations were started his career began to fall to pieces. He had a dreadful argument with the Department about keeping his School open and they ended up demoting him. Then he was made redundant. I wasn't surprised. There were hardly any kids left to teach."

"God! Why have you never told me all this? I could have helped."

"But Michael, you've only been working here for the past few months. The rumour was that you were not looking forward to working for an older woman. Anyway," she laughed, her smile captivating him, "I hope you don't think I'm too big a bore."

"Of course not." Michael's eyes were beaming at her and he held out his hands for her to pull him up out of his seat. "All I can say is that you're very sexy in spite of your brains and age," he added, laughing as he regained his feet.

"Darling," she smiled, "we'll talk about it later. Here's Liam again with the results."

During the next few days the cell cultures were treated with solutions of Zymogen drugs, the complex group of growth factors that Michael had discovered. When applied at specific concentrations and rigorously controlled intervals these drugs induced the growth of the foetal stem cells. The research team waited anxiously to see if the cells formed embryos. By the end of the week thousands of tiny microscopic embryos had formed. While many of the minute embryos, comprising only a few dozen cells were deep frozen for future use, others were implanted onto the artificial placentas in the embryonic modules. As the initial implants seemed to be successful, within a few weeks, batches of frozen embryos were sent to all the major cities where Production Units had already been set up. Early in the planning stages of the cloning project it had been assumed that a considerable number of different foetuses would have been available and that a great variety of clones would be produced, both boys and girls, but by the time the Cloning Laws had been passed, Harry's daughter was the last one to become available. Also, unlike other countries where foetal material had been frozen, due to the laws of Emanon, it had been illegal to store, retain or even import foetal material and hence an immense potential source of cells had been lost. However, during the next few months a number of other foetuses had become available, following miscarriages, although no further normal births had been reported. However many of these had to be discarded as their genetic profile had shown that the babies would have been highly deformed or defective. A male foetus had become available a few months later following a further unfortunate miscarriage and a second cloning project had got underway. The President had been delighted when it was reported that a male clone had been obtained.

Soon however, the successfully cloned embryos derived from Harry's daughter were developing well and the new Cloning Factories throughout Emanon were in full operation. Things were progressing well.

## Chapter Nine

Tessa and Sophie had settled in well to their new apartment in Konburg. The twenty-five-storied Rana Mansions, had been taken over by the authorities for the purpose of housing young families and suspected fertile people from across Emanon. It was still run as a hotel with excellent restaurants, games, social rooms and swimming pools all of which functioned normally. Tessa's lounge looked out high over the esplanade along the north shore of Lake Rana. On a clear day she could see the far shore and the tall buildings glinting in the sunlight and the ships and ferries plying their way up and down the massive inland waterway.

Her mother and father had been able to visit her twice, at the government's expense. They'd enjoyed their brief trips to the old City of Konburg seeing all the wonderful ancient buildings and fascinating museums, art galleries and exhibitions. Their history and traditions displayed and explained to local and tourists to the full. Tessa had made friends with other young mothers who had been brought to the Clinic to assist with the ongoing research into fertility. Shortly after her arrival Tessa had met Cara Higgins and her young baby Mel, who had been brought up from Southport. The common bond of single-parenthood brought Tessa and Cara close and they helped each other in many ways during the first few weeks as they settled into their new life in the strange city. Cara had managed to get a part-time job in the fertility clinic and Tessa often looked after infant Mel.

The administrators of Rana Mansions encouraged weekly social events so that everyone would get to know each other and these evenings became the highlight of the week. Tessa and Cara had been attending for some weeks, her friend always taking the opportunity to dress up for the occasion. To night, at the Panda Club dance, was no exception and Cara looked beautiful. Her gown was not cloth, but like an extra skin, that moulded the body with a sleek firmness, yet softness, into a fantasy dream. From her waist, following the gentle curve of her hips, long fibres seemed to grow out and sweep to the ground, shielding, except when she moved, her long slender legs. In contrast, Tessa felt dowdy in her simple, plain dress and the short seal fur cape that her mother had given her before she'd left Dunfooey.

"Look," exclaimed Cara, pointing to a tall man who had just entered and was lingering alone at the doorway. "That's Harry Atkins. He's from Southport. I went to school with him. They took the baby from his wife to try and clone it. His picture's been in all the papers. His wife Greta and I used to be friends when we were kids."

"Call him over," Tessa said. "Ask him to join us. He looks as though he's alone."

Harry had just arrived in Konburg and had been allocated an apartment in Rana Mansions and was delighted to find someone he knew.

"This is Tessa," Cara said, introducing him to the others that were sitting around the large circular table, waiting to order their meal. Harry was soon seated between herself and Tessa.

"I was sorry to hear about your wife and baby," Tessa mentioned quietly when he had settled beside her. "It must have been a great shock, especially with all the trouble about the accident. I read all about it in the papers."

Harry nodded and tensed but as their conversation turned to other casual interests he became more relaxed and appeared to be enjoying the company.

"You like seals?" he asked Tessa, as he passed her a slice of tender pup steak and admired her cape.

"Oh yes, I've always thought seal pups were beautiful," Tessa replied, "nearly as nice as spring lambs. I was brought up on a farm near the north coast so I've seen a lot of both. It's such a pity that they have to be killed, though."

"Well," he said, defensively, "I've been working out on the Rock, so sealing has become a way of life. Just like your sheep and lambs, they have to be farmed, you know. In fact they're the only mammals that still breed normally."

"Oh, I don't mean that!" Tessa was embarrassed as the tone of his voice seemed hurt. "It's a very important job. What would we do without seal meat?" She smiled at him as she put a tender piece of steak into her mouth and dabbed her lips with a napkin, her eyes watching him come back from his dark shell like a hermit crab.

"Do you think the seals are becoming infertile as well?" Cara asked, feeling that Tessa was dominating her old friend. "I read that there was an epidemic of some sort during last spring."

"Oh yes. There was a disease last spring, but it didn't have anything to do with fertility. You often get diseases in the big colonies, but this year they appear to be back to normal." Harry looked down at Tessa, smiling. "Mind you, there are still plenty out there. The whole place is covered with them during the low tides in the late spring."

"So it's a good job we like seal meat," Cara laughed. "Harry will keep us well supplied." The others joined in the laughter, hiding behind the tragic humour of the situation. The Panda Clubs had been saying for years that pollution had long ago got out of hand, that the air, the oceans, the land, all carried the poison that had led to the present crisis of infertility. Only a few people appeared to remain fertile and most of those were now in Rana Mansions, most of them at the dance. Perhaps together they would yield the secret of a cure or produce the nucleus of a new generation of fertile children. They would be well looked after, fed on pure organically grown food and fresh fish and seal meat. Their diet would have no drugs or pollutants, factory produced or GM foods.

After the meal, couples circulated and danced. Harry danced with Cara and they talked about home and his bereavement. They had known each other since childhood and they had a lot of news to share. Cara had become slightly drunk. She clung to Harry as they danced, and he found her body smooth and supple and young.

Tessa sat alone at the table and watched. She was horrified at the blatant way that Cara was using her body. She looked away, remembering the man, Mike, and the dance when she had led the strange hiker into the barn and they had made love on the hay. Now, there was Sophie. But had she behaved ....?

The dance was over and they were all coming back laughing and relaxed. Cara skilfully manoeuvred beside Harry and continued to chat to him as though the others at the table didn't exist. Tessa was not used to the competitiveness of city life, but Harry was nice.

"Have you ever danced with a seal?" she laughed, cutting into Cara's conversation. "Maybe you have mermaids out there on the Rock?"

"Oh yes," Harry replied, turning his attention to Tessa, "we all have mermaid friends out there. However, I haven't danced with a seal yet, but I'm going to now," he added as the music struck up for another dance.

"Have you been to the Clinic, yet?" Harry asked, as they moved around the floor.

"Yes," Tessa replied, looking up at the big man who held her firmly and yet guided her like a gentle giant. She felt confident in his arms and she searched in his deep sea green eyes and through the wildness of his huge red beard that covered his cheeks and chin. "But they only take samples. Blood samples, fluid samples. Temperature, blood pressure. Anything they can measure. I don't think they know what they're doing."

"Do they make you go with others?" he asked anxiously. "There's an awful lot of rumours about what goes on here."

"Oh no!" Tessa smiled. "It's not like that. They just say that we should make friends and if we wish we should try and have babies. But they are really more interested in trying to get live sperm and ova so as to get in vitro fertilisation working again. The test-tube baby technique that was used so successful previously, now won't work as we women don't produce viable ova any longer and you men have no live sperm!" She gave him a playful squeeze around his waist.

"But how are we fertile then?"

"We're not. They think that the life of the sperm and maybe the ova as well, has become very short and they die before an experiment can be set up, or even conception can occur. We were just very lucky that we conceived."

"Cara says that your daughter was born in a van."

"Yes, it was a terrible night. But everything's fine now. You must come and see Sophie. I'm sorry you lost your daughter. But they say the cloning is being successful. Will you take one?"

"May be. They want me to stay here until the clones are born. I would like to see your daughter."

"Of course. Come to morrow." The music stopped and he hugged her tightly for a second and they walked slowly back to the table. Suddenly, Tessa realised that they were holding hands and she looked up at Harry's big friendly face, smiling down at her, and she pressed his large strong rough fingers.

## Chapter Ten

"There you are, Michael," Bernard Langwood said coolly as Michael entered the Director's large oak panelled office, still embarrassed by his young colleague's uncontrolled outburst during the Presidential Conference. Michael had always admired the deep leather sofas and armchairs and the big oak desk, matching the panelling and the heavily stacked shelves on the walls. The Director nodded towards a stranger who was sitting in one of the armchairs drinking a cup of coffee. "I want to introduce you to Mr Joyce." The gentleman, dressed in a dark striped suit and plain neck tie, set his coffee cup and saucer neatly on the edge of the desk and rose slowly, to shake Michael's hand with a cool firm grip. "Mr Joyce is personal secretary to the President," the professor added. "We are very honoured to have him here."

Michael shook his hand firmly, trying to control the nervous shake, as his mind raced as to what this could be all about - this sudden, unexpected call to the Director's office.

"Hello, Dr Rand," Mr Joyce said. He was a tall man with greying hair, proud and confident of his influential position at the Palace. "The President has sent me here to give you his personal thanks for all the efforts you and your team have made on this project. We have all been delighted to hear the success of the cloning experiment and want you to take back to your colleagues the President's special congratulations. President Neilson had asked me to speak directly to Dr Rowlands as well as yourself, but Professor Langwood tells me that she is working at the Fertility Clinic this morning, so please convey her my regards. We are delighted to see that both strands of our strategy are being pursued so enthusiastically."

"We just do our best, Mr Secretary." Michael responded, not quite sure just how to address him.

"Now, the President feels that we should get more public support for this venture and try and recover from the rather negative reaction we had following the introduction of the Cloning Laws. He believes that we should get the support of the parents of the newly cloned children and show the world just how they accept this new method."

"But, im .." Michael glanced at Langwood, who was grinning and nodding with approval. "But Mr Secretary, it is too early. The embryos are."

"Now, Dr Rand, don't worry. Time goes very quickly in these matters. We must quickly restore confidence among the general public. We must gain the support of the Holy Fathers if clone children are going to be fully accepted. We have every confidence that you and Dr Rowlands will overcome the technical problems as you've always done in the past." He looked over to Langwood for support and got a confident grin and nod. "However, we must take steps to look after the political aspects which will come to the crisis point when the babies are born. What are we going to do with all your babies in eight months time? Apparently there are thousands being produced all over Emanon. People will have to be prepared for them. Their future parents, perhaps I should say, foster parents, must think of them as beautiful loveable babies not little Frankenstein's. You know what I mean?"

"Michael, we know you are not very keen on the idea of the Fathers blessing the modules," Bernard said quietly from behind his desk, "but we feel it would create the correct image for the public. Very soon, as you know, the babies will have to be allocated to their prospective parents. You know," he added, grinning at the Secretary, "we already have a waiting list for the babies. Once we publicise them the demand will increase enormously."

"But, gentlemen, I have bad news. We've lost the second clone, the male one. The most recent genetic fingerprints have shown that the children would have severe abnormalities. I had to order termination of them, only this morning. These things happen during gestation. You cannot predict it," he added, apologetically.

"Oh! What a pity. But you still have the first clone? That is going well?" The Secretary spoke, a note of reprimand in his stern voice.

"Yes. But the facts are that we have only a single viable clone left. The first one we got, the female clone, but the foetuses are very small. And it is still much too early to know whether or not there will be any problems. The oxygen concentration is very critical for brain development and I'm concerned about it."

"Which one is that?" the Secretary asked, ignoring the negative aspects of the situation and suddenly looking worried.

"As I said, it was the first one we got. The one from

Southport."

"Thank God," Mr Joyce said, relieved. "The President will be delighted. He promised that the father, a Mr Harry Atkins,- he was out on the Rock, you know, when this all happened. You see, the President, well, in fact, I wrote to him and promised that he could have one of the clone babies. Isn't it lucky, Professor that it's this one that has survived?" It's this Harry Atkins that we want to use for this publicity venture.

"Didn't I tell you that these two always work it out? Karen and Michael make a wonderful team. In more ways than one," he added spontaneously, smiling at Michael and indicating his approval of their budding relationship that had now become common room gossip around the Institute.

"Now, Michael," Langwood added, with a slightly anxious, but authoritative touch to his voice, "the Secretary and I have just been talking about Mr Atkins. As he is now living in Rana Mansions, Mr Joyce has arranged that he would meet him here."

"What!" Michael snapped, incredulous, "here, today? Could I not have been told?"

"Now, now, Michael," Langwood responded. "It's all been done in a great hurry."

"Oh yes," Mr Joyce confirmed, "the President makes these rapid decisions and requests you know. But I assure you we planned to keep you fully informed."

"Michael, we want you to take Mr Atkins up to the Unit and show him round. Explain what you're doing. Encourage him. Make him feel important. He's only a reefer, you know, so he needs careful sympathetic treatment. We've arranged for a photographer and a reporter to join you after lunch and I expect you can let them get some shots of the Modules and a close-up of a foetus or two with the father looking at them. The reporter will know what is needed. They're members of the President's personal publicity team."

"But Karen isn't in today," Michael objected. "The Embryonic Modules are really her part of the project. She should be involved if there is any ...."

"Yes, Michael. That's a pity," Langwood cut in, preventing Michael from admitting to a grievous scientific flaw. "But I'm sure Karen doesn't want personal publicity out of this affair any more than you do. Anyway, as Director of the Institute, I and the Secretary here, acting for the President, will be photographed with Mr Atkins.

It's all arranged. You just get him well prepared and make him understand as much as you can. Make him feel an important part of the project." Without further comment Langwood called through the intercom. "Will you send in Mr Atkins. He should still be in the waiting room."

Michael stood to the side, tense, expectant, angry. The door opened and a very tall and strongly built young man entered. His skin was well tanned. His eyes were deep set under thick eyebrows that matched his red hair. His beard was neatly trimmed, emphasising his strong protruding chin, that was set firm and his lips, like his eyes, challenged the authority of the group. Michael felt his small fragile desk-bound body shrink under Harry's ruthless gaze.

"Ah! I'm so glad you were able to come, Mr Atkins," the Secretary started forward taking Harry by the elbow and guiding him across to Michael. "Let me introduce you to Dr.."

"Dr Rand," Langwood said quickly, taking up the introduction, having also come around to the front of his desk. "Dr Rand is the scientist responsible for cloning your daughter, Mr Atkins, and I'm glad to say that he is willing to show you everything about the experiment."

Harry grasped Michael's hand in a bone shattering grip and held it tight. "Did you cut my baby up into bits?" he demanded without taking his eyes off Michael's or loosening the grip on his hand. "Like I saw they did with pigs on a TV programme."

"Oh! No, no," denied Michael, easing his hand out of the vice. "We have a very different method from the one that is used with animals. We use very expensive instruments and microscopes and surgical apparatus just like in an operating theatre

"It's not like that at all," reassured the Secretary. "The President has sent me to thank you personally."

"We'll show you everything in the unit in a little while," Bernard added a comment to try and lessen the tension that had sparked around the office.

"You know I was very upset when I heard what you had done, without even my consent. I could have killed you that night." Harry was uninhibited and frank, directors, scientists, Presidents, at least President's secretaries, meant nothing to him. "But the President wrote me a nice letter. It was a great help."

He looked down at Michael, sensing the fear that was in his eyes. Smiling, he placed his great strong hands around Michael's

shoulders and shook him gently. "I hear you've done a good job with my wean."
Tension in the room dissipated and a ripple of conversation followed as the afternoon's programme was described to Harry. Photographers appeared and for an hour the office became a studio. Mr Joyce presented Harry with a plaque of the Cross of Emanon while numerous photographs and films of the presentation were taken. Michael was then instructed to take Harry up to the laboratory where in the embryonic modules the young clone foetuses were now visible.
The next morning the newspapers and TV bulletins across Emanon publicised the success of the cloning experiment as the lead story and Harry was suddenly the national star and hero.

Chapter Eleven

Tessa lay naked under the light sheet. She had crept back to bed silently after feeding Sophie and now lay on her back. There was warmth in her heart and her mind was giddy with a whirling of thoughts and emotions that she had never before experienced. Harry lay beside her in a deep sleep, a low rumbling snore coming from his huge, satisfied, exhausted frame. All his hate and anger, his frustration and sorrow, all his love and passion had been poured into her. She had taken it all and had room for more and in return her gentle giant had taken her beyond the stars and clothed her in the magic fabric of the universe. She was in love. Her giant had been brought from that distant Rock by some magic spell to save her, to save the world. She reached out and touched the slumbering muscles on his shoulder and he turned and took her in his arms and his strength came back and they never had been so happy.

"Will you come to the Institute with me today?" Harry asked, as they ate their breakfast and Sophie was gurgling at them over the side of her cot."

"Oh, Harry," Tessa said nervously, "I'm afraid I might be sick. It might spoil it all for you."

"Please, darling. It's really very nice. You've seen the photos. They've made ours a special closed-in incubator. You don't need to go into the factory part. I believe it would do her a lot of good to have both our influences there. Just to touch the glass surface and let our spirits flow in. I believe she misses the closeness of her mother's tummy, the warmth, the spirit, the thoughts."

"I do want to, Harry, you know that. But some of the women here say they won't go back and were revolted by seeing the real things. I'm afraid I might be, too."

"But really," Harry continued, encouraging her, "most of the women spend hours touching the glass and talking to the babies. Some say they respond. Reach out to them. Touch the same place on the inside of the glass. They come out enthralled. Please Tessa, I would really love you to come. You know I think of Greta when I'm there, but I know that it is no use. That is all over. I need you. I love you. Please come with me today."

"All right, Harry," Tessa said smiling across the table. "I love you too, very much. However, if I really can't go in, or stay in for long, you'll forgive me."

But Tessa had no problems and her fears were completely unfounded. From the moment they joined the queue for the afternoon's visiting session, she realised that the excitement of seeing their baby growing and developing was to be wonderful, considered by most an experience not to be missed. Some mothers-to-be claimed that the baby responded to them alone, moving more quickly and excitedly when they were at the module than when anyone else was there. The attendants also confirmed that the babies had favourites among the staff who adjusted the feeding fluid and checked the hundreds of instruments and dials that controlled the micro-environment in the embryonic modules.

Harry's child-to-be had been moved into a separate room and the module draped with cloth so that the pipes and tubes and numerous attachments would be unseen by visitors and the cameras that frequently recorded the progress for the fascinated general public. The original modules had been designed for piglets and similar units were in routine use in the pig factories throughout Emanon. But now room was pleasant and quiet and Harry had arranged a bunch of flowers on the small table that sat in front of the module.

Tessa held Harry's hand firmly as she entered, sure that she would either faint or run out. But when she saw the simple glass vessel with the light green fluid and the small infant turning slowly as if swimming, its arms and little fingers already well formed, its perfectly smooth head round and marked with dark veins, its eyes closed yet seeing, its short plump legs kicking against the side of the vessel, she thought of Sophie inside her and the memory of those first movements and when she knew for sure that the baby was alive and hers.

She left Harry's hand within seconds of entering the room and went slowly over to the module and touched it with her fingers and then her cheek and then pressed her lips on the glass close to the baby's head. She felt sure that the baby moved towards her, its little hands grabbing at her hair.

They both sat silently for a long time just watching their tiny moving daughter, waiting for some sudden change, development, some sign of recognition. Whenever she drifted towards them inside the spherical glass module their hands gripped and Tessa's lips moved close to the tiny form. Sometimes the long flexible artificial umbilical cord floated round to the front of the module. They withdrew slightly back but watched, entranced by the pulsating rhythm of the circulating fluids from the hidden computerised pumping systems behind the screen.

Tessa felt a movement behind her and looked round anxiously, disturbed from her reverie.

"Oh, hello, Dr Rowlands," Harry said, getting up and standing back politely. "This is my wife, Tessa," he added, looking at Tessa and smiling proudly. "She decided to come in today."

"I'm so glad," Karen said, looking over Tessa's shoulder at the module. "She seems to be doing very well. It will be no time before you have her home," she added as she checked on some of the dials at the side of the module.

"You're both at Rana Mansions?" Karen commented. "I heard about you in the Clinic. How nice. Congratulations. I hope you both will be very happy."

Tessa moved closer to Harry, holding his big hand, frozen to the spot as she recognised Karen's face. Photographs and film of Karen and Michael had been top news during the early publicity about the Institute and the cloning project and Tessa had immediately recognised Michael as the man who had seduced her at O'Flattery's.

## Chapter Twelve

Michael and Karen had just come down from the high crags above the cliffs of the Northern Cape and had swum in the blue water off a shelving sandy beach in a little private cove a few miles north of Dunfooey. They were dozing on the sand, the warm afternoon sun drying off the salty water. Michael dreamed in his half-sleep. It seemed a lifetime ago, but this was the beach where he'd met the cuddly farming girl. Had they really danced the night away at the ceilidh in O'Flafferty's Inn at the village? He'd promised to write to her, but there had never been time. Maybe she would be at the Inn tonight. She had been a waitress - she'd served him at dinner - and then later.... She had been young and fresh and exciting and he remembered her, running and chasing in the sand and falling and rolling in the surf.

But now there was Karen. She needed him. The emergency and the unique combination of their research work as well as the personal tragedy in Karen's first marriage had flung them together in a mutual understanding and need. Karen was older and mature, but still beautiful, exciting and sophisticated. They made a good couple among the City's elite. She had good contacts in Konburg where he was a relative stranger and Karen's senior position at the Institute gave her a lot of influence.

"I saw your big friend the other day, the father of the clone," Karen murmured, in a dreamy voice, the emptiness of the place pulling their minds together in some unfathomable fashion.

"Mr Atkins, big Harry. Yes, he's quite a character. Where did you meet him?"

"I had to stand in for one of the assistants and do a routine check of the modules. Harry and his new wife were visiting. She seems very nice, but very quiet. Didn't say a much, but apparently she comes from this region."

"That's right. I read somewhere in the papers that she was a farming girl from this region."

x

High on the hills across the bay Frank Tooley looked through the lens of a powerful telescope from the window of his cottage and saw the couple lying on the sand in the cove opposite. The couple embraced and then dressed. He watched them walk slowly hand in hand up the winding path to the small car park at the top of the cliff. At first the man paid only a casual interest to the couple and would have scanned on up to the cliffs to an eagle's nest, but he hesitated. The stranger's face was familiar. The photographer pressed a button on the console beside the scope and a picture slid out. He looked at it intently and went over to a cabinet containing many files of photographs. Most were of sea birds nesting on the cliff opposite or of seals on the rocks and animals on the hillsides. But some were of people caught accidentally as they relaxed on the shore or walked in the hills, especially if they were entering the nature reserve and nesting region of the golden eagles that it was his job to protect. He flicked through a file of photographs and stopped at one of two young people, a young man with straight blond hair and a girl with red hair and freckles.

"By God! That's Tessa's man. I knew it. I never forget a face. The bastard."

*

Later that night at O'Flafferty's Inn, Karen and Michael had a beautiful meal of freshly caught seafood. They had watched the sun sink over the bay that gave Dunfooey a safe sheltered harbour. Their long walk and fresh air had given them a good appetite. It was late summer and the restaurant was only half full and the landlord, behind the bar, was in a jovial mood chatting to some locals. He was glad to have the rush of the busy summer season behind him. Wine had flowed freely all night and Michael had drunk a lot.

"That man? At the corner of the bar, with the big beard," Karen asked, annoyance in her voice. "Do you know him? He keeps looking at us."

Michael looked round and the man looked away abruptly.

"No. I've never seen him before. God, I've only been here once." Michael was agitated and felt a little guilty. He had looked forward to seeing the young attractive waitress again. What was her name? He privately tried to recall it, as he drank the strong wine and ate the delicious fresh seafood. Memories of the exciting evening he'd spent with her stirred his passions beyond his control. He saw now clearly why he had meandered around the region, stopping here and there, but knowing unconsciously that he would reach Dunfooey sometime during their brief vacation. However it was the end of the season and she was not on duty. It would be nice just to say hello.

Did she remember him? But the man, he had never seen him before. Michael glanced across to the end of the bar again. The man was gone. "He's away. I think he knew we were taking about him."

"Let's walk to the end of the harbour and then we'll turn in," Karen said, suddenly wanting to get out of the restaurant, to bring Michael back. He had been too silent and had drifted away from her. He had drunk too much. She felt that there was something strange here. "We have an early start in the morning."

They walked slowly, hand in hand, along the stone harbour. The moon had just come up over the mountains and a bolt of silver streaked across the water breaking into the darkness and reflecting from the shining hulls and masts of two Tall Ships anchored in the bay. They kissed and he held her tight. Michael stirred. She was there. It had been here it had started, at the end of the harbour, after the dance. Their bodies had clung together, never wanting to part. He looked up and saw the dark roof of the barn behind the Inn and he pulled Karen closer and kissed her again and again, reliving his passion from the past.

They made an early start in the morning with Karen driving the treacherous route up to Dunfooey Pass and then down onto the central plain and on towards Konburg. Michael was quiet and seemed asleep, but his mind was in ferment. While he was settling the bill, the Landlord had passed him an envelope, marked 'Confidential.'

Hastily he had opened it in the toilet while Karen was packing the last items into the car. His hands shook as he unfolded the single piece of paper and sweat broke on his forehead as his eyes scanned the printed message.

"THE GIRL YOU RAPED HAS HAD A BABY. YOU BASTARD!"

## Chapter Thirteen

"Oh, Harry," Tessa said excitedly as they walked down the long corridor from the Clone Production Unit to the front entrance of the Institute, her arm fondly clinging to his and her fair freckled face looking up at him with the love and joy of an expectant mother. "It's so beautiful. Now that I've got used to the idea of it all, the tubes and glass and dials and all that, it's just the baby I see. Every day it's more beautiful and to think that tomorrow I'll be able to hold her."

The corridor resounded to the rapid movement of feet, numerous heels clicking on the tiled floor, mingled with the excited chatter of the expectant parents. Except for Harry and Tessa, the first group of parents-to-be had been selected by a random computer draw of the applicants. It had become clear during the past few months that the government's attempts to achieve more natural pregnancies by bringing fertile people together in the Fertility Clinic had failed. But now, even for the young couples at Rana Mansions, the tragedy did not seem so bad. The cloning had been successful and the first hundred babies would be born within the next few days. There was an expectant air around and publicity had been in general very successful. There had been television broadcast chat shows with expectant parents. Cameras had zoomed in on foetuses at every stage of development. Mothers had been seen fondling the glass modules. The tiny babies had been filmed responding to mock caresses and kisses. Anxious fathers-to-be looked on proudly, their hands on their wives' shoulders staring at the glass modules or making embarrassed glances at the cameras. Throughout Emanon, the demand for a clone baby had been enormous and the nation waited with renewed hope for Delivery Day.

The crowd in the corridor tightened up as Tessa and Harry approached the main exit. There was a commotion ahead - aggressive shouting and pushing from the people coming behind.

"What's happening?" Tessa shouted above the noise, stretching up, pulling on Harry's shoulder, to see over those in front.

"It's the Omega Corps," Harry shouted down from the vantage point of his massive frame that was head and shoulders above the rest.

"Why do they want to interfere now?" a neighbour shouted

across to Harry. "I thought they'd been banned."

"They are," Harry responded. "But they still have a lot of support."

Harry had pushed his way, Tessa following in his wake, through the crowd to the front. The crowd gave way to them recognising Harry as their spokesman. After all he was the father of the clone. Everyone knew him. He had defended the clone on broadcasts across Emanon. Now he was not only the father of the clone, he was their big strong leader and defender.

Outside at the top of the steps they could see a large crowd blocking their way forward. White placards were held high that were slashed with blood-red messages and claims - MURDERS - NO SOULS - END OF EMANON - STOP CLONING - GOD FORBIDS - POLLUTION OUT - BRING BACK FERTILITY - SAVE WILD ANIMALS - OMEGA CORPS WILL FIGHT - SAVE YOUR SOULS - JOIN THE OMEGA CORPS - NEILSON OUT - WE NEED OMEGA - WE NEED OMEGA - WE NEED OMEGA - GOD'S WILL BE DONE.

Large white banners, with the golden Crosses backing red Omega signs fluttered in the breeze above the heads of the crowd.

As Harry and his friends looked out over the crowd, waves of impassioned chanting, the hooting of horns and the beating of drums came to them from beyond the closed iron gates that led to the big square in front of the Institute.

"Where did they come from?" Harry said to one of the guards who was trying to hold the crowd back.

"They suddenly arrived about ten minutes ago - in buses, coming from all parts of the city. They most have been gathering in secret in the suburbs and had a well co-ordinated plan. Look at the buses over there." He pointed across the square where dozens of buses were parked. "They're well organised. We only were told something was wrong about an hour ago. We got the gates shut just in time."

"Those gates will never hold them, if they start to get rough."

"But I didn't think they'd be so fanatical as to attack us."

"It's not surprising. The Omega Corps have always wanted to stop cloning. They've been waiting for an excuse. With all the publicity, they know the first births are due soon. If they get in they'll wreck everything. Surely the guards are going to stop them."

Three youths dressed in white smocks with a red OMEGA sign stamped on their foreheads were attacking the gates. The noise and screaming increased to a high pitch. Tessa felt her legs turn to jelly and she gripped Harry's arm tightly. "Look!" she cried in horror, as she recognised one of the women attackers, noting the red OMEGA sign on her forehead and the blond hair tied back with a red sweat band. "There's Cara!"

"Didn't she got arrested for stealing drugs from the pharmacy at the Clinic," Harry shouted back over the noise. "She was always a bit wild, even when at school. Maybe."

The guards were struggling to hold the gate closed, but the lock gave and the gates swung open and the crowd surged in. More guards had gathered on the steps trying to keep the attackers from the unprepared group of parents-to-be that were jammed in the narrow doorway and corridor.

"Get back!" The guards shouted as they fought with the first wave of attackers that rushed up the steps. But it was no use. The weight and force of their onslaught quickly overcame the efforts of the guards. They fell back on the steps, the Omega group climbing over them up the steps towards the door.

Harry and Tessa were in the front row. Others, horrified at what was happening, tried to force their way back into the building against the outward flow of the people inside. Harry pushed Tessa behind him and stepped forward to the edge of the top step.

The first attacker to break through the line of guards was a lithe youth about half the weight of Harry. He rushed Harry with a pole that had been used for a banner and would have split open his head if Harry had not ducked just in time. He spontaneously sidestepped the onslaught and caught the thrashing pole in mid air, ripping it from the man's hands. Grabbing it in the centre with both hands about two feet apart, he crouched down into an attacking stance. The youth came on up the last step, propelled by the momentum of those following. Harry swung the pole under the youth's chin. There was a loud crack and scream as the man fell backwards on his friends. Harry now threw his full weight behind his pole-weapon and tore his way through the attackers on the steps. To the right and left he inflicted severe damage on the necks and heads of anyone that came within his range. But then the pole snapped and throwing it aside he grabbed the nearest attacker by the throat and the groin. Holding him high above his head, he threw him down on top of the attackers who were still struggling with the guards at the bottom of the steps.

By now Tessa and the others had regained the shelter of the building and one of the big doors had been closed. Knowing that he could not delay the attack much longer, Harry retreated up the steps and slipped in just as the other door was banged shut. Tessa ran to him, stretching up to kiss him and wipe blood from his cheek. She felt his great heart pounding beneath his sweaty blood stained shirt and torn jacket. She smelt the scent of fear and hate rising from the core of his being.

"They would have killed the clone!" he stammered, recovering from the shock and spontaneity of his actions.

"Well done, Harry," someone called from down the corridor. "No one else could have stopped them."

Outside a siren screeched as a number of police cars raced up the central avenue and into the square. Within minutes, the skirmish was over and the attackers were away mingling with the crowd, nursing their wounds.

The crowd was now peaceful and had struck up a chanting religious hymn. A Father, dressed in his long white gown, the ancient golden crosses hanging from around his neck, was speaking from a podium in the centre of the square. The demonstrators, subdued, gathered round in a quiet, respectful, peaceful protest.

The Omega Corps had planned a night long vigil to pray for God's mercy and the salvation of Emanon.

Chapter Fourteen

The journey back from Dunfooey had been the worst that Michael had ever encountered. There was a tension in the car and there was hardly a word exchanged as they drove through the winding mountain roads until they reached the main highway to the South. He had drunk too much on their last night at O'Flafferty's Inn and once again he'd over indulged in the seafood that he could never resist. His stomach ached and whenever he managed to escape to the privacy of a toilet he would reread the message from the bearded stranger at the bar. It must have been the stranger at the bar? He wasn't sure. The message was clear. He had read it time and again. The large unsteady print floated before his eyes. The words RAPED .. BASTARD .. BABY .. became imprinted on his mind.

    Could it be true? He was fertile! Tessa O'Malley was the name printed on the back of the photograph. It was her photo, that beautiful fresh freckled face, that flame of red hair, that he'd dreamt about often and which had drawn him back to Dunfooey. It was only a dream, a fantasy, a nightmare that would pass with his hangover. Now he loved Karen. Their relationship had been accepted by all their colleagues in the City and through her he had become fully integrated into the hub of Konburg society.

    Karen was beautiful, clever, exciting, liberated. Tessa was just a cuddly colleen. He would never see her again. Karen needed him. He had helped her get over the tragedy of Claude's death. She loved him. He loved her. Together they could do so much for the world, now that their clone was ready.

    Michael looked at the photo again, into the smiling blue eyes that shone out from the colour print. He put the photo back in the now tattered envelope and switched on the computer console on the desk in front of him. He knew he was going to do something that was illegal, but the situation required action and he had access to the genetic fingerprints of everyone at the Clinic. It had been early the first morning back at their apartment, while he lay tossing and turning, still disturbed by the fear of discovery and what the stranger may be planning to do, that he realised that if the allegations were true then Tessa and her child would have been brought to the Fertility Clinic in Rana Mansions.

First, he searched the computer directory for the name O'Malley in Dunfooey and found Tessa's registration Number and proceeded to question the data bank. Within a few seconds the flickering screen settled and the words

O'Malley TESSA - DUN234854F

appeared at the top. Gradually the screen filled with a series of bar lines. He tapped a few more keys and the picture reduced in size to the left hand third of the screen.

He thought for a moment and tried a few more questions and then the screen flickered again and the centre box on the screen filled with information.

O'Malley SOPHIE - DUN4762134F

followed by the bar lines of Sophie's genetic fingerprint.

Michael compared it carefully with Tessa's. There was considerable similarity, but some differences.

He looked at the keyboard again and typed in his own name and registration number. He sat tensely, waiting the few seconds as the computer flicked through the data bank searching for his own records.

MICHAEL RAND - ELD366921M became visible in the right hand window on the screen and then ever so slowly his own black bar lines drew themselves into the empty space.

His hands were gripping the edge of the desk and his eyes staring intently at the screen.

God! Just look at those, he thought, always amazed at the precision and sensitivity of the genetic fingerprinting technique. Without taking his eyes off the screen he typed PRINT SCREEN and the printer beside him hummed into action. He tore off the paper sheet, folded it carefully and put it into the envelope with Tessa's photograph. He had just switched off the computer when there was a loud hammering on the door and voices shouting.

"Michael," Liam shouted as he unlocked the door, "the Omega Corps is attacking us. Come quick! Some of the parents are trapped at the gateway."

They dashed down the corridor to the windows overlooking the square at the front of the Institute. From their elevated position they saw the crowd of small white figures surging around the front gate. There was fighting going on and the alarm bells were ringing. Was there a fire? Had the Omega gang already broken in on the lower floors?

"We'd better not use the elevators," Michael shouted as he ran to the stairs and began to bound down two steps at a time, the others following. On the third floor he left the staircase and ran along the corridor following the signs to the EMBRYONIC MODULES.

"We must protect the clones," he shouted back, encouraging the other staff to keep up with him. He pushed through the swing doors into the production unit and looked around. The staff in charge of the unit had fled when the fire alarms had gone off but the babies in the modules were moving around as normal, completely unattended.

"Here," Liam shouted, always ready with a practical suggestion. "Pull this deep freezer across the corridor. They won't get across this easily. Pile up those tables and chairs on top."

"These damn fire doors don't even lock," Michael swore, trying to wedge a stool in under the handles to jam the swing doors closed.

Their amateur defences were just about complete when the alarm bells stopped, leaving their ears humming, and Karen came running along the corridor, her loose white coat flying out behind her.

"It's all right," she shouted. "They got the front door closed just in time. The guards were useless. If it hadn't been for Harry Atkins they would have got in."

"Are the parents all right?" Michael asked.

"Yes. We'll have to get them out from the other side or take them by helijet from the roof. Security are dealing with that now."

They walked quietly around the modules looking at the tranquil scene, the silent floating babies, ready and waiting to be born.

"What sort of world are we bringing them into, Michael?" Karen asked, as they looked at a baby that was pressing its tiny hand against the inner glass surface, nearly begging to get out. She clung to Michael's arm and he felt her body still shake from the excitement and fright of the last intense few minutes. They were now on the ground floor foyer and the would-be parents were standing talking in groups, concerned, relieved and frightened.

"There's Harry," Karen said, as they came toward the group. "You'd better speak to him."

"Ah, Harry," Michael said, holding out his hand to the big man who was standing talking to a small group awaiting their turn for the elevator to the roof. "It's nice to see you again. I hear you saved us all."

Harry turned round and recognising Michael grasped his hand with friendship, remembering how welcome he had been made the first time he had visited the Institute when Dr Rand had shown him around.

"Why, Dr Rand," he said in a deep voice, looking down at Michael, "it is nice to see you again. I guess you need to get some better security here." There were a few words about the incident and then Harry followed with: "Can I introduce you to my wife? We're going to take one of my baby daughters, you know."

Tessa was chatting to some friends but turned towards Harry as he spoke across the corridor to her. "Tessa, come over here a minute, I want you to meet the Doctor who started all this. Dr Rand, this is Tessa."

Their eyes met, locked in a memory trap that seemed an eternity. All the events of the past year flashed through their minds, like a giant wave crashing on a rocky foreland or tossing their clinging bodies on the crest of the savage surf. Their eyes spoke silent words of recognition and understanding. Horror and fear crept into each with their spontaneous private assessment of what would happen if their secret was ever discovered.

"Hello, Dr Rand," Tessa extended her small hand and Michael held it briefly, "we're looking forward immensely to getting the baby born."

"It's going to be very exciting. I hope everything goes well."

"I've got a daughter of my own," Tessa volunteered, her arm clinging to Harry's as though for protection from herself, but her eyes holding Michael's in a moment of reprimand and challenge. "She's called Sophie," she added, as the elevator arrived and the group moved in and she was away.

"She comes from Dunfooey," Karen said, as they watched the door close. "You remember I spoke about her before."

"Nice lass," Michael commented, turning away and joining the group of staff that were gradually filtering back to the laboratories to tend the modules in the final run-down to Delivery Day One.

Chapter Fifteen

Cara had taken her last two pills of Myana just before going to the Panda Club's dinner on the evening she had introduced her friend Tessa to Harry. Throughout the evening she had been floating on air, the feel of her glamorous evening gown, taking her back to the exciting hyper lifestyle of the nightclub circuit that had been her previous secret life in Southport. The strong wine had helped and she felt she was the most attractive and sparkling woman in the room. Harry would be such a catch. Her drugged mind had bubbled over the bounds of reason and she believed that Tessa was competing for what was rightly hers. As she sat watching Tessa and Harry move around the floor during their last dance, she imagined and felt the grip of those strong arms around her own waist. Her body quivered and she longed for the return of those short moments of ecstasy during their brief contact, earlier in the evening. She had eventually found someone, a lonely innocent man, who failed her in the early hours, and in the morning she was depressed and lonely and there were no more pills and she was full of hate.

    She had taken a job in the Clinic, hoping to steal some drugs, and had spent a few weeks in the Donation Unit, helping to co-ordinate the supply of semen for the cross fertilisation experiments that were in full swing in one last attempt to achieve successful pregnancies. She had been addicted for many years and her need was urgent. On the morning following the Panda Club dinner she had been caught stealing drugs from the pharmacy and had been arrested and eventually admitted to the rehabilitation clinic in Belfast.

    It was there that the dedicated Fathers had come to her rescue. She had strayed from the paths of God and had ignored the holy commandments. They reminded her that she had been washed in the Holy Waters of Shanna when she was an innocent child and her soul ached to be back among the fold of the Family. The doctors in the clinic purified her blood and cleansed her body and the Fathers took her mind and spirit and washed them free of the evil forces that had darkened her life.

    Soon the ravages of pain and distress left her body as it became pure and free of the toxins that had poisoned her. Now she was ready to be "reborn". The Fathers took her, along with other patients to the Great Falls of Shanna where the waters of the inland lakes mixed with the bitter salt of the ocean. To this holy confluence, the people of Emanon had come for thousands of years to purify their bodies, their minds and their Souls. It was here that Cara had been Reborn.

    Cara had now a mission in life and she had joined the Omega Corps, as encouraged by the Fathers during her illness. Their demonstration in Konburg had been a great success, except for the unfortunate incident when some headstrong youths had tried to break into the Institute. That had not been in the plan. The Omega Corps was to capture people's Souls not split open their heads. She had seen Tessa on the steps and had decided that she must talk to her before it was too late.

    She rang the bell twice and waited. She knew that Tessa was in the apartment and had seen Harry leave a few minutes before on his way to the gym for his nightly workout. She should have at least two hours with Tessa. She was probably tending to baby Sophie. Cara looked forward to seeing the infant again after these long months since she had left Rana Mansions. Her own baby, Mel, had been taken from her by the social workers. He was with foster parents and she hoped that soon she would be allowed to get him back.

    "Why, Cara!" Tessa exclaimed as she opened the door, shocked to see her unexpected visitor. "It was you I saw at the demonstration."

    "Oh, Tessa," Cara said, her voice pleading for forgiveness and friendship. "Please can we talk? I do so want to explain what has happened."

    "Of course, come on in. You must see Sophie," Tessa said, leading the way into the lounge. "She's grown a lot. I've just put her in her cot but she's not asleep yet. Come on."

    Cara took Sophie in her arms and kissed her forehead. "Oh! She is beautiful. She's growing so quickly. It's months since I've seen her." Sophie's small hand grabbed Cara's long blond hair that fell in curls down to her shoulder and the infant gurgled with delight. She had always been happy in Cara's arms and it seemed as though she had remembered her. "Look," Cara said, taking a parcel from her bag allowing Sophie to tear open the colourful wrapper. "Look what Auntie Cara's brought you. What is it?" She waited briefly for a reply, but Sophie gurgled even more with delight, hugging her new furry toy seal pup to her chest and kissing its nose.

"It's a seal," Cara said precisely, "it's a seal. A lovely cuddly seal."

"Oh, Cara! That's lovely," Tessa said taking her daughter back and putting her into the cot. "That's very thoughtful of you." They sat and chatted while Sophie played contentedly with her seal for a while and then went to sleep. It was like old times.

"Now, tell me. How are you keeping? We've heard nothing since you were taken away. I'd no idea that you were so sick. What's happened to little Mel?" Tessa asked, encouraging Cara to feel at ease, suddenly anxious to help. She knew that it must have been difficult for her to decide to come back after what had happened.

"It's a long story," Cara replied, wanting to talk, "but I'm better now. Fully cured. I'll never take Myana or Zoss again. I got hooked on them as a teenager and just managed to keep it secret until that terrible night. You must have thought me awful."

"Well to be honest, I did feel you were over sexy and you certainly couldn't leave men alone and were always talking about them. I did become suspicious about your night duties at the clinic, when you used to ask me to mind Mel for you. But I didn't ever dream that you were on drugs."

"I'm fine now. I'm cured. Tessa, I do want to apologise for deceiving you. I'm so sorry for what I did. Also, I've good news."

"What is it?" Tessa asked, expecting to hear that she'd got little Mel back from the orphanage.

"I've been Reborn."

"You what!" Tessa exclaimed, surprised. It was the last thing that she could imagine happening to Cara. "You went back to the Falls and went through the Pool?"

"Yes. The Fathers were so kind to me and they brought me back from hell. I was all alone and now I'm part of the great Family. Oh Tessa, you should join us. I know you're a believer, but to be a full member of the Church, to have the spirit move in your body every moment of the day, it has made me such a different person. I can feel God in me at every turn. He is helping me, guiding me. I've such a wonderful feeling as though my whole body was on fire with an inner joy."

"Oh, Cara, I remember going with our School group to the Falls when I was twelve. I went across gripping the rope in case I'd drown. But other than getting very cold and hating the Fathers for holding my head under the water for far too long, I didn't think much about it. We all laughed about it coming back in the coach. But it was a good holiday." Tessa remembered her brief excursion to the Great Falls of Shanna that was an essential part of every child's upbringing in Emanon and although she held the beliefs and teachings of the Fathers in high regard, she would never had thought of getting Reborn.

"Listen, Tessa, I've talked to the Fathers and I want to help. I'm on probation for another six months and then I'll get Mel back. The foster parents are very nice and I am allowed to see him everyday now."

"I know," Tessa said, "I've visited him occasionally. He's doing very well. It's good for Sophie to see him."

"Thanks, they told me you'd been. That's partly why I felt I could come and see you." Cara eyes were full of tears and she held Tessa's hand, seeking friendship and forgiveness. "Tessa, soon you and Harry will plan to bring home one of the clone babies. By the way, how is Harry? I've never got asking you how he is," she added, interrupting her theme and realising that she'd moved too quickly towards her mission.

"Those friends of yours would have killed him this afternoon, given half a chance," Tessa remarked, her voice tinged with anger.

"Oh, Tessa, I'm so sorry about this afternoon. That was never meant to happen. Those youths got out of hand, but just at the start. I'm so glad Harry's all right. He's such a wonderful man. I know he'll be good for you."

"But what were you saying about the clone?" Tessa sensed that Cara had more serious things to say.

"Oh, yes," Cara hesitated, a little put out of her stride and realising Tessa had fathomed the real reason for her visit.

"We get the baby home in a few days," Tessa continued, excited and delighted at the prospect of having a baby sister for Sophie.

"These clone babies, Tessa, you know they have no Soul. The Fathers say they should not be brought up with normal children. You know that without a Soul, they will be filled with Evil. Do you think it right that she should be brought up with little Sophie?"

The freckles on Tessa's fair skin merged into a flood of red rage. "Look Cara," she snapped, leaning over the coffee table between them. The cup and saucer she was holding slipped from her hand and brown liquid spilt on the carpet. "Damn it!" she added, getting up to clean the messed floor. "The clone babies are just like any others. I've seen them for the past months. They're beautiful. I love her just as I would if she was in my own tummy. I feel and think about her just like I did when I was carrying Sophie. It's nonsense what some of the Fathers say. You know that the cloned embryos were all blessed by the Fathers at the very beginning."

"But, Tessa," Cara continued, making the sign of the Cross at this blasphemous statement as she helped to pick up the pieces of broken crockery. "They weren't the real Fathers. They were just the group that are in the hands of the Masters at the Palace. You know well enough that many Fathers don't agree." She remained silent for a moment, letting the tension in the room subside. Patience, the Fathers had taught her, was a virtue.

"What I mean, Tessa, is, if you need any help. We don't know what will happen ... if things go wrong. The Fathers think that perhaps if they were brought to the Falls and cleansed in the Holy Waters of Shanna and Reborn that it might help."

"Oh Cara," Tessa said, speaking from the kitchen, "you've been through a lot. I know you only want to help. It'll be all right. There are going to be hundreds of new babies in a few weeks time and I'm sure we'll manage. You know that both Harry and I are very committed to the Church, always have been, but the extremist elements are doing more harm than good. There's no need for the Omega Corps to become so aggressive and militant. They're only making the Palace authorities more rigid and restrictive. What the Corps did to the production units in Southport was disgusting. They broke in and killed all the little embryos when the first batch was started. Now the factories are guarded and secure. What's the point?"

The evening had gone so quickly. Suddenly the front door opened and Harry returned from the gym.

"Come and see who's here." Tessa called, as she heard Harry at the door.

"Why, Cara!" Harry greeted her as she rose from the chair.

"Cara thinks we should get the baby Reborn at the Falls," Tessa remarked as she came back into the room with a fresh pot of coffee.

"Oh, that might be an idea," Harry said calmly, sitting down and pouring himself a cup of coffee from the jug on the table that had survived the accident. "But we'd better wait till the summer. It's a bit cold for it at this time of the year."

"Well, there really is no hurry," Cara took up the theme without pushing it with Harry too much. If she could get the real father of the clone to lead the way the Holy Fathers would be delighted with her. "Perhaps next spring on a Holy Day we could have a big service for all the clone babies."

"Then you've joined the Omega Corps?" Harry queried, disregarding any further talk about Rebirth. "That was a disgusting affair this afternoon. I hope it's not the policy of the Corps to be violent. I thought they'd decided to be non violent after that catastrophe at Southport."

"Harry, I fully agree," Cara replied. "We only want to do what's right. There are lots of people very concerned about what's happening and cloning may not be the answer. The Fathers want much more funds to be put into research on the cure for fertility instead of factories to produce more clones. The real reason for this afternoon's demonstration was to launch a campaign for the Omega Fertility Fund. All the money collected will go into research for fertility. You know that we all want to get back to normal breeding - what we're doing now with all these production units producing babies by the score everyday is just unnatural. It's not what the vast majority of people really want."

It was getting late when Cara left. Friendships were reformed and she promised to come back soon to see Sophie and the new baby.

## Chapter Sixteen

During the past few months Karen had leaned more and more heavily on her growing relationship with Michael. She had looked forward to their short vacation just prior to the planned birth of the clone. The past months had been full of disappointments. Firstly, there was the complete failure of her team at the Clinic to find any evidence of fertility. Then the repeated failure of most of the cloning experiments on all those early foetuses and thirdly the continual worry about whether their only success, the little girl clones, would be all right. The foetuses were so small. Had the oxygen tension been right? Humans had never been produced in modules before. There should have been more research. Now it was too late. Her research on a cure for infertility had failed. Michael had been right. There seemed to be no drugs that would work. The pressure and strain of having a dual commitment had been too much and she felt she was losing her grip on the team and her authority was drifting away.

But Michael had been there, supporting her and pulling her back from the verge on long sleepless nights after days of tragedy and disappointments, her mind continually plagued by the doubt the clone girls might not be all right, that they too would die or be abnormal, like all the others. It was Michael's more youthful enthusiasm and the continued support of Bernard, who in spite of his age and increasing infirmity, were the lifelines that kept her going.

Of course, everyone at the Institute had been tense as the date of the birth of the clone babies drew nearer. And then Michael had been away a lot. The building of the new clone production units in all the major cities was now nearing completion. Michael was in constant demand to give advice and ensure that the cloning programme was implemented correctly throughout Emanon. Had she been too demanding, too dependent? Now he needed her support, her patience and understanding, especially as the great day was so close.

She would leave early tonight and prepare a special meal for Michael. He would be late at the Institute, checking the final details in preparation for the first deliveries.

"I think that's everything ready for the morning, now," Karen called across the theatre to a nurse and moving out into the neighbouring maternity ward. "Have you got the labels and the cots all marked, Sister?"

"Yes, Dr Rowlands," the middle-aged nurse replied, a little exasperation creeping into her voice. She'd never had so much fuss and talk about looking after babies before. "Everything is ready for the morning, Dr Rowlands," she repeated, collecting a large batch of labels and checking once again that they were in the correct numerical order.

"You know we mustn't get the babies mixed up," Karen commented, talking more to herself than the nurse.

Back at their apartment, Karen took from the deep freeze the box that they had brought back from Dunfooey. Michael had talked about the seafood of the region many times before they had visited the Inn at Dunfooey and now she knew why. The O'Flafferty's speciality had been the gastronomic experience of their vacation and she took care in selecting choice specimens of starfish, prawns, crab, oysters and other precious fruits of the sea. Long strands of green and brown seaweed, chopped up and cooked gently, added both flavour and colour to the tastefully presented dishes that were ready and on the table just a few minutes before Michael returned.

"Hello, darling," Karen called from the kitchen, as she heard him entering the apartment. She threw her apron in a heap in the corner and came out to meet him. She had chosen to wear an attractive low cut gown. "Is everything all right for tomorrow? Are you tired?" She kissed him on the cheek.

"Come on," she added, "I've got a treat for you tonight."

"Why, it's just like the Dunfooey speciality," Michael laughed, and squeezed her hand in appreciation of the effort she had put into the meal. "How did you remember?"

"I talked the waiter into giving me one of the plastic models they had on their display counter. You'd hardly know the difference."

"You mean this is plastic?" He was momentarily taken aback and lifted a piece of crab, just to make sure.

Karen laughed, delighted that she had obviously pleased him. "Let's have something to drink."

It proved a wonderful meal. The wine loosened their tongues and they talked and flirted while the trials of the day and concerns of tomorrow were far away. Michael was so attractive and entertaining. He thrilled her with his quick comments and humour. How could any woman resist him?

The starfish had a wonderful flavour and they both indulged as they had done at the Inn. Michael remembered the first time he'd tasted it when Tessa had given it to him as a special treat.

"That girl, Tessa," Michael volunteered, through a mouthful of green seaweed and sliced prawn, "I remember her now. It was a few years ago when I was hiking over that way. She worked at the Inn. Gave me some starfish. I ate far too many of them, practically made myself ill." They laughed and teased.

"She seems a very nice lass. Do you think she remembered you?"

"Oh, I doubt it." Michael replied, wishing now he had not raised the subject. "She'd see thousands of tourists during the season out there."

"Even if she did, she'd be too shy to say so anyway," Karen commented. "I've spoken to her a couple of times but she seems very quiet."

"Well, I suppose it is a big change to be brought from a small place like Dunfooey to a city like Konburg and with a baby less that a year old."

"Is it?" Karen questioned. "I didn't hear what age the child was. She just said she'd a daughter called Sophie. I'd assumed she was much older." The wine had loosened her memory and unconscious interactions flashed through her mind.

Michael continued to chew on the tasty seaweed salad and took another chunk of crab meat and a sip of wine and another starfish slipped down leaving a delightful twang on the edge of his tongue. There was that silence again.

Karen felt a chill in the air and pulled her wrap closer around her bare shoulders.

"Michael," her voice was suddenly stern and mature and hurt. "Do you know something that I don't about Tessa and Harry?"

Michael took another long sip of wine and began easing apart the shell of a clam. There was more silence.

"Michael," Karen was demanding and pleading at the same time. "Please Michael. Talk to me. I know there is something wrong. Ever since we left Dunfooey there has been something on your mind. You've been different."

Michael continued to chew the clam and refilled his glass and then reached across to recharge Karen's as an afterthought.

"Thanks," she said dryly, "but don't drink so much. We've a

big day tomorrow," she added, wishing to bring the situation and conversation back to the present, back from the past, whatever it was.

"Karen," Michael said after another long silence, while she dried a tear from the edge of her carefully shadowed eye, leaving a dark blue smudge on her cheek. "We must talk."

"I want to talk, Michael," she snapped back, "but you just sit and say nothing. Just how long will you going to keep this secret you've got to yourself? I know it's there. What is the matter with you?" She was now standing beside him, her long slender dark fingers gliding through his blond straight hair, pressing into his scalp, searching for his thoughts.

Michael got up and holding her by the bare shoulders, kissed her on the forehead and said, "Karen, I have something to show you. Come into the study." He led her by the hand out of the lounge and down the passage to his small study. It was cool in there and the freshness of the air sobered them up. Besides this was a place of work and reason and reality. He fished in his briefcase and took out an envelope and spread the contents on the desk.

Karen looked across, switching on the desk light.

"The Innkeeper gave me this before I left Dunfooey last week," Michael said in an unsteady voice.

Karen looked at the photo, recognised the fresh smiling face of Tessa, a face full of vigour and delight and smiling with joy. She turned the photo over and read the words written on the back. She bit into her lower lip and clenched her fists as she read, time and again, the frightful printed words.. RAPIST ... BASTARD!

"Did you rape her?" she accused.

"Of course not. She was as willing as I was. She wasn't a virgin. That man, the chap we saw in the bar, he's probably jealous, but he's right about the baby."

He unfolded the computer print out and spread the pages of the genetic fingerprints so that Karen could see them.

"I ran a computer search at the Institute and found this," Michael said after a few minutes.

"That's illegal," Karen said, horrified. "You should have asked permission. You know that," she reprimanded. "What is it?"

"On the left is Tessa's. In the middle is her daughter, Sophie. On the right is mine." He pointed to each in turn with a ruler and then handed it to Karen. She placed it carefully on the sheet and knowing how to read a genetic fingerprint, she checked off, band for band, down and across the page. Neither spoke. Slowly she slid the ruler further and further down the page until it reached the last bar line. Then Karen looked up.

Tears were in her eyes, her eye shadow was now a mess streaking down her smooth light brown cheeks, smudged and wet, where she had wiped her eyes with the back of her hand in an unconscious action. Her mind was a whirlpool, thoughts and memories racing back and forth, round and round the events of the past year, Claude, embryos, death, birth, Michael, Tessa, Harry, Sophie, Omega, flashed through her mind. Where would it all stop? How could she survive without Michael? Everything was just getting right again, but now her life was falling apart. She saw Michael in a different light. Rumours about him must be true. Had he really reformed since she had come to live with him? He was away a lot, travelling to the production units across Emanon. Never once had he invited her to go along. The Modules had been her design. She knew more about them than he did and yet somehow he had become responsible for them. He had become the expert. She had been left behind, searching for anti-infertility drugs that probably didn't exist.

"Bastard is right!" her voice came as a hiss from the depths of her being and the words spat at Michael as they stood face to face in the small room.

"No!"

"You still want her, don't you? Don't you? That's why you insisted on going back to Dunfooey, when I would have liked to visit my folks in the South."

"No!"

"What would have happened if she'd been there? Slipped away in the middle of dinner for another speciality!"

"No! Karen. It's not like that."

"What's it like? What's she like? Bitch. Bastard. Are you going to try and get her behind Harry's back? That big man will beat you into pulp."

"I'm sorry, Karen. I was young. It was a mistake. It's not like that any more. I promise. I admit I was curious to see her again. But now it's you I love. We're so suitable for each other. She means nothing to me."

"Just a good cunt, I suppose. And of course, there's your daughter!"

"But Karen, don't you see? I'm fertile. Maybe we can have a

child. That's why I'm telling you all this. I love you. I don't want to keep any secrets from you. Not now, not after all we've come to mean to each other. The future holds so much for us. Please believe me. I love you!"

"Please, Michael," she wept, looking at him, their faces a few inches apart, sweat bursting from their foreheads and their bodies shaking with anger and passion. She was holding him with her right hand and the other hand crept up his forearm to his shoulder. "Please, Michael, please never leave me. Never do that again."

Michael stooped over her, looking into her pleading eyes, sparkling with tears in the brightness of the desk lamp. His gentle fingers stroked the tears away from her cheek and then he passed his hand downwards, his fingertips lingering over her bare shoulder and arm, their eyes still glued together in a silent search for truth and love, until his trembling hand slipped in under her low cut flimsy gown. Their lips touched. She clung to him and they both wept.

## Chapter Seventeen

Harry and Tessa had been invited to the first Delivery Day. They had taken their seats along with the other parents-to-be in the viewing gallery looking down through the plate glass window into the operating theatre. Tessa felt as excited as an expectant mother while Harry's eyes were fixed on the silent green gowned figures, expecting every second to see the glass module being brought into the theatre.

The buzz of casual conversation ceased abruptly as the first module was wheeled in on a trolley, and the delivery team gathered round. TV cameras hummed and tubes were connected and valves turned on or off. The fluids drained away and the baby settled in the lower half of the module, splashing in the residual warm green liquid. The top half of the glass dome was removed and gentle gloved hands carefully picked the infant out.

Tessa held Harry's hand, childlike in her dependence on him. He had become her father figure in the strange new world of the city. Her strong gentle loving giant had made life bearable in the loneliness of the crowded life of Rana Mansions. It was so strange to watch from the gallery the birth of the child, their child, to watch the pink gloved hands of the nurse take the baby out of the fluid in the half module, like a transparent carefully broken egg. The cruel slap on the back forced air into the lungs as green fluid was coughed out and soiled the sterile garment of the nurse. Memories of the pains when Sophie had been born on that fateful night far away in the mountains returned to her. Her muscles twisted and turned and strained and her whole body trembled, leaning for support against Harry's solid side.

She knew that beneath the quiet exterior, Harry was far away with Greta at this moment of the birth of his child. Tessa and Harry had talked a lot about his earlier love for Greta and their plans and hopes. But it had been the tragedy of Greta's death that had brought them together and she understood and waited for him to return.

They had glimpses of the baby move. Its tiny arm struggled against the nurse and they heard it's first cry through the loud speakers in the gallery. Harry pressed Tessa's shoulder tightly and they were at one and the baby was theirs. It had been so easy compared to Sophie's birth, no pain or struggling, no agony or torture, no fear, no uncontrollable screaming at the last pangs of birth. Was this the future? Was this what God had planned.

In every home throughout Emanon, women looked at the television screens that showed the birth and cries of the first clone baby and a vision of the future flashed around the world. Would anyone ever choose the old way again? Now the dangers of childbirth itself had vanished forever. They had seen it before from other countries on the TV, but now it had come home to Emanon. Their world had changed. This was a new beginning. Even the Holy Fathers with their pent-up passions and their extreme followers who feared for the children's Souls were subdued by the reality of what had happened. At the same moment, across the whole of Emanon, and beyond, millions of people, fathers and mothers, single men and woman, were on their feet and cheering the successful birth of the first Emanon clone baby.

Harry and Tessa waited anxiously as the staff in the theatre, excited by their success, congratulated each other and they saw the Director appear briefly to have his photograph taken holding the infant. The parents-to-be had been told that the babies would have to be examined carefully before they could see them. But within minutes Harry's name was called and they moved down to the nursery where they saw the little infant lying peacefully in a cot. Tessa held her briefly and Harry looked at the tiny face, unbelieving that he was her father. He saw an immediate resemblance to her mother. "I'm glad we will call her Greta," he said quietly, as Tessa put the infant back into the cot.

"Yes, that will be nice. She'll be our Little Greta," Tessa replied.

"We shouldn't disturb her for a while now, my dear," the sister in charge said, "but you can come and see her tomorrow. You'll get her home in a few days." It was a quiet dismissal, an anti-climax, to all the waiting and worry. They left the Institute and with a few other new parents, walked along the esplanade enjoying the fresh autumn breeze that blew across the Rana.

Chapter Eighteen

Like everyone else at the first delivery, Karen had held her breath, instinctively, trying to will the infant to breathe. The child must live! Her eyes glanced upwards and she saw Tessa in the gallery above, and for a second anger and jealousy surged through her limbs. But then she looked back at Michael who was completely absorbed in the birth as the infant gave its first cry, oblivious to the turmoil in her mind resulting from his revelations of the previous night.
 The staff gathered around excitedly for a moment, admiring the beautiful baby, now wrapped in a warm white blanket. Both Michael and Karen were offered congratulations and handshakes from various colleagues. The swing doors of the theatre suddenly burst open and Professor Langwood who had been watching the television in his office came in, his face glowing with excitement and satisfaction, his limp magnified by his haste.
 "Well done, my dear," he said, grasping Karen by the hands and hugging her tightly. "I knew you'd manage it. Where's Michael?" he looked round as Michael came across the theatre. "Excellent, Michael. It couldn't have been better. Now we really can save Emanon. At last we are back on the world stage as one of the surviving races - long live the Celts!"
 "It will be a woman's world, though," Michael laughed, picking up the concern that they all had felt due to the large number of failures they had had with the other cloning experiments. Even with the new pinhole surgery techniques of being able to remove biopsies of the now, extremely rare, early foetal tissue, none of their attempts to clone again had been successful. However, Michael had been pursuing a new line of research involving the possibility of the transfer of sex chromosomes and he had now high hopes that soon he would be able to convert the clone girls to males, but this was still secret work that he had not even told Karen about as he was afraid that the authorities might stop this line of research that the Fathers would certainly object too.
 "Karen," Bernard said, taking her by the arm and still holding Michael by the hand. "The President rang through immediately he heard the first cry. He's delighted. We are all invited to the Palace for a reception and dinner tomorrow tonight."

"But."

"Everything else is cancelled." Bernard laughed, his face still glowing in the heat and humidity of the theatre. "We'll take the helijet from here. We'll leave at six. Look your best, my dear. It's all publicity, you know." He spoke generally around the theatre for a few minutes, congratulating everyone on their efforts. He admired the new baby briefly and then posed for the press, holding the tiny infant, anxiously supervised by the Sister, whose protestations were ignored. Then with a cheerful wave, he was gone, hobbling through the door on his bad leg.

Now, one by one, the modules were brought into the theatre, and the surgical teams, working in two hourly shifts, continued to deliver the new babies throughout the day. Each time there was an anxious moment, until the baby's cry shattered the silence. During the first day of delivery only three stillbirths were recorded, a much better rate of success than had been expected.

By late afternoon rows of cots lined each side of the nursery and a buzz of excited activity filled the ward.

"That's been a busy day, Sister," Karen said as she paid her last visit to the ward. "Have you been on duty all day?"

"Yes," she said, obviously tired and nearly exhausted from the strain of the continuous flow of deliveries. "But these technicians! They just get back the empty modules to clean up and I think they're a bit annoyed because the nursing staff is taking over. I understand. They've been looking after them for months and then suddenly we're in charge. But we'll have to stop the technicians coming in. They're in and out all the time. We'll have to make a rule. I'm convinced the babies know them," the Sister added, disappearing down the ward to a child that was screeching.

Karen looked down the line of cots at the tiny faces, some peaceful, others crying and frustrated at being cast into a strange hard world of clothes and sheets after the warm smooth fluids of her modules. She felt a yearning to lift one up and hold it in her arms, to feel the small face press against her breast and know that it was hers. She longed to love it as her child, to watch it grow and guide it. She hesitated at a cot, looking down at a peaceful infant, sound asleep, and was tempted to nurse it.

"Now, now, Dr Rowlands," the Sister reprimanded as she rushed hurriedly back from the far end of the ward. "Don't disturb her. We've only got that one settled. You're as bad as the technicians.

These babies will be spoilt."

"I'm sorry, Sister," Karen said. Indeed, she would like to spoil one of these babies. Why had she not decided to take one? The first two batches were all booked and it would be months before Michael and she could get one. They had never discussed it. But they should have a child. Especially now! It would help keep them together. Tears came to her eyes and she left the ward, hurrying along the corridor to the privacy of her office, banging the door closed. "Oh, Michael, Michael!" she said to herself, recalling her pleadings in the early morning as they lay recovering from their feast of anger, frustration and love. "Why must you be like that?"

Chapter Nineteen

Before dawn the next morning the new parents were queuing up at the entrance to the maternity wards. Nurses were coming in and out, with trolleys and babies' bottles and soiled nappies. The parents strained to see through the momentarily opened door.

Tessa and Harry waited tensely trying in vain to get a glimpse of their daughter. The queue moved slowly forward as the nurse at the entrance checked each parent's name. She gave them the number of the cot that their daughter was in. Once in the ward Tessa and Harry walked directly to their cot. Mothers were lifting their infants and fondling them and the fathers standing back uncertain, some more anxious than others to hold the little fragile figurines.

Harry, already well used to handling Sophie, held his new daughter proudly and confidently and Tessa reached up with her handkerchief and wiped away tears that streamed down his cheek.

The infants were gurgling and crying. The parents talked and laughed and the atmosphere in the nursery was happy and relaxed. Suddenly from the cot next to Tessa's there was an anxious call.

"Nurse, Nurse!" a young mother shouted above the bubble of conversation and noise. "Nurse, come quickly. This is not my baby."

Suddenly there was silence and all eyes swung to the centre of the disturbance.

A junior nurse rushed over to the couple and the Sister came out of her office, striding forward urgently, "Now, now, now. There's nothing wrong," she volunteered, intent on taking control of the situation that she had feared would occur.

"Look," the distraught mother said anxiously, anger simmering beneath the surface of her tense voice. "Look, there are two labels on my baby. One has worked its way up the arm and was hidden by the sleeve. There's another number on the label around the wrist. They're not the same."

The Sister moved in rapidly and took the infant from the mother's arms without a word. The parents were now gathering round and the babies, sensing the strange vibrations in the room, were screeching with all their might. Within a second the ward had changed from a happy relaxed nursery to a crescendo of screaming babies. The noise increased dramatically when the Sister turned the baby over and skilfully removed her nappy and exposed the bare bottom to the cold chill of the fresh air.

The parents looked, their eyes staring, unbelieving, at the number on the baby's bottom, still red and sore from the recent tattooing.

"There you are," the Sister said proudly, "there's been no mistake. That's the number on her birth certificate. Isn't it?" she asked confidently. The mother, embarrassed and confused, searched in her handbag and retrieved the sheet of paper and checked carefully the numbers with those tattooed on the child's bottom.

"It is the same," the father agreed, "but why are there two labels on the arm?"

"Oh, that's just a simple accident. Probably happened after bath time. It's been all very rushed this morning. I'm sorry about that," she said authoritatively, dismissing the incident as a minor inevitable error. She wrapped the nappy back around the squirming infant who was still screeching. She gave the infant back to the mother and then said loudly above the noise, "I think you should put the babies back in their cots for a while and let them settle. They're very easily disturbed and they're very tired. Remember they're only a day old," she reprimanded and the parents dispersed, while the crying gradually waned as the babies were tucked into their warm cots.

"I didn't know they'd been stamped like that," Tessa said, looking up to Harry as their daughter fell into a peaceful sleep.

"It's just like they do with the piglets," he said sadly, recalling the horror vision of the TV programme on his way back from the Rock that now seemed a lifetime ago. "But I suppose it's necessary. They do all look so alike. The nurses must have an awful time telling them apart."

"Poor little thing," Tessa said, envisaging the labelling session when rows of babies, their tiny bare bottoms exposed, were stamped with a lifelong number. "It must have been sore. But I suppose it's compensation for the easy birth. I've always wondered just how much pain a baby feels when it's born. It's pretty bad for the mother," she added.

"She's so tiny compared to Sophie," Harry said. "I never realised just how quickly a baby grows."

"Oh, but she is a very tiny baby," Tessa emphasised. "Sophie was much bigger when she was born. I'm surprised that the doctors haven't said something about their size. They're so petite," Tessa said, looking around the nursery, which was now quiet. Parents were sitting patiently beside the cots, chatting in whispers or just watching with loving eyes their tiny daughters, dreaming of the time within the next few days when they would get them home.

## Chapter Twenty

Michael had been daydreaming about the invitation to the Palace for some time. He recalled how during his first visit he had been in the shadow of Karen and old Bernard but now his fame had streaked ahead as the cloning technology had hit the headlines and his name was on everyone's lips. He relished in the expectation of being the guest of honour. Of course Karen would give the glamour and sparkle to the occasion and he would give all credit to her work in the design of the artificial placenta and the embryonic module, but he felt sure that everyone now accepted that he had been the driving force behind the cloning initiative. After all it had been his discovery of how to clone from foetal tissue that had spelt success for the project.

He had dreamed of this for years. He relived the moment, felt his heart thump and his clenched fists during those fleeting moments of intense silence before the babies gave their first cries. During Delivery day he'd experienced a rare moment of transformation and a vision formed in his mind that gave his whole life a new purpose. His whole being vibrated with an excitement, that was secret and private and was his alone.

"Isn't this a wonderful place?" Michael said, pressing Karen's hand and looking down at the vista of the Palace and beyond, as the helijet descended toward the landing pad.

"The sunset from here is fantastic. But it's not as good as from Dunfooey." she added, surprised by his childlike enthusiasm for the Palace and the whole evening. They had known unofficially for some time that an invitation to the President's Table would come following the successful birth of the clone and Michael had been excited by the prospect much more than she had been.

Unlike his previous visit to the Palace, this was a private affair and only a few selected guests were to be present.

"Do you think he'll have the Archbishop present?" Michael asked across the passageway to Bernard.

"Oh, yes. My old friend, Longfellow," Bernard replied, smiling, "I'm sure he'll be here. We were at college together, you know. He was a great sportsman. Not a bad chap really. Always wanted to become a Father, though. We used to argue for hours about science and religion. We'll probably have a good chat about old times over dinner."

Michael swallowed hard. He had always thought that the Professor was as opposed as he was to the Church. They had long agreed that these old fashioned beliefs were not consistent with recent scientific discoveries. But now Michael wondered if Bernard's attitudes had changed and if the dinner was really to allow the President to achieve a political reconciliation between the Church and the Council of Masters following their unilateral introduction of the Cloning Laws. Such a pact could effectively tie his hands in developing any of the more advanced aspects to the cloning programme that had been stirring his imagination during the past weeks and months with the exciting possibilities of genetically engineering the little girl clones, a scientific and social challenge that he found resistible.

Michael was silent as the party walked through the Terrace, but he admired the well laid out flowerbeds and the view of the lake, the setting sun reflecting golden from the water and glinting from the windows of the tall building clinging to the waterfront in the distance. His hands glided over the rough stone of the statues that held the secrets of the long history of Emanon.

The President met them at the foot of a massive Cross and Michael noticed that Karen had spontaneously deflected and even Bernard had bowed his head reverently. The President stepped forward, his hand extended in friendship and welcome. Michael found himself accepting tradition and bowing his head towards the stone images as the President moved towards him with his hand extended.

"Congratulations, Dr Rand," President Neilson said warmly, shaking Michael's hand firmly. "This is a tremendous achievement. I hear from all parts that your production units are in full operation and that babies will be available in all parts of Emanon within the next few months. We are all....." He caught a glimpse of Karen standing to the side and proceeded. "Ah, my dear Dr Rowlands. How nice to see you again," he said, taking her arm and moving her towards Michael. He held both their hands in a fatherly gesture between his own. "Both of you have done a great service to Emanon. I want you both to know how much we appreciate the efforts you've made." He hesitated for a second, and then continued. "And I was so glad to hear of you're forthcoming marriage. I hope you will be very happy. You will be of great support to each other." He looked at them again with a fatherly smile and pressed their hands in his and looking around, called, "Archbishop! We must make this the marriage of the century. The Palace will be at your disposal."

There was a spontaneous round of applause from those standing near. Karen felt a cold sweat break on Michael's hand and they both trembled.

"Now, Michael," the President continued, "I have a little something to give you. An honour that I know you will hold dear and that will show the world just how important the success of the clone is to Emanon." An attendant came forward with a golden tray in the centre of which was a small ancient box that was studded with precious jewels and golden lace work of ancient designs.

Slowly the President lifted out of the box a golden chain, careful so that the medallion appeared last.

It was only then that Michael realised that they were at the centre of the stage with cameras, reporters and lights focused on them. The ceremony was being seen in all parts of Emanon. The President now spoke in a louder voice to capture the attention of the others and addressing the cameras.

"I speak to all of Emanon, in recognition of this great day. This Day of Delivery will go down in history as the day that Emanon was saved, and to honour all those involved I am appointing Dr Rand to the ancient and noble Guild of the Masters of Emanon." He placed the chain and the bright golden Cross containing an embossed M over his head.

Lights flashed and cameras buzzed. There was polite clapping and handshakes and many words of congratulations. This was so much more than Michael had expected. A prize perhaps, a large grant for further research, but to be made a Master, the highest honour in the land, was far beyond his expectations.

Bernard grasped his hand, his round plump face beaming with pleasure. "My best student! Always knew you would do it," he said. "You've both done well," he looked at Karen, noticing a shallow smile on her face. "I don't think you've met Archbishop Longfellow," Bernard said, introducing his old college friend-cum-enemy.

"Well, congratulations, my young man. Bernard has been telling me great things about you." The Archbishop wore a light grey suit and roll neck white shirt. He was taller than Michael and had broad shoulders and an athletic frame. Michael remembered how well he'd carried himself when dressed in the elaborate robes of the

Holy Orders. "We now must work together and ensure that the children are accepted into society. I will do everything I can to have them accepted into the Church. I was very concerned to hear that the Omega Corps had attacked the Institute. I'm sure that phase is over now. There are always a few extremists, you know, when matters of great importance come to the fore. But God seems to be on your side. Success will breed success. The little ones will be Reborn. God has given us a sign. He has pointed a way forward."

"Dr Rowlands," he continued, switching his attention to Karen who was holding Michael's left arm and had kept close to him during the brief period following the award. "I remember your lecture at the conference extremely well. Those were very exciting results and ideas about the causes of infertility. How is your work coming along? Is there any chance of a cure yet? I pray for this, day and night, as surely, this must be God's ultimate plan."

"I've been so busy with the cloning that there has been little time for the basic research recently," she stammered, taken aback by the directness of the Archbishop's remarks. It had been months since anyone had mentioned her work on infertility as it had become clear that her research and attempts to find fertile couple at the Fertility Clinic in Rana Mansions had been a complete failure. But how could she explain her important role in the cloning project? The embryonic modules that she'd designed and had been used for years in the agricultural field had been the basis of the success. But, now the general public were not interested in farm animals. It was the clone babies that were important and Michael had been the person to make that possible.

"But you know, Archbishop," she said spontaneously, trying to defend her lack of success in the way scientists always do. "We need more money. Most of the resources go into the cloning work and the best scientists have all been absorbed in the new production units. There has been so much to do. Finding a cure is costly in time and funds. We urgently need more money devoted to the search for a drug."

"I will have to see what I can do," the Archbishop volunteered, sensing concern in Karen's voice. "I hear that the Omega Corps have established a Fertility Fund. Yes, indeed. Why not?" he continued, thinking out loud as they moved inside, following the President and the first lady to dinner. "This would give a focus for the Omega Corps and keep them out of mischief. Is that not a good idea, Michael?" he said, looking for spontaneous support and at the same time probing behind coolness he saw lingering in Michael's eyes.

"That would be a great help," Michael smiled, greeting the suggestion with subdued enthusiasm. "In fact, I want Karen to concentrate on her research now that the first batch is through. You know I could not have succeeded without her help."

"It was a very successful collaboration," Bernard intervened. "Indeed, successful in more ways than one, if I may say so." Everyone laughed and were relaxed as they took their seats around the President's table, already anticipating a grand wedding feast in the Palace.

It was a select and influential group that had been invited to dinner and Michael was relieved to see that Harry and Tessa were not present. For some days it had been praying on his mind that Tessa and Harry may have also been invited as the President had previously been so keen to see that Harry was involved as father of the clone. But Harry would have been out of place in such company and although Tessa was all right for a brief encounter on the hay, she would have been terrified at the thought of sitting around the President's table. In contrast, Karen was in her element, completely at ease and the centre of attention. She was radiant and glowing and he was so proud of her. They were just right together. Yes, she should go back to her research for a cure for infertility. That would keep her happy even though he had lost hope in that direction. There was another route. There was a lot could be done with the clone now it was established. The whole field of Celtic genetics was now open before him and as a Master of Emanon his influence would grow by the hour. The new technology meant that a whole new society could be designed and cloned. As one of the few scientists in the Guild of Masters, he could lead the way. Well-designed babies would become a reality. Under his guidance, the Celts would lead the world.

His appointment as a Master had to be sanctioned by the Holy Fathers and by the end of the evening Michael had agreed that in future a Father would be present at each birth of a clone baby. The child would be washed in the holy waters from the Great Falls of Shanna. She would be blessed and in this way, a Soul would enter and transform the baby. Later they would be taken to the Great Falls of Shanna to complete their Rebirth.

It was all against Michael's basic principles and long held

views about the religious dogmas of Emanon, but these myths were hard to prove wrong. Bernard and Karen were happy enough with the scheme and the President had obviously sorted this out with the Archbishop beforehand. Moreover he was fully aware of the unspoken commitment he had given to the Fathers on willingly accepting the Chain of a Master of Emanon. He felt the weight of the Holy Cross in his lap and fondled the cold heavy gold chain as he chatted to the President's wife about his youth and mountaineering exploits.

The evening was long and the wine had flowed freely and by the time they left the palace Michael's mind was in turmoil. Thoughts and visions that had lapped around his subconscious when he had first seen the babies being delivered now crystallised. Would this gold chain that encircled his being, anchor him to the past or give him the strength to haul Emanon into the future?

There was great joy in success and fame and Michael lay awake well into the early morning and did not notice that Karen had wept herself to sleep.

Chapter Twenty One

Harry had looked forward to having Little Greta home. Unfortunately, his expectations and hopes for a healthy vigorous child, contented and happy like Sophie, were soon to be shattered.
    Within a few days of the first deliveries of the cloned babies it had become obvious that they were weakly, highly strung and very easily "upset". Rumours had spread around the clinic. They said that some nurses had been rejected by the clone. Indeed a few nurses had consistently induced a chorus of cries and shrieks of distress when they entered the ward. Others were popular and the babies lay quietly and contented when they were on duty. "They'll do better when you have them home and they get more attention," the nurses would say, and parents were encouraged to take their infants home as soon as possible.
    Tessa and Harry had been allowed to move into a larger apartment pending Greta's arrival. But Little Greta was very fragile. She didn't suckle her bottle for any length of time and cried a lot and put on weight very slowly compared to what Tessa had experienced with Sophie, whom she had breast fed.
    "She doesn't see me," Harry said, concerned, as he held the infant in his arms and looked into her eyes, trying to get her attention.
    "She sees all right," Tessa said, reassuring him. "I've seen her reach for things, but I don't think she responds to us, yet. She's not...." Tessa hesitated as she did not want to continually compare Little Greta's progress with Sophie's, and she knew how disappointed and upset Harry was about the rumours that his daughters were not only going to be midgets but may also be retarded. Tessa went on, "the doctors have said not to worry as they have everything under control and it would just take time for babies to settle in after leaving all their sisters. They probably miss each other. Just like identical twins, but even more so."
    Tessa regretted what she had said. Doctors were a sore point with Harry. Gradually after the birth of the clone, his resentment of doctors returned to an even greater extent.
    "They always say they know," Harry murmured, trying to keep his temper. "They should have been able to tell that something

was wrong before getting so many babies started. They rushed into mass production before they had a clue as to what they'd be really like."

"They were so sure of themselves," Tessa agreed. Trying to avoid another angry outburst, she added, laughing sarcastically. "They even made that Dr Rand a Master. Unless things improve the President will look a real fool." Tessa had been horrified at the realisation that Dr Rand had been her 'Mike' and was Sophie's real father, but had buried this fact deep in the back of her mind. It was impossible. They just looked alike. Surely he would have said something, contacted her, by now. She may just have imagined that he'd recognised her that day at the Institute after the Omega attack. Anyway, who would believe her against the word of someone like Dr Rand. And if he really wanted, he could take Sophie away from her. He was so powerful now. Harry need never know who Sophie's father was. It was best to forget him. It would upset Harry and she loved him so much now. Harry had accepted Sophie as his own daughter and they were happy except for the nagging worry about Little Greta.

"I'm sure it's all Rand's fault," Harry snapped. "When they were born, it was all his clone. He never once referred to me or Greta. Now the newspapers are saying there was a defect in one of the parents and that the doctors had never been told. My God, Tessa, we had never been asked. Of course, Greta had gypsy blood in her. Thousands of people have. It was all in her records. They just never damn well looked. They were in such a hurry to get the foetus that they never asked us anything about her parents or grandparents. The foetus was just taken in such a hurry. Greta was left to die. If they'd asked Greta's parents anything they'd have been told her father was a gypsy. Now they blame me! God it's a good job they are sending me back to the Rock in a few weeks. If I get near Rand again I'm liable to throttle him."

"But she is beautiful," Tessa said quietly, to humour him, lifting Greta and bouncing her in the air. "My beautiful petite gypsy girl."

Little Greta had eventually gone to sleep in Harry's arms. He got up to put her into her cot, moving very slowly and carefully, trying to prevent her from waking and having another bout of crying.

"Something will have to be done," he said, coming back from the nursery. He sat down, stretching his long legs, half across the small room. "I'll have to go back to the Rock in a few weeks and I can't leave you to look after Greta and Sophie. It's far too much to expect of you. How are you going to manage when I'm away?" Harry's special leave was now nearing an end and he was planning to travel to Southport for a brief visit to his parents before leaving for his three months period of duty.

"Don't worry, Harry," Tessa assured him, "I've asked Cara to come and stay for a while. Soon we will be allowed to go back to Dunfooey and live with my parents. It will be better for the children there in the mountains. Little Greta might do better there. Cara has relatives in a village near Dunfooey and is thinking of going to live there too, for Mel's sake. We'll be all right," Tessa continued, enthusiastically, "once we get to Dunfooey, mother will help to look after both of us. I'm so glad that they're allowing us to go back home, now that the Fertility Clinic is being closed."

"It's a shame. After all the hope that the fertile people would have more children it has all failed. Isn't there a feeling of hopelessness in the Mansions. I'm glad to be going back to the Rock," Harry said, "but I'll be back in the spring," Harry said quietly. Part of him was excited by the prospect of being back at his work on the Rock. But deep down he knew that he was going to miss Tessa and Sophie and his own restless Little Greta.

There was a weak cry from the nursery and then a demanding screech and their hope for a quiet evening, chatting and planning, vanished.

At first Harry nursed the baby, but she continued to wail. Tessa and Harry fell silent, their eyes telling of their continual frustration and exhaustion that Little Greta's arrival had brought to their life. Eventually, unable able to stand the noise of the tantrum any longer, Tessa opened the door into the outer landing. She saw the large number, Level 19, painted on the wall opposite. She looked up and down the corridor. No one was around, but she'd expected that any moment doors would open and angry and frustrated neighbours would scowl and tell her to keep the damn thing quiet. She came back and nodded to Harry. He carried the infant, wrapped in a warm blanket, down the long corridor to the central foyer where a number of landings merged. There were already a number of parents in the foyer nursing their infants, most of whom were screeching and crying. The parents moved close, touching the infants together and gradually the noise subsided and Rana Mansions became quiet again.

The parents nodded, some smiled, some scowled and they moved carefully back to their apartments, hoping that that would be the last 'upset' until morning.

Chapter Twenty Two

Karen had stayed late at the Institute after everyone else had gone. She had a key to the Pharmacy store. She slipped in, switching on the light in the dark room and searched along the shelves. She soon found a pile of small cardboard boxes that were covered in dust and hadn't been touched for years.

Back in the lab Karen took a small bottle from her coat pocket containing a sample of her urine. Within minutes she had carried out the test. She remained calm. She discarded the solutions and pocketing the remainder of the test kit, left the lab and hurried home. Karen made herself a simple meal and then settled down in an armchair, relaxed, looking back over her dairy of the past few months and trying to remember the details of her relationship with Michael. There were nagging thoughts at the back of her mind that excited her even more than the recent knowledge that she was pregnant. She realised that if Michael could father two children in such a short space of time when the rest of the world was infertile, it was no mere chance. There must be a common factor. A link between what happened to the girl Tessa and herself. Yes, it must be more than just having sex with Michael. There must be something else. The timing was right. It could have been sometime during their vacation around Dunfooey or just after coming back to the city. There was a link. She was sure of it.

Later in the evening, she did the test again on a fresh sample and it was still positive. How would Michael react? When would she tell him? He had been strange during the past weeks since the birth of the clone. He was tired out and the strain of the past year was telling on him. He needed her support as much as she needed his. She felt sure that the effects of the publicity and all the fame would pass and he'd soon be his old self, dedicated to his science. They were reconciled about his brief affair with Tessa and were already planning a big public wedding in the Palace and arrangements for the event were well underway.

At the Institute there was so much work to do now that they had found the growth defect in the cloned cells of the little girls and had to try and correct it before further batches were started. It could be done, but it would take time and the whole cloning programme would be held up, perhaps for years, unless another embryo or foetus could be found.

Oh, but how a child of their own would keep them together! It would give a fresh direction to their research. Perhaps it would make Michael as interested in finding a cure for infertility as she was instead of being so possessed with designing babies. Certainly the birth of her child would ensure more support for her own researches, especially now that she had a real clue to what a cure might be.

It was well past midnight by the time Michael arrived back from the Meeting of the Guild of Masters. He had been drinking again. It had been a wonderful evening and he had met all the leading Masters of Emanon. He had been elected onto the Council of Masters and his speech about his vision of the future of Emanon had got a great reception. His new position entitled him to wear the ancient garments of the Guild and he'd brought them home to show Karen. He was anxious to lay them out on the bed and to try them on.

She thought he looked ridiculous dressed up in the ancient garb, that had been passed on for uncountable generations. He was excited, like a child playing with new toys. "Take my photograph." "Do you like this one?" It was early morning before his excitement had abated and they went to bed, Karen exhausted and Michael, finally satisfied, asleep.

Karen was awake and up early. She'd been sick again and another test showed a positive result. She would have to tell Michael at breakfast. He would be away for five days visiting Production Units in Southport and other cities around Emanon. She couldn't wait until he'd come back.

Michael was alert and fresh at breakfast, looking forward to his trip to the other cities. He was sure to be especially welcomed at each of them by the city Masters. He was drinking his third cup of coffee when Karen felt she could hold back her news no longer.

"Michael," she said, the urgency in her voice immediately attracting his attention. "I've something important to tell you. Will you put away those papers for a minute? Please."

"What is it?" he snapped, his mind now focused on the business of the day.

Michael, I'm pregnant. You've made me pregnant. You're fertile. We're going to have a child. Not just a clone child, but a real child. Oh, darling, isn't it wonderful? We now have a real clue to a cure."

Michael's cup of coffee stopped half way to his mouth. His hand trembled and coffee spilt over the rim onto the light grey jacket of his suit.

"You're sure?"

"Yes. Definitely. I've done three positive tests and I've been sick every morning this week."

"That's wonderful," he said as he came round the table and clasped Karen in his arms. They kissed and she held onto him tightly and the tears streamed down her cheeks. "Oh, I'm so glad you're happy about it. I so much want a child. I had given up all hope. There were so many disappointments with Claude for all those years. Now suddenly I'm pregnant. I just can't believe it."

"Now listen, Karen, you be careful," Michael instructed, showing genuine concern and as much delight with the unexpected news as Karen. "Go and see Dr Stirling this morning. Get everything confirmed and arranged. We must be sure everything goes correctly, this time."

"There's plenty of time for that, darling, first we must find the link with Dunfooey." She knew that Michael was too smart to miss the obvious connection and had assumed that he would be already speculating and getting excited about the various research options were opened up.

"Oh, I don't think there's any connection. It's just pure chance. We'll talk about it when I get back, but in the meantime you go and see Dr Stirling. You must register the pregnancy. It's the law."

"Can't you cancel this trip, just for a day or two."

"No, I can't. I'm sorry. This trip is very important. The programme is all arranged. I'll be back by the end of the week and I'll ring you every night. I promise."

They kissed again at the door as the driver carried Michael's case to the waiting car and they waved enthusiastically as the car sped off to the airport to catch the early plane to Southport.

Karen returned alone to the house and sipped her cold cup of coffee. What had he meant? 'Correctly, this time.' 'Dr Stirling.' He was head of the Institute's surgical team, not her private doctor. What did Michael mean? . Of course, there was the Cloning Law, which clearly stated that all foetuses were the property of Emanon while the emergency lasted and that the Palace could decide whether to continue or terminate a pregnancy. Karen realised that the novel pin-hole surgery operation provided additional hope that a small amount of foetal tissue could be removed while still allowing the baby to come to term. But would it not be too early for that yet? No, Michael would soon grasp the importance of the connection with Dunfooey. Surely he must see that a vital clue was staring him in the face. Although he might have to admit that he had also an illegitimate daughter that was unimportant compared to finding a cure.

Chapter Twenty Three

Michael had a first class ticket and if lucky he would have plenty of room to work or relax during the short flight to Southport. His head had not cleared completely after his heavy drinking the previous evening and the bombshell that Karen had planted on his breakfast table. He was delighted. He was fertile. But how should he proceed. Karen clearly wanted to have the baby, but was that the best choice?

His Master's Pass gave him a speedy transfer through the passenger lounge and he had settled into his luxury seat in good time for take off. He had chosen a window seat and on checking in he had asked if the neighbouring aisle seat could be kept free, so he had spread his papers and items over it. He was glancing over the morning papers awaiting take-off, when a voice in his ear pulled him abruptly out of his private world.

"Excuse me, sir."

Michael looked up into the smiling eyes of a glamorous hostess who was bending down towards him. An aura of perfume enveloped him. Dark brown eyes, smiling from the fine smooth tanned face, melted away his initial irritation at being disturbed.

"Good morning, Katrina," Michael said, noting her name on her lapel badge. He returned the smile, expecting to be offered some breakfast.

"Good morning, sir," said the hostess, smiling again as she bent closer obviously wishing to say something personal. Michael stretched forward over the spare seat to hear her above the noise of the idling engines. "We have a little problem, sir, and I wonder if you would mind helping. I know you're a Master, sir, but I wonder if you would be so kind as to help."

"But of course, my dear," Michael responded without hesitation and inhaled another lungful of delicious scented air. "What can I do for you?"

"Well, sir, the flight is full this morning except for this vacant seat."

Michael spontaneously began to gather the papers he'd spread out on the neighbouring seat. "Oh, I'm so sorry," he murmured, feeling a little guilty and embarrassed, momentarily assuming and hoping that she wanted to use the spare seat beside him during take off.

"That's all right, sir, but one of the passengers is a rather large gentleman. He really should have reserved first class. I hope you don't mind." The hostess smiled again and added, "I knew you wouldn't," as though she had known Michael for a long time.

"Of course not," Michael laughed, accepting the misunderstanding between them but smiling back. "There's no problem. I'll just clear away these papers."

Within seconds, Katrina appeared again through the doorway and came down the aisle. Michael froze in his seat, his hands clasping the armrests. At first he had the sensation that gravity was pressing him into the back of the seat, but it was the sight of Harry Atkins that had appeared, his head of red hair ducking under the arch of the doorway. Harry came plodding down the aisle, his hands grasping the tops of the seats in order to steady himself against the motion of the plane. Katrina stood in the aisle, smiling and waiting for Harry to get into his seat.

"This is more your size, sir." Michael watched her smile at Harry, the same synthetic smile that had melted him a few moments ago. "I hope you'll both be comfortable. It was very good of you, sir." She flashed a special smile at Michael and was gone down the aisle.

"My God, it's you." Harry said, as he squeezed into the seat and struggled to find his seat belt. Michael moved to the left, making room for the extra bit of body that entered his domain. Harry's elbow strayed close to Michael's chin as he eventually fastened the belt just before take-off.

"I didn't expect to see you here," Michael managed to say, avoiding the roving elbow.

"That's better," Harry added as he got settled into his seat. They both glanced out the window as the plane soared to its cruising height and then banked into the sun as they flew southwards away from the towering blocks of the city and out over the deep morning blue of Lough Rana. "They had me in a small seat at the back and I could hardly breathe. Hope you don't mind? When I go out to the Rock they always give me a double seat. I don't normally travel on these commercial lines. Our Company helijets have much more room. Have you got enough room?" he added looking sideways at Michael who seemed to have shrivelled in size. Michael was glad that Harry had folded his massive arms across his chest and he was no longer in danger of getting accidentally decapitated.

"How's your little girl?" Michael hadn't seen Harry since the morning of the first delivery day and then only briefly. He remembered catching a quick glance of Tessa as she had looked down from the gallery at him.

"Oh, Little Greta's giving us a terrible time. Not growing at all. I think she's wasting away. No sleep again last night. That's why I nearly missed the flight this morning."

"God, it's all been most unfortunate," Michael sympathised, defending the official line on the tragedy that had plagued the first attempts at cloning. "It was always a gamble. We just hadn't enough time to check out everything before the pregnancies stopped."

"What will happen now?" Harry queried. He had heard rumours that more embryos were being aborted, and that some of the staff in the Production Units had objected. "Are you killing off the rest of them?"

"Oh, now, Harry. We don't just kill them off. We terminate the cultures. We close down the modules. You must try and not look on them as real pregnancies."

"I'm sorry, Dr Rand, but this all brings back to me what happened to my first wife. All your modules contain my daughters. Have I no say in what happens to them?" Harry felt his heart pounding in his chest. He knew he must stop pursuing that trend of thought that made him so angry. Certainly not here. But Rand was the man who had murdered his daughter!.

"I understand what you must feel, Mr Atkins, but you must not live in the past. Your new wife, what's she called?"

"Tessa."

"Surely Tessa and you have a new life ahead of you now. Hasn't she got a baby girl?" Michael sensed the smouldering anger in Harry's words.

"I know. I'm very lucky to have found Tessa. She's wonderful and really helped me through the bad patches after my wife's death. And Sophie is just great. She's a beautiful child."

It was obvious from the tone of Harry's voice that Tessa had never mentioned the fact that he was Sophie's father. In spite of his promises to Karen, Michael thought a lot about Tessa and Sophie and he hoped that someday he'd be able to meet with Tessa and occasionally dreamt about seeing his daughter, but the fear that a scandal would jeopardise his career prevented him from making contact.

"But my little Greta will never grow up to be like that," Harry added, his tone half-blaming Michael.

"If only the Law had been made earlier we may have had more success." Michael said in self-defence. "It's such a pity that your little girls are so retarded," Michael remembered the day well and how they all waited anxiously at the Institute for the foetus to arrive. "You see, I think it was the lack of oxygen during the long delay after your wife's accident. You know she was on a life support machine for days. Not the ideal conditions for foetal development. Even if the child had been born it may well have turned out the same. It means that we need to get foetal tissue very young to do this cloning successfully." His words had been partly said to put the blame on Harry, but suddenly he realised what he had said. The revelation that had been staring him in the face for months, now forced his hand on the life of his own future child. He knew that the surgical teams were still on stand-by and could move as soon as a pregnancy was reported. Karen would visit Dr Stirling in the afternoon. They must take a foetal biopsy directly. He squeezed past Harry, "Excuse me, excuse me. I must make an urgent phone call. Excuse me. I'll be back in a minute."

Michael had just returned to his seat when Katrina brought them their light breakfast on a disposable plastic tray.

"She's a lovely girl," Michael murmured, nodding at the hostess as she moved away down the aisle and he started to pick his way through the small plate of prawns. -Then the truth suddenly dawned. He saw it all clearly. His being fertile, the relationship of Dunfooey, Tessa and Karen, were all tied together by a link that could only be associated with seafood. Could seafood really be the cure for infertility as Karen had tried to tell him earlier? But more urgently, this was an opportunity for cloning his own child? Of course he could understand Karen wanting to have the baby. But his vision of a clone society, his ambition and the thought of his son being cloned had momentarily clouded his reason. But, yes, it was better to go ahead. The cure for infertility could be dealt with later.

Later that night from his hotel room in Southport, Michael tried a number of times to phone Karen at their home, but was unable to get a reply. There was no answer from her office at the Institute. He shook his head, exasperated and took another long sip of white bubbly wine from the tall glass that was on the bedside table. "I'll try again in the morning," he said, glancing over to Katrina who was watching him over the edge of her long narrow wine glass. "I can't do much more now," he added, satisfied that he had done all he could. "You're very beautiful, my dear," he smiled into her eyes as he slipped under the sheet beside her.

## Chapter Twenty Four

"I gave you a call," Karen said, as the door to the apartment on the 19th floor of the Rana Mansions opened. "I'm Dr Rowlands from the Institute. Maybe you remember me?"

"Of course," Tessa said, smiling through the tiredness in her eyes. "I've seen you often. Have you come to see Little Greta? Do come in."

Karen followed Tessa into the small lounge and she sat down on the settee. She waited for a few minutes while Tessa lifted the screeching infant out of the cot and tried to quieten her by offering her a fresh bottle of milk.

"How's she keeping? Is she still very fretful?" Karen asked, knowing only too well the difficulties that the parents had been having with the clone babies.

"It's the others," Tessa replied. "I'm sure it's the others. They're quiet when together, but are so demanding when they're alone with us. I hope to take her back home to Dunfooey soon and maybe she'll forget the others there."

"Look, Tessa, I'm sorry for intruding into your private life but I must talk to you. It's very personal. Do you mind?"

"No, of course not."

"I've been in hospital. I was pregnant. They wanted me to let them take some of the foetal cells for the cloning programme. You may have heard that they have developed a prenatal operation, using pinhole surgery, that allows a small section of foetal tissue to be removed. I thought it was too early, but they said it wasn't and of course I had to agree. It's the law. But, unfortunately, there was a post-operative complication and I've lost the baby. They say I probably would have had a miscarriage, anyway, even if I hadn't had the surgery."

"Oh, I'm so sorry, Dr Rowlands. I thought you looked pale. Can I get you something to drink, a cup of coffee, perhaps?" Tessa offered, covering the strained silence that followed Karen's comments.

"Thanks. I'm all right, now. I half expected it. I kept thinking that I'd be special. That they'd allow me to be different. But of course they couldn't."

"Did your husband - you are married now?" Tessa added, blushing slightly, realising the complexities of the situation. "Did he not try to stop them?"

"He says that he tried, but I'm not sure how hard. The rumour at the Institute is that he gave instructions by phone to follow the regulations. As a Master of Emanon he could not be seen to break the Law." Karen said softly, tears streaming down her cheeks.

"Actually, Dr Rowlands, Harry told me that your husband had travelled out to Southport with him and that he'd been very upset and made an urgent phone call from the plane about something."

"I can guess what it was about." Karen said coldly. "I believe it was taken early, despite what I was told. It was taken so that Michael can perfect the cloning technology. The younger the foetal tissue is the better. It has always been the procedure with animals. We've known that for a long time but never paid much attention to it. When there's no shortage of material the question never rises."

"Oh! How horrible," Tessa said. "I'd have thought that your husband of all people would have been able to have stopped it."

"No, Tessa. Dr Rand is not my husband and I never want to see him again. I heard from a relative who works in the hotel in Southport that he'd spent the night with some young woman even when he knew what was happening to me. I cannot face him. I will never go back to him."

"I don't think he's a very faithful man?" Tessa said quietly, looking at Karen and sensing that her secret was known.

"But Tessa, I didn't come to talk to you about myself. I want to talk to you about something else, something very personal. I hope you don't mind?"

"What is it?" Tessa sat forward on the edge of the settee.

"I think you know Michael. Did you not meet him in Dunfooey last year?" Her voice was quiet and direct and she looked searchingly into Tessa's eyes, pleading for honesty and friendship and understanding.

Tessa hesitated. She was embarrassed and confused. She had forced herself to forget Mike. Of course he had swept her off her feet during that hot summer evening when she had allowed herself to fall under his spell. Briefly she had hoped that he'd have come back. He'd had a magic that she'd never quite forget and when she'd seen him again accidentally at the Institute it had stirred her imagination beyond reality. It was her private secret, not even Harry knew about it. It was something from the past, something to be kept as a dream. It was Sophie that was real. She was the real living expression of a heady youthful moment of passion that now gave her and Harry so much joy and love. It was Sophie that had brought them together and had welded a loving bond between them.

"Yes. He was holidaying around Dunfooey. I was a waitress in the Inn." Tessa admitted. "But everyone believes that Sophie is Harry's child. I wouldn't want Mike to interfere. How did you know?"

"We visited Dunfooey a while ago. Someone recognised him, someone who must be very fond of you. He told him you'd had a baby, and that he'd raped you!"

"Oh, No! That'll be Frank Tooley. He's a dear, sweet friend. We're cousins," Tessa smiled. "I can just imagine him. He'd frighten him on purpose. But he's never told me."

"Well, Tessa, that's not important now. The thing that I want to ask you about is related to my pregnancy as well as yours. You see, I believe that it is very strange that Michael has made two of us pregnant inside two years when practically everyone else is infertile. Maybe there is something special about him or there's something special about us, but more likely there's something in common about what led up to the pregnancy."

"I see what you mean." Tessa was curled up on the big chair, making room for Sophie and Little Greta beside her.

"First, we were both at Dunfooey. We were staying at the same Inn as you had worked at."

"Yes. We made love in the barn at the back."

"That might not be so important. But can you remember what you ate during your time with Michael? Had you anything unusual?"

"My God, it was a long time ago. Why yes, we did have a special meal at the Inn on the evening of my day off, after we'd been on the beach. We had the seafood speciality of the region. Mike loved it. I remember he asked for a second helping."

"Exactly. Michael loved it. We had it too. He was so fond of it that we brought some home and we've had it a number of times. I made a special meal to celebrate the birth of the first clone girls and we ate a lot of it that night as well. You see, Tessa, it fits exactly with the time I conceived."

"You know my grandfather always said that seaweeds were

good for making babies. It's an old wives tale of the region."

"He was probably right. I've looked up the records and nearly all the last pregnancies have been from coastal regions. Harry's first wife was from the south coast. You're from the north. The spread of infertility has been mainly from the cities. There must be something in one of the rare exotic sea foods that is an antidote to infertility."

"But what can we do? There are dozens of possible fish or seafoods that may contain a cure. It could take years to find it. It could be very rare and expensive, local people very seldom eat it."

"Maybe so, Tessa. But we have to try. I want your help. You know the people at Dunfooey. I want to set up a laboratory there and sample and test the local products. Talk to the local people. I believe that the clue to curing our infertility must lie around the coasts. There is something in the sea that we must find. You see, Tessa, for years my research has been trying to find a cure for infertility. Unfortunately we still don't know what the cause is. Only that there is a defect in the very basic process of meiosis, such that viable sperm and ova cannot be formed."

"There is something in the environment, probably a pollutant or toxic chemical in the water supply. For centuries our industries have been polluting the environment, and I believe that the effect can be overcome by a component of sea food, probably one of the exotic shell fish."

"But why has this work stopped at the Institute? Surely the government would want to get a cure?" Tessa queried.

"Well you see we are not making any progress here. There is no sign of viable sperm or ova in all our testing. What I want now is a new laboratory in a region where we have direct access to seafood of a greatest variety. And also I must get away from here."

"Well, Dunfooey's the place. There is a great variety of sea foods all around the coast."

"Also, Tessa, I cannot work in the Institute any more. Now that Michael has been made a Master of Emanon he has become impossible to work with. I know that already he has started genetic experiments on the girl embryos, trying to improve them. I disagree with him and so do the Fathers. But Michael has convinced the President and the Council of Masters that his route is the only way forward. His powers of persuasion and charm are very strong and they don't seem to be able to resist him. They are so blinded by the glamour of our nation being at the forefront of the cloning technology and leading the world that they are oblivious to the real dangers."

"Look, Dr Rowlands," Tessa was beginning to relax and feel part of a great new adventure with this stranger who had come to her, revealing her deepest secret, but needing her help, "I'm going back to Dunfooey next week. We've decided that Little Greta and Sophie would be better brought up in the fresh air of the mountains than here in the city. Harry has gone back to the Rock. I'll be glad to get back home. But why don't you come too. You need a rest. You can have a holiday. Stay with my folks, or at the Inn, if you'd prefer. You can meet Frank Tooley. He's a marine biologist and is the warden of the nature reserve. You'll like Frank. He will know all about the sea foods."

From the moment she had entered the apartment, Karen had taken a liking to Tessa. Ever since learning of her affair with Michael she had been jealous of her. She realised that Michael had gone back to Dunfooey with a secret hope of seeing Tessa again. Karen had often wondered what would have happened if Tessa had still been there. Would he have taken her again? She had watched Tessa jealously. Tessa had everything, a beautiful daughter of her own, Sophie, and now Little Greta and that big strong faithful man, Harry. But face to face, Tessa was gentle, open and honest.

Karen reached for baby Sophie and held her up. The infant responded to her smiles and gurgled with delight, "Da, da," the infant managed to utter, stretching out her hand to catch hold of Karen's dark hair that hung over her left shoulder. She tried to imagine Michael as the father of this beautiful child. She had his bright blue eyes and there was a hint of the roguishness on her lips that made Michael so devastatingly irresistible.

"She's like her father," Tessa read Karen's thoughts, "the nice bits," she added, laughing.

"You know, if the new clone boys survive, she'll be their half sister," Karen said, dreaming aloud. "I wonder will they ever meet? She's going to have a difficult life."

"My family at Dunfooey half believed that Sophie was a miracle as I'd kept my pregnancy a secret for so long. There were even rumours that she was the second coming, the new Christ! I half believed it myself for a while. I must tell Harry. He will understand. But I'll not tell Sophie until she's grown up or until she asks. She will believe that Harry is her daddy."

"Yes, Tessa," Karen said, preparing to leave, "I will come to

Dunfooey. I'll ask Archbishop Longfellow about funding a research lab there. He did say something about the Omega Corps raising funds for fertility research, but I don't know what its being used for. Perhaps I can get the Corps to fund a research facility that will be independent of the government." Yes, this was the way forward. She could not stay in Konburg and be near Michael or the Institute when her sons were growing in her modules without having any control of them. Her new knowledge of Michael's private dreams made her sick - God knows what he intended to do with them, now that he'd developed genetic manipulation techniques to such an advanced level. With other countries now entering the race, the previous international collaborations and scientific exchanges that had made the technology possible, were vanishing. Nationalistic urges for survival had become the predominant focus of government support. When the cards were down and survival was the big issue, the aim was no longer merely to clone a human, but to clone the 'best' human, the best Emanon, the best Celt, the best Scot, the best Welshman, the best English man, the best German, the best Arab, the best Jew. Every ethnic and so-called nationalistic grouping would want their own special genes to survive. The selfish genes that had helped to made biological evolution a success and nationalism inevitable, now saw an alternative method of reproduction that would eliminate individual freedom and risk and provide a platform for nationalistic excesses that never before existed. What had she done in building the Embryonic Modules? She was amazed at just how rapidly they had become exploited by the most primitive biological urges. Now Michael was already planning to correct the defects in the little girls. He had told the President that he could replace their gypsy genes! And then he had other passions and desires. He was convinced that he had a special role to play in the design, salvation and perfection of the race of Emanons, produced and engineered to his ideal specification. Karen could no longer be part of his fantasy and yet the ageing President was pouring money into the scheme, convinced that Michael was on the right lines to save Emanon from extinction. The old man was enamoured by the success of the initial attempts and convinced by Michael's promises for the future. Although international collaboration had now practically ceased, President Neilson was enraged by the fact that the Emanon-based technology, developed by Karen, was now being used in other countries, apparently with great success as they had started to clone from foetal tissue much earlier. Michael had convinced him that the scientists had been right, that the old Church dogmas had held Emanon back. Now the President saw that every effort would have to be made to catch up before his nation was too weak to prevent take over by neighbouring countries, greedy for their rich resources of gas and grass.

Yes, she would go with Tessa. She held Sophie tightly, kissing her on the cheek. Oh, how she wanted a little baby, to cuddle and love! Why had she not been allowed to have her baby? Would Michael follow them to Dunfooey. Would he try to claim Sophie? She must protect her. Help to educate and raise her so that she would be able to handle the future. Even if they found a cure for the infertility, Sophie would be one of the few young normal people by the time she'd grown up. Sophie responded to the cuddles and kisses with beams and gurgles of delight. Tears were streaming from Karen's eyes when her private reverie was interrupted by the shrill of the doorbell. Karen froze. Had Michael followed her?

"Oh, that'll be my friend, Cara." Tessa said, sensing Karen's shock. "She said she'd call. You'll like her." Tessa got up carrying little Greta to open the door.

Cara came in, as usual, a bundle of energy, enthusiasm and dedication. Sophie reached for her with recognition and affection and Karen, embarrassed, wiped her eyes and felt a pang of jealousy as Sophie cuddled into Cara's arms.

"Cara is the organiser of our local Omega Corps committee," Tessa said, having introduced Cara as her oldest friend in Konburg. "You know the Corps is organising the Fertility Campaign that was set up by the Archbishop."

"Oh, how interesting," Karen said, looking at Cara with in a new light. "I'd heard that the Fathers were going to support the Fertility Programme, but the Council of Masters have ridiculed it saying that previous money had been wasted. I have not heard much about the Omega Corps since some hooligans attacked the Institute."

"That's most unfortunate," Cara interrupted. "We've now become better organised and the rougher elements have been controlled. We just want to see fertility back again and if clone people are going to be part of normal life they will have to be Reborn. It stands to reason." Cara was simple and direct and her enthusiasm and belief were infectious. Tessa explained what Karen was intending to do at Dunfooey and suggested that the Omega Fund might help.

"Why, certainly," Cara volunteered on behalf of her committee. Her active mind had been tossing over a possibility that would be attractive during Tessa's brief outline of Karen's situation. "In fact, Dr Rowlands, our committee had just been speaking about you the other evening. We were wondering if you would be willing to become our President. Your name would attract a lot of support."

Karen was taken aback by the directness of Cara's suggestion but she had quickly realised how important it was to tap into the Omega funding that may well now become the only support for the fertility programme.

"Why, Cara, that is kind of you." Karen sensed that Cara's suggestion was instantaneous rather than planned, but she admired the rapid assessment of the situation that the Omega leader had made. "I'd be honoured to be the President of your campaign. I think it is best if everyone knows that there is a chance of a return to normal fertility, even though it may be some years away yet."

"There's a committee meeting tomorrow and I'll put your name on the Agenda. Your support will be a great boost to our movement and it's just what we need. We must stop this evil that will ruin Emanon." They talked more about the move to Dunfooey and agreed that their discussions about a laboratory there should be kept secret and that they would delay announcing her joining the Omega Corps until she was well settled into her new life in the north.

Chapter Twenty Five

The journey from Dunfooey to the Great Falls of Shanna had been exhausting for Little Greta who although now ten years old had remained very fragile and petite. Whole families, including a number of other clone girls as well as the few normal children like Sophie and Mel had been brought on the journey to attend the special Rebirth ceremony.

Their tiredness vanished as they approached the ancient city of Tanark and the atmosphere in the coach became carnival-like. To Sophie, the city was enormous compared to the tiny village of Dunfooey. She sat in a window seat beside her adopted aunt Karen who pointed out the various building they passed. "That's the university, right along the banks of the Shanna. You'll go there someday. I know you will." Her aunt Karen had said as they passed the university campus and Sophie sighed, "but it's so big!" Karen had been helping to teach her and knew that young Sophie was very intelligent. As the coach approached the centre, the magnificent granite cathedral with towering spires and sparkling windows loomed above them making her gasp with wonder and she could not take her eyes of the great stone monuments covered with intrigue designs that guarded the entrance to the wide avenue up to the main square. The streets were packed. People from all parts of Emanon thronged along the wide pavements or sat in coffee bars under shades shielding them from the bright sunlight. Everyone was in light summer shirts and frocks and the sound of music seemed to be everywhere. The crowds were happy and rejoicing. Groups were singing and chanting hymns and choruses. Soon the party from Dunfooey were settled into their hotel. Sophie and Greta's room had a small balcony that gave a narrow glimpse of the Great Falls Shanna in the distance. She enjoyed her first shower and although refreshed and eager to go out was soon curled up in a clean crisp sheeted bed with Little Greta sound asleep in her arms, dreaming of tomorrow.

Without breakfast, and dressed in long white towelling robes, they joined the queue at the top of the stone steps leading down the steep gorge to the black pool at the foot of the Great Falls, the dawn mist still clung to the cliff face. As the sun rose and illuminated the chasm, they could pick out far below the tiny figures of the Fathers immersing the little children in the cold flowing waters. Cries echoed up the cliff face, countered only by the chimes of bells from the cathedral. As the queue moved downwards Sophie could see the Fathers in their purple robes, their Holy Crosses dangling around their necks on golden chains. Would they really put a Soul into her little sister? Would she become well and be able to talk? Sophie had great expectations for the effect of the Rebirth on Little Greta and was certain that it would be a success. For weeks and months she had prayed every night that the miracle of Rebirth would make Greta normal. In spite of her backwardness, Sophie loved the gentle petite, dark haired girl, who had become so popular with everyone in the village. Of course, like all her sisters, Little Greta was prone to tantrums, but provided they remembered to give her the tablets she was a happy child and although she had never learnt to talk, read or write, she was agile, alert and attractive.

As they neared the edge of the river Sophie drew back and held Karen's hand, watching Harry who was carrying Little Greta. Sophie prayed and pressed Tessa and Karen's hands tightly as they watched Harry step into the water. Harry knelt before the waiting Father and reached up his little daughter.

"Oh, Father," Harry said in a well rehearsed phrase, "Take this child Little Greta for the Lord's desire. Give her a Soul; and make her well. Let her grow in God's image and be perfect in his Eyes."

The Father took Little Greta and raised her above his head.

"Oh, God," the Father said, his the gold chains and crosses catching the reflection of the sun. "Bless this little child, Greta. Breathe into her your Soul. Let the Holy Waters of Shanna wash away the sins of her ancestors that she bears for us all to see. Remove Oh Lord we pray this burden from the child and free her from them and free her from all the sin. Give her a new life with Thee. God we all ask your forgiveness. Allow your spirit to enter the child and make her well." He leaned down and immersed Little Greta completely in the flowing waters of the pool and held her there for what seemed to Sophie a very long time. Tessa and Harry also immersed their bodies completely in the water and laid their hands on the little figure that was struggling and screeching with terror as the Father lifted her up again, water dripping of the soaked robe.

"God Bless you all," the Father said, "and the child," he smiled, passing Little Greta back into Harry's arms and moving to the next family in the queue.

Before starting the long climb back up the stone steps, Sophie was allowed to get a brief dip in the Holy River and was given a gentle touch on the head by another Father. Of course, she knew that she already had a Soul, but still, she thought, a special blessing could not have done her any harm. She climbed back up the hard steps, slightly disappointed by size of the Great Falls of Shanna, and wondered if a miracle really had happened.

As they emerged from the changing rooms at the top of the cliff, now dressed in their holiday clothes, the atmosphere brought Sophie back to normal. Here there was a marked contrast to the religious ceremony down at the Holy Pool. In the great square in front of the cathedral was a market and fair, with stalls and games and roundabouts and everything to make a child happy. Mel and she ran off into the crowds, enjoying the freedom and excitement of a day at the Fair. Sophie wanted to take Little Greta along but the child cried when she was removed from the other group of clone girls she was playing with and the parents said, "Oh, leave them alone, they're happy together."

But for the adults, however, the official business of the day was not yet over. Although the practice of the Special Rebirth had been started by the Omega Corps, eventually after a lot of debate and discussion, the scheme had been agreed by the Archbishop and the President. Rebirth, they reckoned may produce the miracle that the public wanted. However, the Palace authorities had another reason for favouring Rebirth as they knew now that the long-term future of the clone girls would present a major social problem. In spite of their small size the little girls had developed an aggressive streak especially when they managed to get into groups. Parents in city areas were finding them very difficult to control and there were reports that the little girls formed gangs and frequently ran away and caused trouble, even at the age of five. The longer they were allowed to stay with individual families the greater the problem would become. In fact, clone girls had already become a considerable embarrassment and expense and many parents were demanding special tax allowances and financial help for looking after them.

The authorities used the occasion of the Rebirth Ceremony to interview the parents and specialist teams of social workers made every attempt to encourage them to hand over their little daughters to the new residential homes that had been set up in all the major cities. The new National Institution for Clone Girls would provide everything for the girls as they grew and developed into adults. It was now clear that although petite, they would probably mature physically and lead an active and healthy life. Lectures were given, films shown, and there were numerous private discussions between officials and worried parents. Brochures about the Residential Homes and the future problems were freely circulated. The Fathers spoke strongly in support of the government's new initiative and encouraged parents to think about returning their little girls to the authorities.

Tessa and Harry had rejected out of hand the suggestion that they would return Little Greta. Harry, after all, was her real father and he had a special letter from the President himself. She could never be taken away. Moreover, they both had a strong faith in the Rebirth and were convinced that with their continuous prayers that she would soon grow into a normal child. Out in the isolated regions around Dunfooey, Little Greta had become part of the larger family circle. There was ample help to look after her and friends to share the burden. The defective and deformed had always been treated with a special love and affection in isolated rural communities and Little Greta had been accepted for what she was, a simple, unfortunate but loveable and beautiful child.

Frank Tooley had taken a special liking to Little Greta and took her with him over the cliff top to see the sea birds. She would point to the birds and look at the sea and was always happy out in the open air. She learned to gather small living creatures, such as spiders, insects, snails, small shellfish and worms from under seaweed on the rocky shore pools. Although she could not talk, she delighted in finding things that were moving and alive and brought them to Frank with great grins of delight. 'Fank', as she called the warden, became her substitute father as Harry was nearly always away.

Little Greta cuddled close to Sophie on the journey back to Dunfooey and pouted and was clearly annoyed at being taken from her sisters, whom she's been playing with a lot during the trip. She was aware that some of them were not on the coach, but did not understand that they had been handed over to the authorities as some parents had been convinced that they could be looked after better in the state homes. Sophie was still certain that a miracle would happen very soon after the Rebirth Ceremony and that Little Greta would wake up some morning, talking and playing normally with her. It was going to be lovely having a normal little sister and she'd heard so much about the Rebirth and the importance of the Soul, that she had no doubts about the future cure. It was just a matter of time, just whenever God decided to make it happen.

By the time the coach slowed to a halt in the Dunfooey Square, Little Greta had recovered much of her previous happy disposition, especially when they started the decline from Dunfooey Pass into the valley and she recognised places that she associated with home. She was first out of the coach as the doors swung open and dashed along the platform crying, "Fank, Fank," and sprang up into the arms of Frank Tooley who was faithfully awaiting their arrival with his old van to take them up to their mountain farm.

Sophie laughed, looking out the window, glad to see her little sister happy again. "She's happy to be home again. She's going to be all right. I think the miracle's going to happen tonight."

Chapter Twenty Six

Tessa was sure that they had a good case for keeping Little Greta. They waited, anxious along with the remaining parents of the clone girls, for the 'hearing' before the visiting Committee in the Town Hall. They had letters from local residents, officials, local Fathers, doctors, all supporting their claim that they were suitable parents for Little Greta. Although the long awaited miracle had not happened everyone around Dunfooey wanted to keep Little Greta.

Little Greta had grown more than they'd expected, but they knew that this had been due more to the drugs supplied by the authorities than to the now forgotten Rebirth. They were sad that she remained so very retarded. The social workers visited them often, at first once a year but now more frequently as Little Greta entered her teens and had begun to wander away on her own if any opportunity presented itself.

"Good afternoon, Mr Atkins," a stern official said, glancing down at his pad as Harry, Tessa and Karen entered the interview room, Little Greta jumping agilely onto Harry's knee.

"I see you're the real father of the clone girls," one of the officials said, as he checked through the wad of paper before him

His colleague asked; "What do you object about the Residential Home where we look after the clone girls?"

"I don't like it at all," Harry snapped back. "The children would be better off if they were with real live parents, like us, not just nurses and attendants who are not really interested in them."

"Oh, now, Mr Atkins, that's unfair. The staff of the Home is very caring and highly selected. They are dedicated to the girls."

"But I have had a letter from the President saying that I could have one of my own daughters. There it is. In writing!" He slammed the old letter in front of the Chairman and held it firmly with his strong fingers pressed on the desk.

"We know about your famous letter, Mr Atkins, but the situation has changed. When it was written the President or no one else could foresee the problem you now face with Little Greta. Does she not miss her sisters dreadfully? Surely you've experienced this, like everyone else?" the chairman continued.

"That was long ago. When they were babies and were in

contact every day or most days. Once they are separated and given some other interests they soon get used to being apart," Harry responded.

"I suppose it's like you getting used to being away most of the time. You're on the Rock a lot of the time, killing seals, aren't you?"

"I'm a gas engineer, not a sealer." Harry objected.

"There are plenty of people around the farm to attend to Greta," Karen interjected, sensing that the interviewers were alienating Harry and trying to provoke him.

"Oh yes, indeed. There are a lot of interesting people around here. I see that you were once a scientist. Involved in some of the early cloning experiments apparently. Retired to the coast now, I see. I suppose you feel a little guilt complex about the clone girls. We understand, it was all such a rush. A tragedy, I agree, but a bit late now to worry, my dear."

"The child is very happy out at Dunfooey. There's good fresh air and she's developing as well there as she would in an institution," Karen responded, ignoring, but furious at, the young man's comments.

"But surely, Dr Rowlands, as a scientist, you should see through this falsehood. These clone girls will be happy anywhere as long as they are fed and looked after. The adults at Dunfooey who dote on her are making use of her. You are all using her to help fill in the enormous gap in your lives left by infertility. We must be honest with ourselves and look to the long term situation."

"That's untrue," snapped Tessa. "We love her, for herself. I have another normal daughter and she loves her, like a real sister "

"I agree, my dear," a grey-haired woman official spoke for the first time, looking sympathetically at Tessa. "It's like that now, but what about later? When she's older. How will you manage when she's twenty or thirty? When she's sexually mature and uncontrolled and frustrated. What will happen when you are old and there is no one to look after her. Then the transition to the Home will be even more difficult for her. Already we know that she runs away and here there is always the danger of the cliffs and the sea. In a few years she'll be terribly difficult for you to manage."

"That can be kept under control. All we need is a good garden fence," Harry said. "She's happy with us now. I know she is. Please let her stay." Little Greta beamed a radiant smile across the desk at the lady who spoke and mouthed a weak "Fank, Fank".

"But, my dears," the grey-haired woman took the lead again, trying to break the aggression of her younger colleagues, "you know that the natural way for clones to live is together, just like the clone boys. You've seen the films. In their special Residence, they are so content together. You don't want to have to keep her chained up and fenced in your back garden like a dog or a pet. You'll always be afraid that she'll escape and get lost. I expect you already have her electronically tagged in case she wanders away?" she queried, looking at Harry, directly, waiting his answer.

"Of course we do. But at your Homes, you drug them. I know you do," Harry snapped. "My little Greta is not going to be drugged to an early death. I believe that your plan is to eliminate the clone girls once the general public forgets about them. If not, they'll be used for genetic experiments."

"Now, Harry," Karen pressed her hands firmly on Harry's shoulders, trying to soothe him. This was Omega talk, dangerous, probably true, but based on rumour and gossip and superstition. It would alienate the officials and produce the impact that she feared most. They turned aside and conferred briefly. Then the chairman turned back and addressed Harry.

"The Committee has decided on this case. You, Mr Atkins are obviously of an extreme disposition. You are away most of the year killing seals or mending gas pipes and have no actual responsibility for the your daughter. In fact, the man she reacts to most, is this man Tooley. He has no experience with backward children. Tessa, you have your own daughter to look after as well as ageing parents. The outlook is poor. Other friends of the family have no legal responsibility to the girl and their involvement cannot be seriously considered. We note here a report that states that one of the supporting parties, Dr Rowlands," the chairman glanced at Karen, "is the mother of the clone boys and that she abandoned them in order to live in the wilderness and has become a health fanatic. We feel that the outlook is not good. You know that the other foster parents have now all agreed to return their children. We believe that it is best for her and everyone else here."

"I'm sorry, my dear," the woman official said to Tessa, whose eyes were full of tears. "I do think it is for the best. She's not your real daughter, after all. She distracts you from giving your full love to your daughter, Sophie," she added looking at the page. "What a nice name! How lucky you are! I always wanted a daughter."

Tessa clung to Little Greta.

Karen tried to speak. But the Chairman said sternly, "I'm sorry, the interview is over. We know this is very difficult for you, but please. It is best if you make the break sharply. She will get upset if you fuss, so please allow the child to come with us. You can say your goodbyes at the coach before we leave. She will need to be prepared for the journey."

"No! No!" Tessa screeched, clinging to Little Greta, tears streaming down her cheeks and her words echoing through the Hall. Father Seamus came into the room, hearing the interview was over and gently took Tessa's arms from around the child.

"Please, Tessa," he said, his voice kind and sympathetic but firm and confident, "it is for the best, my dear. There is nothing more we can do."

She kissed Little Greta on the forehead and flung herself into Harry's arms.

Later that afternoon they gathered at the station as the coach prepared to leave. Tessa looked through the windows trying to recognise Little Greta but all the clone girls who had been collected from various parts of the region were dressed identically in blue tunics. Their shining black hair had been shorn. The clone girls were holding hands and looking only at each other, giggling, happy, innocent. The coach moved away, stirring up a cloud of dust as it made its way up the gorge to Dunfooey Pass.

## Chapter Twenty Seven

"Fank, Fank." Little Greta had taken to wandering alone among the trees and shrubs that bounded the far end of the grounds of the Home. The morning sun shone through the bare branches where the leaves were just beginning to burst out. Little Greta held her face up towards the warm sun and squeezed her eyes closed against the glare and it felt good.

"Fank, Fank."

She liked the isolation of the wood and the peace and silence of the place. Although she felt content at the Home and her many sisters were nice to be near, she always enjoyed a short spell alone in the woods as it brought back happy feelings. This morning she had slipped away after breakfast with her little plastic bag. The wood was full of perennial flowers and she'd picked a bunch as well as finding a few lovely black backed beetles under small stones that she could manage to turn over. There were slimy slugs that she looked at and watched move slowly, but didn't touch. Time did not mean much to Little Greta and for how long she watched a slug sliding down the stem of a plant on its way to a fresh pasture she'd no idea. For Little Greta, life was like that. Time did not exist. But somehow she found herself, without thinking, lured back at intervals to the white room where she would join the queue with her sisters and be given a small pink tablet that made her feel good. She'd just had one after breakfast and the good feeling still lingered and there were plenty of beetles this morning to put into her little bag.

The path she was following led to the high wire fence that surrounded the grounds of the Home and sometimes she would hold on to the wire and press her face tight against the mesh and peer out into the outside world.

"Fank, Fank," she said to no one in particular, remembering pleasant feelings and seeing pictures in her mind of mountains and sea.

This morning she came across a small hole in the fence and saw on the other side some attractive stones that must conceal more lovely beetles. Little Greta was not escaping; she was unaware of the fence being there to keep her in or to keep others out. It merely separated her from the stones she now urgently wanted to turn over.

They were good stones, some were too large to move but the others had never been touched and hid enormous beetles. There were other good stones further down the lane and she moved on beyond the fence and into the outside world.

"Fank, Fank," she said as she found more spiders and snails and came across a meadow rich in spring flowers, blue bells, cowslips, anemones and violets and the masses of daisies and buttercups and dandelion. Names did not mean anything to her, but the smell was nice and the colours and the way they held their little heads looking at her made her happy. "Fank, Fank," she said to them as she carefully picked some flowers along the edge of the path.

Suddenly the path opened out into a large field at the end of the wood and Little Greta tried to focus her eyes against the glare of the sun at people moving in the distance. There was something on the ground. She thought it was a black and white beetle. Little people were chasing it.

"Fank, Fank," she said to herself as she saw them kick it and then chase it again. Suddenly the beetle came rolling in her direction and she wanted it for her collection, but as it came closer and closer it became bigger and bigger.

"Fank, Fank," she cried, running towards the ball that came to rest as it rolled into the long grass at the edge of the pitch a few yards away. Little Greta jumped on top of it before it could run away. It was slippery like a big wet white snail and she clutched it to her well-formed breasts, lying still for a moment panting with excitement.

"Fank, Fank," she panted as tears of delight streaming down her cheeks at her conquest and capture. Suddenly there was a noise behind her and she rolled over on to her back still clutching the ball to her chest. She looked up at a group of boys. They all looked the same, dressed in short white pants and yellow shirts and big hard muddy boots. Their short hair was fair and their eyes a bright blue. They all looked at her with the same shocked expression. Was she looking in mirrors, Little Greta wondered, and then remembered that all her sisters looked the same but she had never seen them form this position.

"Fank, Fank," she scowled, afraid they might steal her beetle.

"Who are you?" one of the boys said, coming forward and reaching down to get the ball.

"Fank, Fank," Little Greta cried, struggling to hold on to her prize.

"Give it to me, silly," the clone boy shouted, grasping the ball and trying to pull it from Little Greta's surprisingly strong hold.

"I think she's one of the loonies gypsies from the Home," Donal said, coming forward to help his clone brother. They all laughed, embarrassed and conscious of the innocent sensuous posture of Little Greta as she lay provocatively on the ground, clutching the ball just below her breasts. Without thinking, Donal jumped on top of her and tried to prise the ball from her firm grasp.

"Fank, Fank," she cried, and struggled more furiously against the clone boys who were all now trying to help Donal retrieve the ball. She felt her clothes tear and the touch of damp muddy hands sending conflicting messages to her confused and simple brain. "Fank, Fank," she cried, petrified, but at the same time laughing, as it was ticklish. Fank used to tickle her, and she loved to laugh. Now they all laughed as she squirmed and twisted. She was hysterical. There were tickles everywhere. Her arms were around Donal's neck, pulling his hair, her lips forced against his face suddenly bit into his ear. There was a fierce shout and a big man dressed in black appeared above them. He pulled Donal off her by the collar of his yellow shirt.

"Fank, Fank," she was whimpering now, exhausted after her excitement. Her terror returned and a big woman was fixing her torn blouse and helping her stand up.

"It's all right, my dear," the woman said. "These boys are very naughty. Don't cry now. I'll take you home."

A boy was brought over by the man in black and for a moment stood facing Little Greta. His ear was bleeding and he held a white cloth to it, looking at it frequently wit tears in his eyes.

"Say you're sorry," the man in black commanded the teenager, whose lips barely moved in response.

Little Greta remembered that it had been fun playing in the grass, struggling for the ball and smiled at him, forgetting the terror and tears.

"Fank, Fank," she said looking aside for her plastic bag that had gone astray in the fray.

"I'm sorry," Donal said clearly, after further prompting by the warden. It had been the first time that he'd seen a girl so close and as he watched her turn away with the woman his eyes followed the gentle swing of her small but perfectly formed hips. They were nice. The man in black cuffed his ears and pushed him back to the football game.

## Chapter Twenty Eight

Michael felt an overwhelming sense of history as he gathered the velvet of his long purple Presidential robe around him and took the first steps up to the platform for his inauguration. Followed by only his page, a clone boy, he was at the end of a long procession of all the Masters of Emanon who had led with dignity from the doors of the Great Hall. It was a colourful sight that flanked him as he ascended the marble staircase to the huge platform and ancient throne seat. Since the early foundation of Emanon as a united nation, the various Kings and Presidents who had governed the island had commenced their reign from this carved throne.

Today Michael had a deep sense of personal fulfilment as he saw the second of his main ambitions become a reality. The first had been sixteen years ago with the successful birth of the initial batch of clone boys. Their success and his single-handed control of the complex cloning programme had revolutionised Emanon. His captivating manner and ease of persuasion, sheer ability and hard work had impressed the ageing President Neilson, who was convinced that Michael had saved Emanon by dedicating himself to the clone boys.

Some years ago Michael had become the chairman of the Council of Masters and now when illness eventually overtook the old President, the Masters unanimously elected Michael as the successor.

The huge circular dome of the Great Hall of the Palace, with its tier upon tier of balconies was filled to capacity. Today, any dissent that existed between the State and the Holy Fathers was buried beneath the splendour of the occasion. All the senior Holy Fathers with their ceremonial garb were there as well as the Masters and Mayors of the various cities throughout Emanon who had come to welcome the new President and to mourn the passing of their late and highly respected leader.

For the first time during a state occasion, the clone boys were in evidence. They sat in long silent rows in the centre of the auditorium looking directly up at the platform and watched enthralled as their father, in his flowing purple robe that was edged with gold, took his place on the throne. They watched, on the edge of their seats, as the Archbishop presented the blessed golden Seal of

Emanon to Michael.

Michael took the seal and held it high over his head and looked down at his sons in the centre of the auditorium. "On accepting this Seal I give my life to Emanon and swear in the name of God to guide and govern this land and to protect it for so long as I live."

"Blessed art Thou that God has chosen," the recently appointed Archbishop intoned, and smiled obsequiously at Michael from under his tall glittering mitre.

"To lead and guide us."

"To lead and guide us," Michael repeated, his voice crackling with emotion.

"To protect and defend us."

"To protect and defend us," Michael's eyes glanced down to the auditorium and caught for a fleeting second those of Sean, the young clone boy, the son that he had come to know best.

"For better or worse."

"For better or worse."

"Until death do us part," The Archbishop's voice, stern and deep, echoed around the walls of the great dome where ten thousand breaths were held and not a muscle moved.

"Until Death do us part," Michael knew that by saying these words he had committed himself to Emanon for life. But the words drifted across his mind like a cloud from the past and he smiled down at his sons.

The clone boys sat in silence, their eyes focused on their father as he took his vows and they knew the future was theirs. He had taught them well. They knew their history and their uniqueness. Their father had told them that Emanon was theirs. He was going to open the gates to their great future. They would be the founders of a new race, controlled and pure, free from the weaknesses of the any primitive genes. They had seen the Production Units, the wards full of new clone babies. The nurseries and the schools were thriving and busy, training and preparing the new generations of clone boys. Throughout their life, Michael had prepared the first batch of clone boys for their future role as leaders of the new society that he believed was the only way forward for Emanon. Now they were ready and their minds and love went out to him as he stood enmeshed in the mysteries of history and the unknown future.

For a brief second, Michael's eyes scanned the high galleries.

He knew that Karen would be at the ceremony. He had admired the way that she had built up her research at Dunfooey and had resisted obstructing her progress, half knowing that she would fail, half hoping that she would succeed. Initially he had laughed at the role that Karen had played as President of the Omega Fertility Campaign. How could a little amateur laboratory hidden away in the mountains solve this major problem that had defeated even the best brains in many other countries where there was also still no sign of overcoming the infertility crisis. Michael had had a small team of scientists working on the problem for many years with no useful results. No, he was confident that he had been correct. Only nations that had taken on the new cloning technologies would survive the reproductive disaster of the last century. For years, Karen's 'private laboratory' had been the laughing stock of most scientists and only the respect that many of her earlier colleagues and his fear of the scandal that might ensue had prevented him from closing down the small Omega unit at Dunfooey. But now, rumours were rife that she was having success and the Church was increasing their support for her work.

The religious ceremony over and the inauguration completed, Michael bowed to the Archbishop and moved to the rostrum to speak to his people. The clone boys tensed and edged forward in their seats.

"People of Emanon," Michael said, his voice quivering slightly at the enormity of the occasion as he looked out over the vast gathering. His eyes returned and settled on the centre group of clone boys and he could feel them so close, so supportive, so strong. "For many of us, this day is saddened by the memory of the passing away of our beloved President Neilson and we all praise his great contribution to Emanon over so many years." There was a tremendous round of applause, although some present considered that the uncontrolled and rapid industrialisation and economic growth that had taken place during his Presidency, had probably been responsible for the loss of fertility and the excessive degree of pollution that had ruined many parts of Emanon. "Today we must welcome the new generation of clone boys. Over the past few years we have all grown to love and cherish them like our own." There was a polite, but restrained round of applause, all eyes on the rows of the boys with their neatly combed fair hair and light grey suits, especially tailored for the occasion.

Spontaneously, the clone boys stood up and bowed to the President and the rest of the audience and sat down again to a greater round of applause.

"We know that those of you who have had the opportunity of acting as aunts and uncles to the clone boys have found them most rewarding and now that their numbers are increasing daily, soon every couple will be able to adopt a clonit. Of course, occasional visits of the boys to your homes is not like having a family or a baby of your own, but we all know how important it is for the clone boys to be together." Many years ago, Michael had devised a scheme whereby each small group of clone boys, which had come to be called a clonit, could be adopted by an aunt and uncle who would be allowed one day every week to be spent with them. The clonits were spoilt and taken out and played with and became a very successful substitute for a family.

Michael had intended to take the opportunity of his inaugural speech to send out a message to Karen and the Omega Corps that if their work on fertility was really being successful then under his Presidency they would have his support and that the old Fertility Laws could be changed. "Some of you will have heard the rumours of a new cure for infertility and if this proves to be true, I'm sure that the Council of Masters will welcome this and do everything necessary to bring a new generation of Emanons into harmony with the large numbers of clone boys that now exist." In reality, Michael had little hope of a cure being found but he knew what the general public wanted to hear.

"But we must never look on the clone boys as merely fill-in people or children for the gap in the generations of normal children. To day we have among us a vast number of clone boys who will become our leaders in the generations to come. Just as we know that plants can reproduce by vegetative reproduction as well as by sexual methods, and that both progeny live in harmony, so I believe that it is possible for us all to live in harmony. Soon we will see the clone boys becoming adults in our society. In the future, these young clonemen may have to accept future generations of normal children being born again. I pray that God will guide me during my life to provide a secure and happy future for all of Emanon."

There were rounds of applause and the clone boys clapped enthusiastically and all the audience stood up as the great procession led by Michael descended the grand staircase from the platform into the heat of the auditorium. There was clanging of cymbals and the strains of traditional music as they moved slowly in their flowing robes out into the sunlight of the new age.

Chapter Twenty Nine

From all parts of Emanon, festive groups had converged on Konburg. The city was packed to capacity with sightseers and holidaymakers. Banners and flags flew from every window. Bands played at every corner and there were numerous stalls and fairs and amusements for all. The weather was wonderful, with bright blue skies and long warm evenings and the atmosphere in the city was exciting and infectious.

Karen had been nominated along with Harry and Tessa and a few others including Frank Tooley, to represent the Dunfooey region at the inauguration of the new President. They brought Sophie and Mel along as this would give them an opportunity to see the city and enjoy the experience of the great celebrations that would follow the inauguration ceremony. Karen had had considerable reservations about accepting the invitation, but was now glad she'd agreed to come as she'd enjoyed showing Sophie around.

Karen had enjoyed her chosen life in Dunfooey. She had watched Sophie grow and develop into a beautiful young woman, gentle, reliable and caring. Tessa's family had accepted her as one of their own and Karen believed that she had been able to pursue her work on the search for the fertility cure as well at Dunfooey as if she'd remained in Konburg. Archbishop Longfellow had been as good as his word and had established a Church Trust that would support her laboratory for an extended period of time. With Frank Tooley as her chief assistant, they had built up a excellent team and had retained secret international interactions with similar minded groups in other countries who were also struggling to overcome the infertility problem.

Their reserved seats were high in the fourth balcony under the great dome of the hall and the figures below in the auditorium looked small and toy like. The platform was still empty but gradually the auditorium filled up with important guests, many dressed in ceremonial robes. The centre portion was a reserved area and shortly before the proceedings started a large group of clone boys entered in single file and quietly took their places. In the distance Karen watched, intrigued by their appearance. How they had grown, their fair hair glistening like their father's in the sunlight and their shoulders straight! Each wore a light grey coloured suit and they sat without speaking. Karen watched them intently.

"They do look well," Tessa whispered, sensing Karen's reaction to the appearance of her sons. "Don't you want to tell them who you are?"

"No!" Karen replied, emphatically. "You know I can't do that. Not even after all these years. It's too late. Michael would only say that it's because he's President that I've now come forward. He'd claim that I had gone away and neglected them. I know what he's like. He'll twist anything to his own advantage. Tessa, they frighten me. Somehow I believe they know that I'm here. Look!" She grabbed Tessa's arm and motioned towards the clone boys in the front row far below.

Five of the boys sitting in the centre of the row had turned their heads and were looking directly up at Karen. Their eyes, tiny dots in the hall below, seemed to hold Karen's in a visual vice.

Tessa picked them out from the surrounding crowd of heads. "You're right! They're looking directly at us. No, they've looked away. It's just coincidence," she added, not wanting to accept the obvious.

"Now others are looking," Karen whispered, still clutching Tessa's hand. Another group of five clone boys turned their heads in unison and looked directly up at their balcony, quickly picking out the small group from Dunfooey, whom they held firmly in their gaze for a few long seconds.

"Michael must have told them about you," Harry said. "They obviously recognise you."

"Maybe they just sense you're their mother," Sophie said, who had also now picked out the group that were looking upwards. "There's a rumour that the clonies have telepathic powers. We're going to have an awful time at college with them if they tell each other answers and think things behind our backs." Sophie had heard gossip about the clonies and, like others of her age, was slightly concerned about starting college at the same time as the clone boys, who despite being a couple of years younger had already passed the entrance examinations.

After her experience prior to the start of the ceremony in the morning, Karen had considered not attending the garden party in the afternoon, but the thought of seeing her sons at close quarters and finding out what they knew about her was overpowering. The registered guests were invited to visit the beautiful grounds and formal gardens of the Palace and at various locations lunches were served and wine and champagne flowed freely. Later it was planned that the new President would walk among the guests and everyone hoped for a chance to see him.

Karen approached the afternoon with the expectation of a mother seeing her son for the first time. All the emotions of pregnancy and childbearing flooded through her mind. What had she missed by leaving them? Should she have stayed and helped Michael? Would they have been different if she had influenced them as much as Michael had done? There was a flux of thoughts and emotions that she had never experienced before and she knew that the clonies were near and conscious of her. As she walked through the wooded gardens with the group from Dunfooey, sipping the ice cold champagne and looking innocently at the ancient trees and shrubs, Karen was always conscious of the small clusters of young men in grey who moved silently among the shrubs. Sometimes their paths crossed and their eyes met and there was silent recognition or at the most a faint smile or polite nod, and so Michael-like, a fine fingered hand gently brushing the fair hair from his forehead.

As the afternoon wore on there seemed to be an increasing number of clone boys in the vicinity of Karen's group. They seemed bolder and smiled more openly. Had she seen that one before? He was there a moment ago. No, it was another one. They were all so alike that she became dizzy and confused. It was a warm afternoon. She was thirsty. The champagne slipped down easily, she felt safe and protected, holding onto Harry's arm. They all talked cheerfully. Sophie and Mel were holding hands, walking among the trees, chatting to new friends of their own age.

By mid-afternoon the guests began to converge on the main lawn in front of the Palace surrounding the curved marble steps leading up to the main entrance.

At four o'clock all eyes were on the main door of the Palace and a cheer went up as it was pulled open from inside and held for a second forming a black hole in the brightness of the afternoon sun. For a brief moment the cheer weakened and then burst out again in tumultuous applause as Michael, dressed in a white silk suit, stepped out into the sunlight. Karen, relaxed and flushed with the sun and the champagne, broke from Harry's arm and clapped and cheered with the rest, overtaken again by the captivating person that she had once loved. Tessa was also cheering and clapping and her eyes were glistening with tears and she glanced at Karen and they smiled and cheered again, uncontrolled as Michael took the first steps down towards his people. Sophie, who was standing with Mel a little in front of them glanced back, her face radiant and excited, clapping and cheering, carried along with the mass euphoria of the moment and proud to have someone as attractive as Michael as their leader. Harry folded his arms and his teeth clenched, his thick greying beard thrust forward aggressively.

"I don't know why you're clapping," he snarled at the three women whom he had come to love in so many different ways. "He's a real bastard. I don't trust him an inch."

As Michael reached the bottom of the steps and merged with the mass of guests the cheering stopped and people looked at each other, some wondering why they had been so enthusiastic. Suddenly Karen realised that she was surrounded by clone boys. Somehow, within a few seconds, and a few short steps, Harry and Tessa had separated from her and she was alone in the crowd. She tried to look over the heads of the youths but could not see Harry.

"Hello," one of them said. Karen glanced around to try and identify the speaker but could only guess who it was from the general direction of the sound of the words.

"Hello," she answered.

"You're our mother, aren't you?"

Karen froze. Her face flushed scarlet and her knees shook.

"What do you mean?" she stammered.

"What we say. Are you our mother?"

Karen was lost for words. This direct approach was something she'd never expected. She could not tell from the tone of the voice whether they were friendly or not towards her. She wanted Harry beside her. She looked around for help, a way of escape. Suddenly a fresh voice, familiar from long ago, addressed her from behind.

"Why, Karen! How good of you to come all the way from Dunfooey to be with us today."

Karen flashed around, glaring into Michael's face. She hadn't spoken to Michael since she'd left for Dunfooey many years ago.

"You!" she spat out the word, all her hate and anger pent-up. She was revolted by her recent unplanned enthusiasm for him.

"Now, now, my dear, surely you are not still upset after all these years. Haven't they done well?" He turned to the group of clone boys. "Come, let me introduce you to some of them." He took her by the elbow and moved her close to the boys who gathered round in a tight group. "Boys," he continued, "let me introduce you to someone very important. This is your mother, Karen. I've told you about her many times."

"We've already met," one of them said, his voice colder than before and clearly sensitive to Karen's spontaneous reaction to Michael's presence.

"She left us when we were babies," another clone boy said coldly, Karen noticed a red scar on the lobe of his right ear that distinguished him from the others. "I don't think we need her now. We just wanted to see her. As you said, she's quite good looking!"

A clone boy reached out his hand and Karen gave him hers. It seemed cool and damp. "You should not have left us, mother. That was very wrong," he said and turning his back, walked away. The small group moved past her, each one touching her hand briefly and then they were gone, leaving Karen and Michael facing each other, alone in the midst of the crowd of embarrassed guests.

Karen felt a great lump gather in her throat. Her heart pounded. Her eyes were daggers tearing Michael apart. She never knew she had so much hatred in her being as at that moment, but then Harry was at her side and she clung to him. Tessa and Sophie joined them. Michael glanced at them for an instant, remembering. His eyes broke into a smile as he recognised Tessa and realised that the enchanting young lady was really his own daughter.

"It was good of you all to come," Michael said addressing Tessa, taking her hand briefly and glancing at Sophie. Time had moved too far to change things now and he noted that Tessa's eyes still held tears of joy from cheering him. He realised that things could have been different.

"This is our daughter, Sophie," Tessa said, bringing forward Sophie, who was delighted to get the chance of meeting the President.

"My dear, you look wonderful. Why, there are so few young ladies nowadays that we miss your charm and beauty."

Sophie gave him a captivating smile and feigned embarrassment. She had never been spoken to like that before and enjoyed the compliment.

"And I'm her god-father!" a square set man with a red beard stepped forward and grasped Michael's hand in devastating grip. "I remember the day she was conceived," he laughed, his eyes burning like hot colds into the President's.

"Oh, this is Dr Frank Tooley, he's Head of my Marine Biology lab," Karen said. "In fact you may remember seeing him once before. He was at the bar the night we were at Dunfooey, years ago."

Michael's hand and body went limp as his past flooded through his mind. His reputation would be ruined, if they made this public. Today of all days. The public loves a scandal and the glory of his Inauguration would be reduced to a orgy in the hay. They could ruin him. "Nice to meet you Dr Tooley. I'm sure you are doing good work out there in Dunfooey. Have you found that special shell fish yet?" he struggled to free his hand from Frank's vice-like grip. "You must meet the boys. Karen thinks they're due to your shell fish," he smirked, "but I like to think of them as a miracle." He looked around and called one of the clone boys over. "Sean, come and meet Sophie." A clone boy came forward, brushing his fair hair out of his eyes and politely held out his hand to shake Sophie's. "She'll be starting university with you at beginning of term."

Others followed, pushing and elbowing their way between Michael and Frank, and edging out the others and isolating Sophie.

"Hello, Sophie," Sean said. "We look forward to seeing you at the start of term. What will you be studying?"

"Biology," Sophie replied, looking into his bright blue eyes and smiling in friendship. "I've worked a little with uncle Frank in the lab and want to find a cure for infertility." She said spontaneously, and in all innocence.

"That's interesting, you'll have to tell us all about it when we get up to College." Sean replied, retaining eye contact long enough to make her heart miss a beat. "Well, I'll see you later then," and turned back escorting Michael away in the midst of the group of clone boys.

"Oh, Auntie Karry, isn't he sweet? He's only a kid." Sophie said, blushing, looking after the lithe young figure disappearing into the crowd. It would be exciting getting started at university and it will be interesting getting to know the clone boys. But how will we ever tell them apart she thought, suddenly surprised and fascinated by the approving stares of passing clonies.

## Chapter Thirty

"Do you think she'll come?" Sean queried, looking around the small group of brothers as they sat huddled at a table in the quiet corner of the refectory.

"I hope so," Donal mused, breathing heavily through his teeth, his chest heaving with mock excitement. He was sitting erect, straining his head above the others, looking down the length of the restaurant searching for the tall student who stood out from the rest by the attractiveness of her full figure.

"She always smiles at me," Sean admitted proudly. "What I can't make out is how she recognises me so easily? None of the others do. She only saw me for a second or two at the Palace Garden that afternoon and yet she said 'Hello' the moment she saw me after we arrived here months later."

"I've noticed that," Colm said, looking directly at his identical twin who was especially close. "I've watched her. She can look me straight in the eyes and pass on ignoring me and pick you out from the rest of us. Only father can do that. Even the staff at the Home were never really able to pick us out like she can."

"Oh my! But she does look good in those jeans," Donal said, releasing his breath in a long slow hiss through his clenched teeth, still not taking his eyes off Sophie as she walked across the restaurant with her lunch tray to join some friends at a table in the centre of the room. "The way she smiles at you, Sean, is fantastic. She makes me feel all funny. I dream about her every night and I...."

"I know," Sean said, anticipating his brother's words. "It's quite natural. Father told us that we'd find girls attractive, whenever we got the chance of meeting any. But I don't understand her. She's always with that big chap Mel Higgins and although she smiles at me and says a few words, it's always as though she looks on me as a child. I think she is interested in us as children rather than as men."

"She's older than us," Colm said, looking down the room where the other students, all in their late teens, were eating their lunches and chatting and laughing heartily. "They all are. There are none of the others the same age as us. I've read that at our age, two or three years makes quite a lot of difference. If we want to interact more fully with them we must make a real effort to be socially mature.

That's why we don't fit into their groups. We're too young for them."

"Not really," Donal countered, "I could handle her just fine." Some of his brothers laughed, but Sean ignored his comment and took up Colm's theme.

"That's why we want our party to be a success. If our Christmas party goes well, they'll realise that we are mature and maybe we'll get to know them better. All term we have just seen them in classes and then we go our own ways." Sean said.

"Yes, father said that we should try and integrate," Colm recalled.

"Except for the girls, I don't think there is any point," Donal retorted, feeling slighted at Sean ignoring his witty comment. "They don't really want us. That's why we must organise our own activities and not depend on their clubs and sports. We can't compete with their size and weight in sport. Anyway, do we really want to compete the way they do?"

Others in the group laughed and agreed with Donal. Someone said acidly, "You have to join this. You have to join that. You'll enjoy this. You'll enjoy that. I don't see why they should tell us how to enjoy ourselves."

"You'll not be coming to the Party, then," Sean laughed, jesting with Donal.

"You bet I will," Donal replied, still keeping his eye on Sophie who was talking vivaciously and smiling radiantly at the others around her table.

"God, you've got it bad," Sean sneered, "I'm not going to let you near her. You'll ruin it for the rest of us if you act like a lovesick kid."

"Oh, I'm only joking," Donal said seriously, suddenly feeling that the others were laughing at him. He felt the nerve above his left eye throbbing. "All right," he added, with pleading in his voice, "I'll be good. I promise."

The rumours that the young clone students were holding a An end of term's Christmas Party were at first greeted with amusement by the older students, but when the personalised invitation cards arrived the idea seemed good and most of the first year students accepted, encouraged especially by Sophie who was keen to go along.

The clone students lived in a tall block with a large number of small study bedrooms and ample communal areas for relaxation. The common room had been decorated and a buffet supper was laid out on long tables down one side. There was a bar near the entrance and plenty of room for groups to stand and chat or dance to music played by a newly formed band of clone students. Most of the music they played had been written and composed by the clonies themselves. The tempo of the music was lively and there was a good atmosphere at the start of the party.

Sophie and Mel Higgins had continued to remain close friends since coming up to college and he had bought her a beautiful orange dress as his gift for the New Year. Sophie was proud of Mel. He was popular with the rest of the students and was a natural leader. He had a superb physique and was an excellent sportsman. Within a few months he had become captain of the football team and Sophie was delighted that he had encouraged so many of his friends and team mates to attend the party.

Mel had left Sophie chatting with some friends in the centre of the room while he went to the bar for drinks. He glanced back at her as he waited for the young clone barman to serve him. Mel had not realised until they had come up to College just how beautiful Sophie was. He had always just accepted her as Sophie while they had played together in the hills and along the shore at Dunfooey, but now in the strange atmosphere of the big city among their many new friends from all parts of Emanon, he did not see anyone more attractive. Returning with the tray of drinks, he noticed that Sophie had been edged away and was talking intently to a clone student.

"Here's your Martini, Sophie," Mel said, passing a tall glass of deep red liquid across to her. "Hello, there," Mel added, glancing down at the name of the clone student's lapel. "Thanks for the invitation, Sean."

"I'm glad you could come. That was a great goal you scored last week." Sean recalled the success of Mel's team. "I could never kick a ball like that," he added, taking a sip from the long stemmed glass of chilled white wine that he was caressing with his fine delicate fingers.

"Oh, it was just luck, old son," Mel smiled down at Sean and absentmindedly, but in a natural gesture of friendship common among his sporting friends stretched out his huge boned hand and ruffled the boy's carefully groomed hair. Sean spontaneously pulled back and his left hand quickly shot through his fair hair to readjust it, his eyes momentarily blazing disdainfully at Mel.

Embarrassed, Mel turned away, but accidentally his elbow

touched Sophie's as she was about to take a sip of her red Martini. The glass tippled sideways and the dark red wine spilt over her bare shoulders and down the front of her new orange dress.

"Oh, you clumsy fool," Sophie snapped, "look what you've done. You're not on a football field now," she added, immediately regretting having said it, "but look at my dress."

Mel was mortified. "Oh, I'm sorry," he whimpered, flustered, for a moment not knowing what to do.

"Here Sophie," Donal came across from the bar with a large tablecloth. "Take this." He wrapped it around her shoulders drying off the excess wine. She thanked him and gathered the cloth around her throat and over her breasts that were soaked. "Come upstairs and get changed into something dry."

Suddenly before Mel or the others could react to what had happened, Sophie was surrounded by a group of clonies and escorted to the nearby elevator and she vanished as the steel doors slid closed.

Within moments the tension in the room relaxed and the normal buzz of conversation resumed. Except for embarrassed Mel, the incident was forgotten, but he lingered on the periphery of his small circle of friends and kept an expectant eye on the lift doors.

"That was a bit clumsy, Mel, old man," a teammate remarked, bringing Mel back into the conversation. "Sophie will be all right. She'll forgive you, later," he laughed. "I expect you'll have to buy her another new dress."

"Yes, it was bloody stupid," Mel admitted as the flush on his face subsided. "I hope the new one won't be as expensive as the last one," he added, trying to laugh it off, still keeping an eye on the closed lift doors.

In the confined space of the lift, Sophie held the cloth close. Red stains spread through her fingers as the martini seeped through the fabric.

"I must get to a bathroom," she said to the clonies around her. "Oh, I'm awfully sorry. This is spoiling your party. Mel is clumsy sometimes." She was sorry she'd shouted at him in public. That sort of verbal abuse was all right out in Dunfooey but not here in Tanark. It had been very bad manners. She would apologise as soon as she got back. The young clone boys around her in their neat suits looked innocent, embarrassed and concerned. "You're being very thoughtful, thanks," she smiled at them.

"Will a sweat shirt and jeans do? We don't have dresses like that, you know," Donal said.

"Of course. You're very kind. Anything will do. So long as I get out of this sticky mess," she glanced at the elevator number as they seemed to have been in the lift for ages." It had all happened so quickly. "But where are we going?" she queried, as she saw that they had now reached the tenth floor.

"It's all right, Sophie," Donal reassured her. "Our rooms are on the 12th floor. We're nearly there. I've got just what you need."

They left the lift quickly and she felt their firm fine fingers grip her elbows and escort her along the corridor and around two corners before stopping at a door. One of the boys was already fumbling with a key and Sophie was rushed in.

Suddenly the clank of the door closing sent a shudder down Sophie's spine. She glanced around the room. There was a single bed in one corner and a small desk and a chair along the opposite wall. Above the desk were shelves lined with books and a small TV set was fixed to the wall and a computer console stood in the corner. She gasped as her eyes fell on the large picture poster that was stuck on the wall above the bed. It was of herself. She remembered how she had posed for some clone boys at the gym as she'd climbed out of the pool in her bikini. At that huge magnification, the vision of her breasts and her inviting smile made her gasp for breath.

"You're the most beautiful person we've ever seen," Donal said, sensing the horror in her eyes as Sophie took in the implication of her enlarged photograph on the wall.

"We have all one of these," another clone boy added innocently.

Sophie looked around at him. He was just a face, identical to the others. She realised that the name tags that they'd been wearing earlier had been removed. She glanced around the faces in the room. Somehow she knew that Sean was not present. It was strange how she knew him. Suddenly she felt afraid because he was not there. These were all strangers. The room was crowded with them. They were looking at her. She saw her reflection in a mirror and was horrified. The white cloth was stained blood red. She looked at the reflection of the clone boys in the mirror. They seemed to merge into a single figure as she felt her head spinning and confused. There was only one of them.

"Sophie," he seemed to say, "we love you." He stretched forward, his small fine hand took hers, the damp cloth fell free from her shoulders onto the floor. In the mirror she saw the transparent soaked fabric of her orange gown, now stained and ruined.

"There's a shower," the boy said and opened a door to a small washroom. She stepped in and felt the sudden chill of the air on her bare skin as her damp dress slipped to the floor. She was transfixed, watching in the mirror what was happening, but not sensing or being able to participate. Her mind was blank, there was no horror, fear or hate, just sensation and awareness. Hot water and steam enveloped her while scented perfume and soap relaxed her muscles. She knew the boys were looking at her, but it did not seem to matter. She could see them again now through the steam and their eyes were enthralled and worshipping, responding to her every movement as she washed away the sticky stains. Hands roamed over her body, scented soap, gliding smoothly, her long hair hung damp and strewn over her face. She was one of them, their minds fused as they crashed through their climax, flinging themselves in abandon into the shower hugging and caressing her, their wet bodies clinging, the warm water flowing, their minds suddenly open and defenceless. It lasted only a few seconds but it could have been hours. The clone boys clung to Sophie like leeches, their frustration expressed initially in tears and then words of regret, worship and love.

"Oh, Sophie, we're sorry. We couldn't help it. We love you. You are so beautiful. Please love us. We're so alone. We have never known real love, even from our mother. Please be our Queen. We all love you."

For a second, Sophie's mind cleared and she saw inside the mind of the clone. They were only children, lost in a world they did not understand, frightened and alone. The world was against them. They were afraid. She pulled them against her close and felt their trembling lips press against her cheek as she sank again under their spell and the water flowed.

Chapter Thirty One

The atmosphere at the clone students' party had become electric. From the moment that Mel Higgins had spilt the glass of red wine over Sophie's new dress, he had realised that something serious was amiss. The clonies who had not accompanied Sophie upstairs were clustered around the bar at one end of the room, whispering, their eyes diverted. Mel and the small group of his friends who had come to the party joked about the clone boys' lack of interest in competitive sport.

"You remember their first 100 meter race?" someone mentioned, as the group stood chatting after Sophie's sudden disappearance with the group of clone boys when Mel had spilt the glass of red wine over her dress.

"That was fantastic," Jack Rooney laughed. "They all won!"

"Not surprising, when they all get the same marks in examinations and homework. Dr Watson told me that he found three essays that were practically identical. He accused them of copying but it appeared that they had both been written in different rooms at the same time."

Mel kept looking at the elevator doors awaiting Sophie's return, but there was no sign of her and he became more and more concerned. He looked around the room and saw that the clone students had dispersed themselves fairly evenly among the chatting groups and some couples and a few of the clonies were dancing to the music at the far end of the hall.

Time passed. Mel moved around the room keeping a lookout for Sophie, in case she'd come back by another route. He sensed that something was wrong and noticed that Sean had stopped talking to some of his friends and joined a group of clonies who were in agitated conversation.

Mel was sweating now. Instinctively he knew that Sophie was in trouble. He caught a fleeting glimpse of Sean's eyes across the room and he was certain that Sean was concerned as well. He had a look of guilt as he turned his face away. Mel followed him to the side of the room, near to the elevator and approached him from behind. Sean was separated from the other clonies by a few yards and Mel grabbed him around the throat, holding him in a vicious grip.

"Where is she?" he demanded. "Tell me. Quickly."

"Help!" Sean screamed, but his cries were smothered by Mel's hand held firmly over his mouth.

"Grab those boys," Mel shouted. "They're attacking Sophie."

Mel's teammates were like lightning and turned on the clone boys in a second.

"Where is she?" Mel demanded again, holding Sean around the neck to near breaking point and bending his arm behind him until he was screaming.

"We didn't mean it," he pleaded.

"Where is she?"

"Upstairs," Sean stammered.

"Come on, show us, you little bottled-bastard," Mel growled, dragging Sean towards the lift. "If you lot have harmed Sophie, I'll...." Mel was beyond himself, red-faced and shaking with anger.

"What floor?" he growled again as the lift filled up with hefty football players who squeezed in as tightly as possible. "You planned this," he accused, as the elevator started its long climb to the 12th floor.

"No! Really," Sean pleaded, gasping for breath. "It was the others. They did it. I told them not to. I like Sophie. Please let me go. I'll help you."

"I'll throttle you, you bastard. If they've hurt Sophie, you're dead. Who are the others? Come on," he twisted Sean's arm higher, "Come on! Who are they."

"It's Donal. He's their leader. They do what he tells them. Believe me, please. I told them not to."

They spilt out as the lift doors opened and the big men flexed their arms after being so tightly crammed in the small space.

"Take us! Quick!" Mel pushed Sean in front down the narrow corridor.

"It's here," Sean cried stopping before Donal's room.

"It's locked," someone said.

Mel pushed Sean on to the corridor floor and taking a deep breath charged the door like a raging bull. The thin wood gave under him and the door collapsed and he sprawled half into the room. The others charged over him.

On his feet again, Mel tore his way through the others until he was at the door of the shower room and could see Sophie's tangled red hair among the mass of white flesh.

"Get the bastards," Mel shouted as he plunged into the steaming shower unit and took apart the swarm of clonies.

The clone boys were picked up like lice and dragged out of the shower, smacked and beaten and punched until they lay whimpering in the corner of the room.

Mel was in the shower, the steaming water still rushing down. Sophie was crouching, shaking and beyond herself with fear, her eyes staring, not believing what had happened.

"Are you all right?" Mel asked helping her out of the shower and covering her with a blanket torn from the nearby bed.

"Yes, yes," she said, panting, recovering, tears streaming down her cheeks. "I don't know what happened to me. I shouldn't have got into the shower without asking them to go away. I was silly. I don't know what came over me."

"They'll not touch you again. I'll see to that."

"They're just kids, really. They've had no experience of the real world and have been suddenly thrown out of their Home without any preparation of living in a normal community." Suddenly she was sympathetic again. They had been gentle with her and she recalled her vision of how innocent and afraid they were. "They think I am some sort of goddess. They want me to be their Queen!" She had recovered enough to give a weak laugh as she clung to Mel's arm.

"If you ask me they're just a lot of perverts," Mel retorted, still angry and kicked out viciously at the tattooed number on the bare bottom of one of the clonies who had recovered from his beating and was running out of the room, crying.

Chapter Thirty Two

Karen's long dream had come true. She leaned close to the window of the helijet as it circled over the Rock. Ever since her discovery of the fertility extract which had been named, Fex2, from a rare seaweed collected in Dunfooey Bay, she had imagined that the Rock might be a rich source of supply of the new drug.

"But there are acres of weed, I thought it was just a rock," she said, glancing at Harry who sat beside her, smiling with pleasure at her delight.

"They're coming along well," he answered, looking out at the twisting line of dykes that seemed to cling to the line of black rock far below. "We've now dyked in about a mile around the rock itself." He spoke loudly above the noise of the engine as the pilot changed the drive into vertical mode, and they started to descend slowly towards the dome, which slowly opened below them.

"There's the wind-power units," Harry pointed to the long row of windmills that now gave the Rock a continuous supply of electricity. "With the success of the dyke scheme and the growth of plant food we are now nearly self-sufficient. The Company profits are soaring." Harry was proud of the achievements of the Company and had increasingly played a major role in its development.

"But this is wonderful, Harry. Why do we hear so little about it back home? The Rock is hardly ever mentioned on the news or in the press."

"Well, you see, Karen, the Company is in complete control here and we are one hundred percent loyal to the Omega Corps. Our staff are well screened before they are taken on and allowed to work here. So long as we send sufficient seal meat back to Emanon and maintain the supply of gas and oil, the government leaves us alone. But look!"

Karen looked down at the big rock. She hadn't realised that the rock itself was now the nucleus of a huge circular platform supported by concrete pillars built into the surrounding reef. Tall concrete buildings surrounded the apex of the rock that protruded out of the centre of the platform and had been made into the landing pad, covered by a weather proof dome.

"Wonderful, I never realised it was so big. This is a huge

ocean city in mid Atlantic," Karen gasped.

"You only see a fraction of it. Under the Rock, we've made three layers of tunnels and galleries. The Rock itself is just the entrance to a whole new underwater world. The food processing factory and the gas pumping stations are all down there. The more we dig out from under the sea the more of the reef we can reclaim. You'll see it all tomorrow."

"Is the tide coming in?"

"Yes," Harry said. "Within a few hours all the rocks outside of the dykes will be covered. The cycle of tide makes it ideal for growing your seaweed."

They sat silent for a few minutes as the plane hovered above the bright silver dome that gradually opened like a great mouth and they sank through it to settle gently onto the landing pad. They disembarked into the huge rocky cavern to the welcoming smiles from the small group of staff who had come to meet the new arrivals.

"There's Frank," Karen said as she spied Frank Tooley coming forward to greet them. "I wonder how he likes it here. I hope he's got the lab ready," she added, always anxious to get on with the research work. They hugged and he kissed her on the cheek. Since Karen had gone to live in Dunfooey, Frank and she had become very good friends as well as colleagues and she had missed him since he had gone to the Rock to get ready for the next phase of their programme.

The accommodation on the Rock was simple but adequate especially for someone who had become accustomed to living in the relatively old fashioned conditions at Dunfooey. Karen's room was small but the porthole windows gave good views of the ocean. She could sense the sheer bulk and size of the building that she was in. She could see a number of Tall Ships and boats in the harbour, the high walled dykes providing a safe haven in all weathers. One ship had just departed, its bows ploughing into the swell on its way to the main land with another cargo of seal meat and its secret load of Dulce.

The following morning, immediately after breakfast, she went to visit the laboratory that Frank Tooley had spent the last six months getting organised.

"You've done a tremendous job here, Frank," Karen said as they entered the converted rooms that looked out onto the inner quadrangle of the rig towards the ragged rockface of the Rock itself.

"Everything is so fresh and clean. There is plenty of room. I kept thinking that we would be very cramped, stuck in some corner, trying to avoid dead smelly seals and oil."

"Yes," Frank Tooley replied as he sorted out some samples of the seaweed he'd collected the previous day. "It took me days to appreciate just how massive this place is."

As Tessa had predicted her cousin Frank had been willing to help Karen and appreciated from the outset the importance of her research for a fertility drug. Frank was convinced that the infertility had been caused by widespread atmospheric pollution resulting from the combined impact of the decrease in the ozone layer and the effect of the UV light on a number of gaseous pollutants. Soon after Karen's arrival at Dunfooey all those years ago, Frank had arranged for the old barn at the back of O'Flafferty's Inn to be converted into a laboratory and over the years the Omega Fertility Campaign had donated more and more funds to Karen's research. Although, it became well known by the authorities that Karen was the President of Omega's Campaign, it was considered that she was past doing any significant research and although she spoke in public on occasions, few of the government scientists took her seriously. The story had been propagated, and it was generally believed, that following the successful cloning of her son, she'd had a nervous breakdown and had retired to the isolated region at Dunfooey, where she dabbled with pointless experiments on organic farming and a diet of sea food.

However, all this public impression was very far from the truth. Karen had built up a considerable team of dedicated scientists and naturalists based at Dunfooey and had maintained contact with similarly minded scientists in other countries. Like, as had happened in Emanon, many other countries had also hastened down the cloning route of survival rather than the searching for a fertility drug, more afraid of the loss of their national identity than the saving of the human race.

After many years of searching and screening the shellfish and seaweed around the coastline of Dunfooey, Karen's team had isolated a compound that was produced only during a short period in the life cycle of a starfish. The compound was able to induce viable sperm and ova in cloned farm animals. More recently, successful secret trials had been carried out on couples living in very isolated regions and a few pregnancies had occurred. Unfortunately the amount of drug that could be isolated from the starfish was extremely small and it was clear that no largescale use of it was ever going to be possible. Its existence, however, gave the team hope and when its DNA sequence was at last identified, the gene banks of other marine life forms were screened. Frank Tooley had shown that a seaweed, known locally as Dulce, which was occasionally eaten as a speciality, also contained a very similar compound. Extracts of the drug from Dulce was very difficult to obtain but eventually a compound was isolated in sufficient quantity to test. The tests were very successful and the compound, now called, Fex-2, was found to be even more potent than the related compound from starfish.

"Look at this, Karen," Frank said across the laboratory, holding up a fresh specimen of Dulce. The Dulce fields are maturing beautifully and we can harvest tons at every low tide. There are acres of it just for the taking. Also, Karen, the really good news is that the concentration of Fex2 is just as high as what we found in specimens from Dunfooey. Once we get these production units up and running we'll have enough Fex2 to make all of Europe fertile, let alone Emanon." Frank was as enthusiastic as Karen and between them they had made a team that stimulated all their younger colleagues. Over the years she had grown to depend on Frank, as a friend as well as a colleague. She understood more fully now that ever before the closeness that a man and woman can have without the demands of passion and sex. She wondered often just how different Emanon would have been if Frank had been appointed as her assistant at the Institute instead of Michael, all those years ago.

"The sealers can start collecting it as soon as we wish," Harry said, who had been listening to Frank's report. "The Company will employ more men if need be. We can now accommodate them in the new platforms and as long as our quota of seal meat is maintained no one will be any the wiser."

"But how do you keep all this activity secret? Surely when your men go back to Emanon they'll talk," Karen said, anxious that their attempts to mass-produce FEX-2 would not be frustrated.

"Don't worry," Harry answered. "You see, when Little Greta was born, because she was my daughter, nearly all of the rigger's families decided to foster one. They did it because of me and the way the Palace made me publicise the cloning affair. Then, when it became a tragedy and especially when the failure of the Special Rebirth Ceremony was used to force most of the parents to return their little girls to the Institution, the riggers in the Corps became very militant. But they're controlled and highly disciplined now. Secret Omega units that are all over Emanon, are controlled from here on the Rock. In fact as we control about half the supply of seal meat and over seventy five percent of the energy for Emanon, we really control it. The cloneboys haven't got round to thinking about us yet. But they will."

"With Michael becoming President they soon will," Karen said. "His speeches are now so orientated around his clone boys that I think he is losing touch with reality."

"That's clear enough. It goes back a long time," Harry said, recalling his first meeting with Michael, when he was asked to publicise the new clone babies. "When he showed me around the Institute years ago, all he could talk about was the new Clone Age. How wonderful it was going to be. How the Celts would reach their ultimate destiny. There was never a word about trying to find a cure for infertility. He never mentioned your work and you were working on these very ideas in the next lab. My God! The bastard makes me mad!" Harry hit his left hand with his right fist making a solid slapping noise and moved around the room breathing deeply.

"Well, we'll soon have a cure, Harry," Frank said, trying to calm the big man down. "That's when we'll need your Omega Corps."

"And probably your Tall Ships," Karen added. "In a few years the clone boys will have too much control. You've heard what Sophie says about them at college. They are moving ahead too quickly. I don't know how we'll manage. I sense there is something about them that we don't understand. Something about them when they're together. I'm their mother. But they frighten me. I feel they can see inside me. Into my head."

"I know," Harry said, "there's a limited amount of time that we have to deal with the clonemen. We must work quickly. Once the first batch leave university they'll dominate the administration and they'll frustrate all our efforts. They'll take complete control, if we don't stop them."

Chapter Thirty Three


The incident at their end of term's Christmas Party had been very humiliating for the clone boys and had irrevocably changed forever their attitude towards the older students.

"I never thought that she'd do it," Donal said, as he sat in his room chatting with a small group of his brothers early the next morning.

"I know. I was thinking about it. God yes, but that she actually did it took my breath away." Ricky added, shaking his head. "I just kept on wishing that she'd keep going."

"I was too," Cathal interjected. "Could we have made her do it? Mentally I mean, without ever saying anything, just thinking. I guess we all felt the same. It had been all a joke when we started."

"I know. It was like a joke or a dream come true. I could hardly believe my eyes." Donal had been the originator of the plank, and their intention was merely to tell Sophie how much they all liked her and ask her be their Queen. After all she was the most beautiful girl on campus and there had been a lot of talk about Rag Queen's and Beauty Queen's and Donal had thought it would be a clever joke if they claimed Sophie as their Clone Queen. "Do you think we really have that sort of power over the others. Especially when we're together? Can we really control others?"

"We've really only known our aunts and uncles and only seen them once a week or so." Ricky said.

"And the teachers at school. They were all right," Colm added.

"Exactly. You remember when we were quite young at the start of school. The teachers we didn't like seemed to leave. I never thought much about it at the time. It just seemed natural wishing that certain staff would go away. But could we have actually sent them a way. Made them leave. Or rather made them want to leave?" Donal's mind was now working fast, previous episodes coming to the fore, memories and incidents that they had influenced and ignored, just glad that they had happened, all coming out on the surface of their consciousness, a realisation that they had a power that they hadn't recognised, changing them from boys into men.

"We must do some experiments and see how strong it is,"

Donal said, taking command of the situation, his back side still hurt from the vicious kick that Mel Higgins had accurately landed the previous night. "Let's see if we have real control over ourselves. Before we try and control others."

"OK," Sean said, who has sat quietly listening to the conversation and still smouldering with anger at what his brothers had done to Sophie. "Let's see if we can attract Gerry from next door to come in here. I bet he's sound asleep and we won't have any effect on him."

"Good idea," Colm said pulling his hands around his knees and bowing his head in concentration. Donal and some of the others copied him. There was silence in the room.

Sean watched them, smiling to himself. This was another of Donal's silly ideas that would get them all into trouble, yet again. From a young age, Donal had pushed himself forward as the leader of the group and tended to dominate the others. For years Sean had argued with him and often wanted more discussion and agreement by everyone, but mostly Donal got his way and Sean had become pushed to the side, although he was still Michael's clear favourite.

Suddenly the door burst open and Gerry from next door came rushing in. "Are you all right? I thought I heard you screaming."

"You did," Donal replied enthusiastically, "come in. Listen. We've discovered something important!"

"You mean you brought me in here without actually saying a word."

"Yes, we only thought about you."

"What do you do?"

"Nothing. Just think and have confidence. We have to practice and develop this. Let's try and bring in Martin and Joe."

Within half an hour the room was packed with brothers, attracted from various parts of the building. They soon found that the greater the number of clonies sending out their mysterious messages, the more dramatic the effect became.

"When you think about it, we've been using this power for years," Sean remarked, having watched the gathering excitement of the clonies. "It's quite natural to us, but we mustn't abuse it, especially if we can have control over the others. If they find out there'll be real trouble."

"Nonsense," Donal retorted. "If they ever find a cure for fertility, we'll have to fight for our own survival and this will be our weapon that they won't be able to resist. We'll practice. We'll get that bugger, Mel Higgins!" he added with venom.

Chapter Thirty Four

Sophie had felt confused about the events at the Christmas Party. The authorities had dismissed the unfortunate incident with a degree of embarrassment as due to teenage immaturity and blamed the older students for allowing the young innocent clone boys to get drunk. A few of Mel's friends who had helped in Sophie's rescue had been sent down for using excessive force against the clone boys. How much of it had been her own fault, not realising their feelings towards her? Had she encouraged them, provoked them, without being aware of the enormous gap in their lives due to there being no girls around? Her attitude angered Mel Higgins and for weeks their relationship had been strained, but she could not completely condemn the clone boys. She felt the others were making use of the incident as an excuse to reject the clone students and avoid interaction. Within weeks the pattern had frozen and the two communities moved further and further apart, each ignoring the other and avoiding any direct contact.

    In general, the clone boys had a guilt complex about Sophie and avoided her completely. Only Sean had the courage to apologise a few days later on behalf of his brothers for what had happened. His left eye was black and swollen and he still limped. He was anxious for her to know that he had not been involved and had disapproved of his brothers' ruse which had completely got out of hand. There was something about him that intrigued her and they spoke occasionally, but only when she thought no one was looking, especially Mel, who was angered by any sign that Sophie had forgiven the clonies for what they had done. But Sean held a strange attraction to her that she could not understand and one afternoon, in the new year, when a slight skiff of snow lay on the banks along the river, they found themselves walking and watching a few swans picking among the dead reeds.

    "I'm very fond of you Sophie," Sean said after a long silence. "You know we all are, but we all got of to such a bad start that I'm sure things have changed for ever."

    "I know Sean. I like you, in fact I think about you a lot." They walked close, huddling against the cold wind that bore down the wide river from the hills. Mel knows. I can't help it. It's driving him crazy, too. He'll see that I'm not at the touch line watching the game and he'll guess that I'm with you. We'll have a fierce row to night. What am I going to do?"

"Look Sophie," Sean said pulling her close, "I love you. You know that. But it is not only me. All my brothers do. We all think about you every night. Look for you every day. There is something I must tell you. You must keep it a secret. It is very dangerous. You see we can influence people. Like you. They have been practising. Donal is their leader now and you'll have to be careful. Mel is in great danger..." His words were cut off by a sudden shout from the long reeds lining the river side path. About ten clonies suddenly emerged from the thicket and surrounded them. Sophie's arms were grabbed and she was torn of Sean's gentle supporting arm and Sean grabbed roughly and held firmly, his arms twisted behind his back.

"Leave me alone!" Sophie cried, "Stop it!"

"You go back," someone ordered and suddenly she panicked and was running down the path toward the playing fields. Behind her she heard shouts and screams and heavy splashing and knew that Sean had been thrown into the ice cold Shanna.

Chapter Thirty Five

Sophie glanced sideways across the narrow passage between the long row of desks that filled the examination hall. The young cloneman opposite was looking at her. Their eyes met. It was Sean. A thin smile of his memory partially touched her lips and she bent back to the script with renewed vigour. She had been glad he had survived the soaking some years ago.

Tension had mounted to fever pitch during the few weeks before the end of the term. Over the years there had been little success at integrating the two communities and separate clubs and societies had sprung up in the clone community as each year new batches of young clone boys had entered the university. The recent establishment of the Council for Clones and the re-emergence of militants activities on the fringes of the Omega Corps had shattered any earlier hopes of an integrated society.

Today, while Sophie's pen was streaking down the page with a speed of writing that surprised her as the exam questions appeared much easier than she'd expected, Mel Higgins was sitting at the far end of the hall, somehow surrounded by clonemen and isolated from his friends. Mel's eyes did not seem to focus on the page and although he knew that he was writing there was a strange fuzziness in his mind and he had no sense of time. For minutes he would stare into the distance, his curly hair held high by the white sweat band that he now always wore with the red Omega sign stamped clearly on it at the centre of his forehead. Since the dramatic events of that first Christmas Party, his popularity had increased substantially, not only as a sportsman but as a student politician. Encouraged by his mother, Mel had established an Omega Corp group at the university. He soon had an active following and gave increasingly vocal support for the legalisation of Fex-2. But the student Clone Council was vigorously opposed to its use and as government sponsored tests had shown that high doses of Fex-2 could cause cancer in cloned rats, the authorities had prohibited its use.

For some minutes, Mel had been scribbling enthusiastically on his answer paper and an invigilator glanced at the page over his shoulder as he walked down the long aisle of candidates. He stopped abruptly and drew back.

"Higgins, if you continue to do that, you'll fail."

"Bugger off," Mel snapped, turning noisily over to a fresh page and continuing to print in large childlike capitals,

I HATE CLONIES
I HATE CLONIES
CLONIES ARE BOTTLED BASTARDS

The invigilator moved away and suddenly Mel felt his mind clear and the page in front of him came into focus. He gripped his pen and looked at the page aghast. What had he done? What had he written? He flicked through the previous pages of the answer booklet, crumpled up the sheets and stood up. He looked around and saw that he was surrounded by clonies and they were looking at him. Their eyes were like daggers piercing the fabric of his being and suddenly his mind snapped. He was there, their fine hands were roaming over her, touching her, leading her away from him, she was laughing at him, running her fingers through their fair hair, smoothing it gently. He roughly pushed back his chair and began walking down between the rows of clone students, who held their pens ready to continue writing when this distraction had past. His huge bulky frame moved slowly, the curly black mane towering above them, the red Omega sign matching the sudden flush on his face. Mel knew that he shouldn't, but he couldn't help it. He must get out. The atmosphere was sending him crazy. He needed fresh air. He knew he would fail his exam but if he stayed he'd die. The searing pain in his head was unbearable. He felt time was running out. He must get out of the hall to escape from the fierce ache and pounding in his head that was driving him crazy.

Chapter Thirty Six

Later that evening, to celebrate the end of term and the completion of their university career, many students had gathered in the refractory bar, overlooking the Shanna. When Donal arrived there was already a heated argument in progress between a group of clonies and the occupants of a nearby table including Mel Higgins and a number of his friends. All of Mel's friends were now wearing the red head ban of the Omega Corp. Already the table was littered with empty bottles and tongues were well loosened.

"The Palace should stop producing clones and put more money into research for a fertility pill. We would then have real children." Orla said. She was a year older than Sophie and one few young females remaining at the colleague.

"It certainly is very stupid of us to leave all our civilisation to a bunch of perverts like you." Mel retorted, recognising Donal who had just entered.

"Believe what you like, but you can't rewrite history. You can't change the truth. We're here and whether you like it or not we're here to stay." Donal interjected across the void between the tables.

"That's what you think," Mel replied, "you're only here as a fill in. Don't worry, as soon as Fex is available, we'll see that those bloody tin cans that you came in are wrecked. We'll see to that."

"They won't be closed down," Donal answered confidently. "Already the running of the modules is practically in our hands. Even the nursing is all done by clonemen. Now that the President has agreed to setting up a Clone Council, we will now be able to plan for a new social order in order to satisfy the need of the clone, not just your dying race."

"A new society indeed," Mel snapped back. "The President is a fool. Our generation will force the Masters to change their minds. We are going to rule the country. It's our country. We are going to rule, not you lot." Mel was rather drunk and moved to the bar to get his glass refilled. He hated and despised the clone for what they had done to Sophie. "Not a lot of bottle bastards, like you," he spat back at the group of clonies who were clustered around their table watching him intently. Ever since Sophie had come under their influence Mel had loathed them all, especially Sean whom he knew that Sophie had constantly thought about. He had become convinced that she was longing for the excitement of the illicit and perverted contact with the clonies. She seemed to be possessed by them. He could never really trust her not to go back to them. His temper grew as his words flowed freely, condemning and cursing the group of fair-haired young men who sat in front of him, as he now took centre stage from his position at the bar.

The clonemen sat, no one spoke. No one answered him or challenged him. They just sat and stared.

"You're like carrots. Grown for food. All the bloody same. You may as well be farm animals. Look at yourselves, like stupid cabbages, sitting in rows looking at me. Why are you gaping at me like that? Say something, you bunch of bloody tin can bastards. Go away. Disappear. Leave us alone. We don't want you. You're only interested in yourselves. You think that you're a new race. Perfect supermen, but you're nothing but a bunch of perverts."

The clonemen continued to stare at him. Their anger rose at his unreasoned words and Donal kept the pot boiling by interjecting nasty comments about the normals and it was time they were doomed. As the evening wore on Mel became more and more irate and continually returned to the bar for a refill of his glass despite attempts by Sophie to restrain him. To night the Clone knew that this was to be their ultimate test, all their previous suspicions about their ability to influence people was now coming together and their minds fused in a violent ferment of anger and hate.

Mel continued to battle against their irresistible forces, swearing and cursing, flinging abuse at the still quiet faces before him. Sweating profusely, shaking with uncontrolled anger, his words flowed like a fountain, his voice screamed his hate and frustration. Sophie became concerned with his violent and drunken exhibition and she rose to try and calm him.

"Oh you bitch! You clone bitch. Don't touch me. You needn't come to their defence any more. I know what you want. You long for them to gloat over you. Like they did before. Make you their bloody Queen! Worship you indeed. Think you're a bloody goddess. Born to be a fucking queen! You and your bloody clone. I know what you're thinking. Isn't that what you want woman? Isn't it? To have them all to yourself again! Can anything else will ever satisfy you? Will it? Well then, have your bloody clone," he roared at her, becoming more and more excited and violently pushed her forward. She fell headlong staggering across the floor and landed, sprawling across the table in front of Sean, who had sat staring at his hands, rigid, terrified all evening. The rest of the clonies continued to stare at Mel, their silence ate into the very core of their prey.

Sophie's intervention has loosened the final chords of reason in Mel's mind. Sentences were fragmented now but a certain drunken logic still ran through his disconnected ideas. His words seemed to speak back to him, echoing from the distant walls, reflected by the silence and the cold staring glare of the clone. His insatiable thirst once again drove him back to the bar where he filled another glass from the automatic dispenser. Only the gurgle and gulp of rapid swallowing and then the sharp contrasting click as the glass was heavily returned to the table broke the silence. Then turning rapidly, he flung with absolute abandon and fury, the glass against the opposite wall. The glass shattering into a thousand silver shining pieces spread over the heads of those close by. Everyone ducked, some screamed in anger, frightened by the sudden onslaught.

"Ah! That made you talk. You carrots aren't so mute after all." He ranted and swore and laughed with a blood-curdling triumphant roar and as his body shook convulsively, he grabbed a nearby chair and bashed it to pieces against the bar counter. "That's what I'll do to those vats they breed you in," he cried. "We'll bash the bloody modules in." With sudden effortless movement he flung his drunken body across the room, scattering tables and people before him and as though he was on a sports field he charged at the large open window overlooking the angry flooded river that was surging towards the Great Falls.

On seeing Mel losing complete control in the hall, Sophie had realised too late what was happening and had jumped up shouting, "Mel, Mel, stop!" I love you!" Through the rushing surges in his mind, he recognised her voice - a voice of sanity and of hope. "Mel, I love you. Please stop!" Turning on the clonemen she roared, "I know what you're doing. You little scum! Stop it!" Her voice rang across the pandemonium now raging in the hall. Somehow the unexpectedness of her actions broke the commune of minds and the clonies' concentration fractured for a second. For an instant, the explosive pulsations in his head vanished and Mel could see clearly and realised what was happening. But his momentum had carried him onward through the window and as his feet left the ledge he roared, "Sophie! I love you!" He opened his arms and took a high head first dive into the black water.

No one moved. There was a dead hush as broken glass sprinkled on the floor and then silence. A slight smile broke on Donal's lips as he caught Richard's eye across the table. The clonemen looked at the empty gaping window and relaxed.

Chapter Thirty Seven


Sophie was heart broken. She blamed herself for Mel's death and her hatred for the clone increased beyond her wildest dreams. In spite of extensive overnight searches there was no sign of Mel's body and the divers were called off by late afternoon the following day. It was assumed that the fast flowing river, swollen by the recent summer thunder burst, has washed Mel away down stream and over the Great Falls and out to sea. It was expected that his body would be washed up along the estuary within the next few days.

When Sean saw her the next day and stopped to offer her his sympathy, she cursed at him. "You bastard! You should have stopped them. You weak bastard! You sat there like a limpet doing nothing. You knew damn well what they were doing." She was glad it was the end of term as the college was closing down for the summer vacation, and so she gathered together Mel's things and packed his suitcase along with her own and caught the coach to Dunfooey.

Sophie had heard that things had changed drastically during the past term, but she was surprised as the coach was halted at Dunfooey Pass by a group of armed Omega Guards.

"I didn't know things had got so bad," Sophie said to a guard whom she had known as a fisherman from a small isolated village a few miles east of Dunfooey.

"We've just declared independence. Yours is the last coach to get through. The Palace hasn't had time to respond yet. They were not prepared for it at all. They thought that all the real opposition was in the southern region around Southport as this area has been relatively quiet."

"But what prompted this action now?" Sophie asked the young Omega guard who had got onto the coach for the trip down to Dunfooey..

"Last week they sent in a group of so-called social workers and nurses to collect any new babies that had been born here since Fex-2 became available. They say they have to be monitored for cancer and given special treatment. None of us believe that. There were a number of births last year when the first tests were being carried out up in the mountains and the children are fine." The guard smiled at Sophie, and continued. "My sister and Larry Jackson had one, a little boy."

"Did they take him away?" Sophie asked anxiously, knowing the family well.

"No! Thank God! We heard they were coming and smuggled the infant away before they got to the village. He's safe at the moment with a second cousin of mine away up in the highlands. But they've taken all the confidential doctor's records and replaced the local social workers, getting information about all the newly born and the pregnant women. As you know, there's quite a number now, especially up in the hills."

"That's good to hear though," Sophie said. "Fex-2 is working well then. Karen will be pleased. I hope the reports of it causing cancer aren't true." They sat silent as the coach driver made his careful way down the steep road, around numerous hairpin bends providing a breathtaking view of the valley and the ocean beyond. On either side the mountains rose precipitously towards the rugged ridges and away to the west the sky was darkened by great masses of cloud marking the approach of another storm. At places, the road clung to the sheer cliff of the mountain giving way eventually only to broken shale and rock and eventually to upland pasture land. Then through thick forest, it twisted and turned and followed the river that tumbled and surged down the gorge.

"We've beat them," the guard said confidently as they reached the bottom of the Pass, "there's no going back now. The clonies will never get through that Pass, not now that we've sealed it off." Soon they reached the valley floor and were among the rugged foothills that made up the vast coastal range leading down to Dunfooey.

"That's great," Sophie replied. "But you should see the way they can control people. They've been practising on us for the past two years. Last week they demonstrated their power on Mel Higgins. Did you hear that they forced him to jump out the window? It was just plain murder!"

"My God! No I hadn't heard. I've been up patrolling the Pass all week. I am sorry. Poor Mel. Is it really as bad as that?"

"I'm certainly glad I'm finished with college," she continued. "I couldn't stand another day with them near me. They are always there, in my mind, pulling me away, pulling me towards them. I know it. They search my thoughts. I can feel it, just like Karen said about them at the Palace. I experience it too. I don't know why. But it works both ways. Sometimes I can see inside their minds as well. I had proof last week during the examinations. I had only imagined it before, but I knew what they were doing to Mel at the exams. A dream come true. It was in the back of my mind, if only I'd recognised it sooner. But I'd know the feeling again. Funny, I don't feel afraid of them like I used to."

"You'll be safe here," the young guards man said. "We'll not see many clonemen around here, I can promise you that," he added as the coach speeded up on the wide level road on the outskirts of Dunfooey.

The usually sleepy little town of Dunfooey was packed and the coach slowed to a crawl as it approached the centre. The town was decorated with Omega banners flying from every possible location. Crowds were at the station to greet the new arrivals. Sophie could see Harry standing head and shoulder above the rest and rushed out of the coach into his strong arms.

"Oh, Daddy, I'm so glad to be back," she cried, as he swung her in his arms like a child and then she was clinging to Tessa and they were weeping with joy at their reunion.

Karen and Frank Tooley were close by. It was so good to be home. Then she saw Cara Higgins who fell into her arms in tears. "I'm so sorry, Cara, I feel it was my fault. I should have tried harder to stop Mel. He was so high and fluent and seemed to be enjoying himself and at first we were all encouraging him. It was the last night and we'd all been so completely fed up with the clonies that....."

"We can talk later, dear," Tessa said. "Frank has brought the trailer so we can all have a lift back up to the farm." Tessa said, as she climbed up on her father's old tractor and Frank started the engine with a roar and a pall of black smoke.

Tessa had built the peat fire up high and the fresh yellow flames were flickering, sending shadows across the darkened room. Outside the stars were shining sharply in the black sky. They talked through the night and Sophie was brought up to date on the new plans.

"The clonemen developed much more quickly than we ever imagined," Harry was saying, sprawled and relaxing in his chair. "Every time I come back from the Rock they have moved ahead even more. They are now in control of the cities. The papers say that as the eldest group, the originals, those you were at College with, have now graduated and are to become members of the new Council for Clones. It's only in remote regions like around here that they haven't taken over. Even a small number of them can control whole areas with their psychic powers."

"It's when they are in these small groups, twos or threes that we can't resist them," Sophie said. "I think that is why they've been able to dominate their aunts and uncles, even when they were kids. The people who took them as foster children have been under their spell for years. They just do what they're told. I think I managed to break their spell over Mel just as he jumped out the window. In fact the last thing he shouted was 'I love you, Sophie.' I seemed to feel what they were doing. Somehow I can sense what they're up to. I didn't realise it for a long time."

"I think I know what has happened," Karen said seriously, "and it's frightening if it is true. You see the Emanons have always believed that some of them had 'the Gift' or 'second sight' as some people refer to it. I never believed in it and have always looked on it as old superstition. But my mother and father were firm believers and both my grandparents were said to have special talents. When grandfather was a young man he had a travelling show that went around Fairs and he had a famous act that read people's thoughts and then he met Granny whose family was also was in the show business and they developed a joint act in which she sent messages to him while he was locked in a sound proof box." She paused to allow the implications of what she'd said sink in. "When Michael stole my baby and produced the clone, they inherited my gift genes and this has resulted in their mind fusion in a way that couldn't have been predicted. Now, they've become involved with the Palace and run all of Michael's affairs. They act as secretaries and attendants in the Council of Masters, which will soon be, if it's not already under their spell. I'm sure it's the clonemen that are now making the decisions. Just look at the Palace's reaction to Fex-2. They know it works, but still, they ban it. Treat it like an illegal drug. Advertise daily against its use. Push it underground, instead of taking on its wide distribution."

"Is the rumour that it causes cancer true?" Sophie asked, having seen the frequent counter-publicity about the new wonder cure for infertility that was constantly mentioned in the national news bulletins and press.

"Only at very high doses in laboratory animals. At massive doses, over a long period of time it does cause ovarian tumours, in rats. But all drugs have some side effects, especially if abused or at exceptionally high levels. The doses used are far in excess of what we need to use to restore fertility," Karen said firmly, annoyed at the way the Palace had abused the information that her research team had produced in support for Fex-2. "The Church has been arguing for the lifting of the ban, but the Palace takes no notice."

"Still," Harry said, "it will only be a matter of time before they try and penetrate the region. We're safe over the winter, when the snow falls, but by next spring they'll have devised a way of attacking us." He stood up and threw a few more junks of peat on the dying fire. "You see, I don't think that the Clonies can accept the idea that if normal fertility returns then their production units would become redundant and the clone not needed any more. Their overwhelming desire to perpetuate the clone is completely selfish and makes our two cultures incompatible. And it's no use trying to talk to them. If indeed they have the Gift, as Karen says, then they will only make us think they way they want us to. So what is the point? It is either the clone or ourselves."

"I agree," Frank Tooley commented from across the room. "Our agents in the cities tell us that they are now referring to us as 'natives' and we know from Karen's old colleague who's still working in the Genetics Institute that the clone scientists that have just graduated are beginning to design sub-clones that will act as slaves and workers. Biologically speaking, once their numbers have increased to the point when communal mind-fusion is achieved it is as natural for them to behave that way as for us to want sexual partners and families. It's like an insect colony. An ant colony is really a clone. Cleaners, workers, fighters, gatherers, builders, all groups of individuals designed specifically for particular jobs, equivalent to our different organs, such as the kidney, liver, arms, brain. No doubt their scientists will soon find the genes responsible for this so called Gift and they will produce future generations of clones that will have so highly tuned psychic-potential that they will dominate any normal community. With their existing powerful survival mindset, they will become a major threat to other countries let alone the rest of Emanon."

"It is the ultimate expression of the selfish gene," Karen said, agreeing fully with Frank's assessment of the clone's future strategy. "Unlike most other countries, Emanon was too old fashioned in our ethics to take advantage of the new technology, even though most of it was developed here. In fact, in contrast to us, most places have been able to develop numerous clones and are trying to maintain their ethnic balance. But everywhere is struggling to survive at the moment and we can't expect much help from elsewhere. We'll have to deal with situation ourselves. In Emanon, I'm afraid that my cloned sons will do their utmost to get rid of us completely or even worse to make us their slaves."

There was silence in the room. The dawn light through the window brightened and the white mist rolled up the mountain from the distant sea.

"Sophie," Karen said, quietly, her voice anxious and afraid, trying to delay bringing forward the idea. Everyone returned from their moment of private reverie, some knowing that the moment of decision had come.

"What is it, Karen?" Sophie asked, sensing the anxiety in Karen's voice. Over the years Karen had become her second mother and guardian. It had been Karen who had shown her the way through school and helped her pass the difficult examination that took her to university. It had been Karen who had talked to her long into the nights when she had been young and worried about her feelings towards Mel. It had been Karen who had helped her through the trauma following the clonies attack on her at the Christmas Party. Now there was something in her voice that was asking, begging.

"Sophie," Karen said quietly again, "there is something that I feel you and everyone else here should know. There is something very special about you that will help us control the clone."

"No!" Sophie cried. "I'm finished with the clonemen. I never want to see them again. Please don't ask me to do anything." She was tired out from her long journey and Karen suddenly feared that she'd raised the topic at the wrong time. Hopes for her carefully laid plans seemed to vanish. "I just can't." Sophie whimpered, tears of pent-up emotion surging to her eyes.

"Listen, Sophie," Karen continued, ignoring her objections. "There is something that we should have told you a long time ago. Both Tessa and I thought that it would never matter, but now it is vitally important that you know."

"Yes, my dear," Tessa said, reaching over and taking Sophie's hand. "You see, Sophie, Harry is not your real father."

"What!" Sophie cried, shocked and standing up, her back to the fire. She looked from Tessa to Harry and back, for a moment speechless. "Is that true?" They both came over and hugged her.

"Yes, yes. It's true. Even Harry didn't know for a long time. Then we thought it was better that you didn't know. It was for your own good." Tessa cried into her shoulder.

"You know, Sophie. I've always loved you, as though you were my real daughter. We should have told you before, but we thought it best not to. It was many years after I married Tessa that she eventually told me who your real father was and we both felt it was best that you didn't know."

"Who is my father then?" demanded Sophie, her voice quivering, tears streaming down her cheeks, clinging to Tessa and Harry.

"Your father is Michael Rand, the President. You are a half-sister of the clonemen," Karen said slowly, releasing the tension that enveloped the room.

"I was with your father only once. He swept me off my feet and briefly I fell in love with him," Tessa whispered, holding Sophie tightly.

"What! You mean I'm related to that scum?" Sophie cried, breaking from their arms and stepping back into the centre of the room, suddenly feeling accused, dirty, guilty.

"It's true, Sophie," Karen said. "We thought that you would never need to know. For all practical purposes Harry is your father. There were never any official records that Michael was your father. Harry and Tessa had married long before Michael found out about you."

"You mean, they know!" Sophie slumped on the floor, quivering, not wanting to be touched, ashamed. You mean those clonies knew I was their sister?"

"I don't think so. Michael may never have told them. He was always afraid of there being a scandal." Karen tried to calm the turmoil that was tearing the family apart.

Harry crouched down and lifted Sophie to her feet, comforting her.

"I love you, Harry. You'll always be my real father. I love you," she kissed him on his curled greying beard and still holding him around the neck, looked back at Karen. "But why do you have to tell me this now? What difference does it make? How can it help in controlling the clonemen?"

"Look, Sophie," Karen continued, taking her hand and encouraging her to sit down on the settee beside her. "I know it may seem strange that we tell you this, but I have an idea about how to deal with the clone and we need your help. You see, before I left Konburg after they stole my baby I managed to bring with me a copy of the genetic profile of Michael, Tessa and yourself. It was proof that you are Michael's daughter. At that time I thought of using it to ruin Michael if he tried to stop my work here at Dunfooey. As I said he has always been terrified of scandal and Frank's note about him raping Tessa has always plagued him."

"But how can I help?" urged Sophie, recovering and anxious to hear Karen's ideas.

"Well, very simply, Sophie. We want to engineer a virus that will specifically attack the clonemen. I believe that we can make use of one of your specific cell receptor genes, that is also present in the clonemen, to make the virus agent specifically attack them and not the rest of the population."

"I see what you mean," Sophie said after a moment, the implication of the Karen's strategy sinking in. "What virus will you use?" she queried, suddenly intrigued by the biological details of the venture and the prospect of dealing with the clonies once and for all.

"Measles virus," answered Karen without hesitation. "We will make a mutant measles virus that will cause a neurological condition that will allow us to take control of them. It will attack the region of the brain that expresses their gift genes."

"But I thought that measles had been completely eradicated years ago. We don't even vaccinate any more, like polio and small pox?"

"Exactly, Sophie. Measles was eradicated, even in Emanon, about ten years before the fertility crisis developed. But measles is one of the few viruses that provides life long immunity and hence most adults and older people are still immune. But young people like you are susceptible to measles. That's why we also need to make this measles mutant infectious only to the clonemen."

"And there are some measles strains that can cause rare neurological diseases," Sophie recalled her courses in medical virology. "You still have these?"

"Yes, they were kept for research purposes at the Institute and my previous assistant, Liam, has been able to smuggle frozen sample out for us. In fact, Liam is one of our best secret Omega agents in Konburg and has been able to get us the complete profile of the clonemen's genome."

"I remember meeting Liam," Harry said, recalling the time when he had been an important part of the cloning programme so may years ago. "A quiet spoken fellow."

"Yes, that's him," Karen continued. "After I left the Institute, Liam melted into the background and got on with his work. He avoided creating suspicion but has been faithful to me all these years and we have kept in close contact. Anyway, through his help, we now know the genes that we need."

"And, I have this gene?" Sophie said, suddenly sensing the role she was to play.

"Yes. You inherited a gene from Michael that provides a unique cell surface receptor and we can modify the measles attachment genes so that they will only infect the clonemen and a few others. If we can isolate and purify your gene we will then be able to produce the unique cell surface protein or receptor that only you, Michael and the clonemen have. We can then develop laboratory tests that will allow us to test if the system works before releasing it."

"What gene?" Sophie asked.

"The gene codes for a cell surface protein of the salivary glands and by knowing its structure we can make a specific virus attachment protein that binds to your unique receptor."

"I see you will alter the surface of virus so that it will attack only salivary glands with our unique receptor protein. This mutant virus will infect the clonemen and presumably relatives on Michael's side." Sophie's eyes now shone with excitement as she began to understand the subtle role that she could play in the downfall of the hated clonemen.

"We can go over the details tomorrow. But Frank and I have it well worked out in theory."

"What do I have to do?" Sophie asked, anxious now to participate in their scheme.

"We need a blood sample and a small sample of salivary cells," Frank said. "We have already completed the construction of the basic vectors which will allow us to insert the synthetic receptor gene, so as to make it clone specific. The molecular biology laboratory on the Rock is now well established and everything we need is there. We want you to come to the Rock for a while. You'll be safe there and with your experience you can help in the laboratory on the project."

"I see," Sophie hesitated. She remembered the cloneboy, Sean, and his kindness to her and how embarrassed he had been and annoyed at the way his brothers had behaved. "What about Michael Rand and myself, we'll both be susceptible?"

"Yes," Karen said. "I'm afraid that is true. Michael is probably old enough to be immune to measles, but I'm not sure. Anyway, this new virus will have a completely new tropism and will attack you both. There is no other way that we can do it. But don't worry, that why we need to make a vaccine for you. But Sophie," Karen added anxiously, sensing that Sophie was hesitating. "Will you do it?"

"Yes, of course, Karen. When do we sail to the Rock?"

Chapter Thirty Eight

"Damn, Damn!" Michael spat the words down the length of the table as he presided over the weekly dinner with twenty-five of his senior clonemen. "It's that mother of yours! She has never forgiven me for creating all of you. She would never try and understand what I had to do." He held out his glass to be refilled with red wine served by one of the younger cloneboys who attended the table.
"It's the bitch Sophie that we need to worry about," Donal spoke up from the far end of the table. "She blames us for the death of her boyfriend Mel Higgins. He got drunk at the end of term party and jumped out the bloody window into a raging river! We never touched him."
"You remember her, father," Sean spoke from his favoured seat, beside Michael, at the opposite end of the table to Donal. "You introduced me to her at your Garden Party. She was in the group that was with our mother."
"Oh yes," Michael said, recalling the first and only time that he had seen his daughter. "She's very special," he added and took a long sip of wine. "I think it is important that you know now who Sophie is," Michael said quietly after a brief pause. Ever since they had returned from College he had become aware that they could probe his mind, he had sensed it for a long time but now he knew that they were consciously doing it in a determined manner. He took another long sip of the rich red wine and felt the pulsation in his mind clear as the clone relaxed and settled back in their seats, awaiting his revelations.
"Go on, Father. You said there was something important," Sean encouraged, now anxious to hear more about Sophie. They all felt that Michael had peculiar feelings about Sophie, but could not unravel the details of the mystery.
"When I was a young man, about your age, I was on a vacation in the mountains around Dunfooey. I met a beautiful local girl and she is Sophie's mother. Sophie is your half sister," Michael said quietly to a hushed audience. Even the younger generation of clone boys who were serving and clearing away the dishes stopped in their tracks and looked at Michael in astonishment.
"Then I was always right!" Sean said with a smile. "I knew

there was always something between us that was special." The small number of his supporters clustered around him nodded their agreement.

"Why don't you bring her to live at the Palace, Father? She would be better here than being buried out in the wilderness among a lot of natives," Donal spoke up, cutting in on Sean's comments, raising a ripple of laughter from his cronies around the far end of the table.

Michael had thought many times of his beautiful daughter that he'd never got to know, but his life with the clone boys had prevented him from attempting to take her from Tessa and Harry. It would have involved a major legal distraction and the scandal would have upset his plans to move up the political ladder. The threat that Tessa may have accused him of rape was a risk that he'd not been prepared to take and both Karen and Frank Tooley had plenty of evidence that would back up any claim made by Tessa. But now things were different. "Indeed," Michael answered, taking another sip of wine and looking at the long line of portraits on the wall of the previous presidents and their first ladies. "We must think about that, but first we must plan how to regain control of Dunfooey."

"How long do you think the Omega Corps can hold out, father?" Donal asked.

"That whole region is very easy to defend," Michael said recalling his holidays when as a youth he'd hiked around the mountains and coast of the region. "Soon the snows will come and the mountain range will be impassable. It was a clever move for them to declare independence just now. They know that they'll be safe for the winter. We must start training all our sixteen year olds for guard duty and ensure that by next spring all the Emanon forces will be under our control."

"But by then hundreds of babies will be born in the region if Fex-2 works as they say it does," one of the other clone men near Donal spoke up. "We must not allow the natives to imagine that they can start breeding again, even up in the hills."

"We made a mistake, father. The clone guards should have gone into the region directly and not the social workers. We knew terrorists were there."

"Not really," Sean argued, defending his father. "All the reports showed it was in the south that the main Omega forces were located. They moved north only recently."

"I think Sean's right," Michael said, "and you know, I've always said that you must learn to live with the others. If this new drug Fex-2 works and fertility does return, then of course there will be babies."

Sean was sorry that Michael had developed this theme again. He had been preaching it many times over the past months and the number of his supporters had dwindled. "At the moment it's not a question of babies," Sean tried to lessen the tension. "It's the adults we've got to worry about. Surely we can try and talk to them and make an agreement that will suit both our societies. Why can our brotherhood not exist in harmony with theirs?" He had challenged his brothers yet again on this central issue and hoped that this evening he'd get more support, as the unexpected establishment of a no-go area in the northern region had taken them all by surprise.

"That's nonsense, Sean," Donal said sternly, taking the lead in the debate. "What do we need them for? Soon they'll be old and depending on us. We don't want random breeding even if Fex-2 does work. From now on we'll control the population and we know enough about genetics to determine what sort of people we want and need."

"I don't disagree with what you say, Donal," Michael spoke with a slight slur in his voice, having emptied another glass of wine. "I've always said we had a great opportunity to develop a clone-based society on Emanon. Now with your special genes, retrieved from the dawn of time, you will be unique in the modern world. You must not lose that heritage. But Sean is right about the present emergency. It's the normal society that you have to live with before you can secure a fresh approach to the future. But you must defeat the Omega Corps. They will eliminated you if they can!" His mind was confused and his arguments convoluted and contradictory but he had to please both sides. Sean whom he had trained as his heir and loved, and Donal whom he now was afraid off, frightened by the raw emotion that was surging around the table.

"Yes, father," Donal smiled down the table, "I have a plan that will help to do this."

"What is it?" the others challenged.

"We know that the Omega leader is the father of the gypsy clonegirls that are now all in the Institutions. I say we take them and use them as a shield against the Omega. They will never let them be hurt. We can use them as a shield to get through the Pass and once we are into Dunfooey our close-knit clonits will soon take control of

the natives."
There was a murmur of agreement around the table. Sean looked at his father and sensed the confusion that was whirling in his mind. Certainly he knew that once they penetrated the region and got in range of the Omega forces their mind-power would devastate them and they would succumb like the natives in the cities had already done during the past few months. But was it right to use the small gypsy women?

"It would certainly present a problem for them," Michael's mind was reeling. His basic instincts rejected the idea of using these petite clonegirls as hostages. But he had already allowed them to be used for experiments and some had died. However, he sensed that Donal was thinking of something more than merely using them as a shield. Donal had talked about the gypsy girls before. He had boasted about being the first clone boy to touch a girl many years ago and had previously wanted to bring them to the Palace. No, that would be going too far. As President, he could not condone that.

"Listen to me!" Sean stood up, looking down the table at his brother, Donal. "This would be entirely wrong. We all know what you want these girls for. That would be terribly wrong. It would turn the public completely against us."

"Nonsense!" a chorus of comments came back from Donal's end of the table. "The natives in the cities are under our control. What does their opinion matter. There is no need to fear them. Our young clonits are everywhere. The natives will do what they're told."

"That's not all," Sean spoke loudly above the noise of the others. "I know what Donal wants. You all do. We all know how he's been longing for the little girls ever since he caught that one with the football. Some of you were there. You all know the shame he brought on us by his behaviour at our Christmas Party and why he wants to bring Sophie here."

"Yes," Michael spoke up supporting his favourite son, sensing that this was a major moment of decision for the clone and knowing that Sean had always been more sympathetic towards the view of living in harmony than some of the others. "I've heard Donal's remarks about the gypsies before. I think he's only making this suggestion about using them as a shield as an excuse. Is that not so, Donal?" he stood up beside Sean, staring down the table at Donal who was now also standing and glaring, his eyes ablaze at his father and brother.

"And why not?" he flared back at his father. "You created them. What good are they? You've used them for experiments. You agreed that they could be used for clinical testing of drugs. You agreed to genetic experiments on their embryos to try and change them, but all your experiments failed. Why should we not have them here?"

"No!" Sean roared. "What you want to do is wrong. We must not begin our new society on that basis."

His eyes met Donal's down the length of the long mahogany table. The light glistened on the silver ware from chandeliers. There was a moment of silence. Michael knew that a fierce mental battle was underway and tried to support Sean's efforts by every ounce of his being. Mental sparks flew across the room. The small clone boy attendants stood with their backs to the wall unable to avoid the flux of energy that enveloped them. Although Michael had used the clone boys to help along his own career, he had not envisaged the rapid development of their mind-power and the control that they now had over the central activities of Emanon. He knew he was a puppet in their hands and the Council of Masters that had welcomed them as assistants had within weeks become their tool of decision-making. The Palace was now dominated by clonemen of various ages and only a few of the older servants and natives still worked there.

Sean was shaking. He willed his friends to support him, but he knew that they were weakening and could feel them panic and subside under the pressure from the majority around the table. Michael saw that he was losing ground and tried to speak but nothing came out. He wiped Sean's forehead with his napkin and put his arm on his shoulders to steady him, but he slid to the floor, writhing in agony.

Michael looked aghast at his favourite son. He had picked him out as a baby and identified with him much more than with any of the others. He remembered that in the ward during those exciting days after the delivery of the first batch of his cloned sons that he had always lifted baby Sean and nursed him briefly. Sometimes he had lifted others, but as the days had passed and other duties took precedence, he had mainly paid attention to Sean. In the residential home he had called to see the clone boys every day, but had mainly talked to Sean and spoke randomly to the others, smiling and fondling their heads of fine fair hair as they grew into boyhood. He had taken Sean to his house for the weekly visits and had introduced him to the numerous charming companions that he'd had during those years. Sean had given Michael so many high hopes for the future of the clone. As the child grew older, they had discussed and planned the future perfect society, balanced, happy, organised, compassionate, an expression of all the good things. But the real clone was different. It was a thing of its own, devoid of feeling. The aunts and uncles had only been playthings, selected for their selfish pleasure and amusement and forgotten as soon as they had become adults.

    For a moment Michael's mind was free and he saw reality as he looked down at Sean sprawling on the floor at his feet. The mind-power of the clone had been focused on Sean but now turned suddenly onto Michael. His mind was opened like a book to them and they devoured his thoughts. He felt them as though they were leafing through his mind, like turning the pages of an encyclopaedia and reading his innermost thoughts and aspirations. How he had used the clone to get to power. His great desire to be at the top, always at the top, until he had to be President. How he skilfully had allowed and encouraged the clone boys to influence the aunts and uncles of the Masters and the old President himself to give him favours. How he knew, without admitting it, that he had used them for his own purposes. How he had made use of the cloning technology at the very beginning to gain recognition at the Institute and displace Karen from being the leader of the team. Now his mind focused on Sophie and for a second he saw into their minds. He saw the same latent craving that had dominated his own private life but which was now shackled and restrained and unspent in the depths of the clonemen. A searing pain struck his chest and he collapsed on top of Sean

Chapter Thirty Nine

The passage around North Cape was treacherous during the midwinter months and even in early spring sudden storms made any attempt to navigate it potentially dangerous. But there were short spells when the weather was fine and Harry's small fleet of Tall Ships set sail from the shelter of Dunfooey Bay. The crews were excited and in good spirits after being land bound for some months.
Sophie had returned safely from the Rock where the preparation of the anti-clone virus had been completed. They'd had a fast journey back by one of the Tall Ships, pushed on by a strong west wind, which allowed then to slip around North Cape and enter Dunfooey Harbour at the dead of night. The ship had a relatively light cargo, just numerous small vials of virus that would be loaded into aerosol sprays shortly before the planned attack. Sophie had been vaccinated against the new weapon and although the others wanted her to remain in Dunfooey she insisted in joining the team of Omega Agents that would attack Konburg and the Palace. While Frank Tooley remained in Dunfooey to complete the preparations for the defence of the Pass, the other Omega teams left by the fleet of Tall Ships, heading for the various cities around the coasts of Emanon.
Harry made good time on the passage to Southport and was able to sail undetected down the desolate, rugged west coast. They would be seen as the normal early spring delivery of seal meat and did not attract any attention. The voyage was uneventful and they kept well out from land beyond the sea mist as they tacked south. To the west the sky was black with the threat of another storm, but the weather held and soon they saw the occasional island appear on the horizon warning them of the approach of the southern archipelago. Harry knew the region like the back of his hand as he had spent his youth exploring the secret islands and inlets. It was not difficult for Harry to guide his ships into a sheltered bay undetected during the hours of darkness, helped by the lights and markers provided by the local Omega Agents from Southport.
By dawn the deadly cargo and Harry's attack teams were on shore and the Tall Ship had slipped silently away into the night. Harry's cousin, Jose, had become the leader of the southern Omega Corps and had made all the local arrangements for their arrival.

Small boats were ready to take the agents to the mainland and get them to the heart of the city.

Harry had arranged to stay in a safe house where they would see the details of the plans of how the local agents would distribute the virus to have maximum effect, especially at the Clone headquarters of the region.

Late in the evening, Jose brought Harry's father to the safe house, disguised and in secret, avoiding the clone guards that were now patrolling the streets after dark. Harry's father was well known as the founder member of the Omega Corps, and although he was now elderly, he was still a powerful force in the Southern Corps and few decisions were taken without his agreement.

"You'd better stop them, Harry," the old man said after they had greeted each other and he had settled stiffly into an armchair. "They plan to get rid of people like me very soon. Did you hear that they passed a new law, only yesterday, that makes me too old to be of any use to any one or myself? So they say!"

"Don't worry, Dad. They'll be feeling too old for very much themselves within a few weeks once we get our virus released," Harry said, encouraging his father and pleased to see him so well after a recent illness.

"They were never Reborn," the old man said, "that's why they are so evil. Only the first few were taken to the Great Falls, then they abandoned the whole idea."

"That's where the Fathers made the mistake," Harry reflected. "I never believed that blessing the original cells in a bottle would be a substitute for the real immersion," he added, recalling the way that the Church had agreed with Michael that the soul would enter the original cloned cells before the new embryos were transplanted into the modules.

"It worked for the majority of the people, though. They only wanted an excuse to have the children, even for one day a week," Jose said.

"But they are evil! Look what they've done with your daughters." His fathers voice was heavy with disgust and anger. He grasped Harry's hand in his rage. "Harry, it's disgusting, you'll have to stop them. You'll have to stop them."

Within a day of Harry's arrival in Southport, the message came through that all the teams were also in place and the signal was given that the attack would commence the following evening. Omega agents were now ready in every major city throughout Emanon and were well armed with slow release aerosols. The plan was very simple, but hopefully, effective. The slow release aerosols would be hidden in numerous convenient places where clonemen frequented.

Harry's small group had surrounded the block where many of the senior clonemen lived and where the Southern Clone Council meetings were held. It had not been difficult for them to obtain cleaners' uniforms and they were able to enter the building undetected by the clone guards, along with the other natives who were employed as cleaners who now did all the menial tasks for the clonemen. The slow release aerosols were left in convenient places throughout the block, behind curtains, in bathrooms and toilets, under tables in restaurants and bars. The slow release aerosol would make the air infectious to any cloneman or child, and breathing in even a single particle would result in the individual succumbing to the disease.

By breakfast time the atmosphere of the building was saturated with the virus and when the clonemen started to arrive they became infected. Harry's team had by then safely left the building and had separated into small units who continued to leave their deadly aerosols in strategic places. At midday they returned to the safe house to collect more aerosols and to contact Sophie by their secret radio.

"Hello, Sophie!" Harry said in a half whisper, never fully trusting their illegal radio link. "How's it going in Konburg?"

"Very well," she continued, "our distribution throughout the city is nearly complete and aerosols have been smuggled into the Palace along with food deliveries as planned. But, now the empty containers have been found and there is a growing tension in the city. Clone guards are everywhere and some of our agents have been arrested on suspicion of insubordination. Apparently in Konburg all the natives have been conditioned to bow their heads on passing a cloneman. This is just another of their silly laws that they've announced recently."

"Yes, they tell us here that it is dangerous to make eye contact with a cloneman as they can now very rapidly sense our feelings about them."

"Harry," Sophie asked, anxiety in her distant voice. "Have you seen any of the clone girls? They have removed them all from the Home at Konburg.

"Yes, they are all over here," Harry replied angrily. "Dad tells me that the clonemen here are using them as pets."

"It's more sinister than that. Apparently up here in the north, they have been training or conditioning them for some months in a large camp outside the city. Our agents report that large convoys of coaches are now on their way to the Dunfooey Pass."

"Damn," Harry snapped, "and use the little girls as shields, believing that we won't use force against them."

"It's worse than that, Harry," Sophie continued, "we believe that they have been drugged to make them aggressive. They are being trained to hunt in packs."

Harry felt the blood pound through his forehead and his hand shook in anger as he pressed the switch to respond. He knew only too well the aggressive streak that inflicted the clonegirls as they had grown older and how they had had to be sedated to keep them from attacking the staff at the Home.

"Frank Tooley is in charge on the Pass. He'll have to stop them. If they're drugged and all together they won't be easily stopped. Even though they are small, they can fight like little tigers."

"But you know how Frank feels about Little Greta. He won't know what to do. If one says 'Fank Fank' to him, he's lost."

"Get a message through to him, from me. Tell him he must stop them. At all costs....." Suddenly his words were cut off by a loud noise behind him as the door of the room burst open. Harry swung round from the transmitter just in time to see his father slump from his chair. A group of armed clone guards were crouching in the doorway.

Chapter Forty


Donal rose hurriedly from the couch, gathering his dressing gown around himself, angry at the intrusion. "What do you want?" he roared at the embarrassed cloneguard who had stumbled hastily into the Presidential suite. An agile clone girl slipped to the floor and scuttled away to the big bed at the far end of the room.

"What do you want? You silly boy! Why didn't you knock?" Donal had fastened his gown with a large bow and had rapidly regained his composure. The gypsy sat on the bed, cross-legged, drinking from a large glass of red liquid, her eyes fixed hungrily on the youth.

"That little vixen would eat you alive," Donal said, his voice softening, sensing the youth's embarrassment. "What is it, boy?"

"Master," the youth stammered again, keeping half his eye on the small woman on the bed. "The terrorists have attacked. They have left poison gas all over the city and now they've invaded the Palace. Come quickly. You must get outside. The palace is full of gas."

"What!" roared Donal, rushing to the window and looking down over the lawns toward Lake Rana. The staff and guards were standing in clusters looking up at the Presidential suite or talking in excited frightened groups.

"The alarms did not work, Master. The terrorists must have inactivated them. Come on quickly, Master. We must get out of here."

"Come on," Donal shouted back to his pet, who was sitting on the bed, rocking herself, her eyes still fixed on the youth. They ran along the landing and down the curved marble staircase to the front door and joined the other clonies on the lawn.

"Is everyone out?" Donal shouted, taking control of the situation. "Now, what exactly has happened?" he demanded, addressing a senior security guard.

"Early this evening, Master, we began finding empty canisters all over the city. They looked like gas cans, but no harm has been done. Then just a little while ago we found empty canisters throughout the Palace. They must have been smuggled in during the delivery of provisions this afternoon."

"Why was I not told?" Donal snapped

"At first we thought it was a hoax. We knew the terrorists were up to something as we had had reports of an influx of Omega people during the past few days and have been watching some of them."

"Arrest them. Question them. Find out what they're doing. Why have I to make all the decisions here? Can you not think for yourselves?"

"We have already arrested some of them, Master. A woman called Sophie. She was at university. You probably remember her."

Donal's mind exploded in confusion. Sophie. The girl he had worshipped and longed for. The one he had wanted to bring to the Palace. The one he had challenged both Michael and Sean over. Now she had fallen into his lap. The image of her tattered photograph flashed through his mind. Now he would see her again. Now he would make her his Queen.

"Bring her to us, before the great statues on the Terrace. There we will make her tell us the truth. We cannot go into the Palace until we know what they've done." The guards left for the city to collect the captured terrorists and Donal looked around the group of frightened, clonies, calling together the members of the Council. "Let's go to Terrace. There we can decide what to do." They moved off in a group, along the cold marble terrace towards the ancient shrine, their long white embroidered gowns reflecting the cool moonlight of the early spring evening, groups of the cloned pets following them. "Take them away," he shouted, pushing off one who clung to the hem of his gown, crying 'Fank, Fank'. "Put them back in their quarters. Give them something to quiet them."

Chapter Forty One

Sophie had been distributing canisters in the new Clone School that had been opened in Konburg, when she realised that some of the staff were clonies who had been at College with her. As she left the science block, she felt that a clone man had recognised her. She felt it was Richard, but hadn't spoken and hurried on to meet Cara, who was leading the Omega attack at the main door. They had left directly, abandoning their remaining canisters in a wastebasket near the front entrance.
　　She could feel the clonies there in the back of her mind. Suddenly they were alert. Everyone she passed on the street glanced at them. Some clonies, in front of them on the footpath, turned and watched them approach, smiling, recognising, waiting. Sophie knew that her image had somehow been transmitted from clonie to clonie across the city. She was trapped, her mind-pattern shining like a beacon on a still sea on a dark clear night. She told Cara to separate from her and maybe she would escape. "But don't go to the safe house," she whispered as she dropped behind, disappearing into the crowd. Suddenly she was surrounded by clonemen and a car drew up beside them and she was hustled into the back seat.
　　Sophie first became conscious of being on cold stone and opened her eyes to look up at the ancient granite faces of the large statues of the ancient kings that she recalled lined the terrace in the Palace gardens. She sat up and realised that she was on the stone slab that topped the ancient Cairn of Emanon. She blinked her eyes against the strong spotlights that illuminated the whole terrace against the blackness of the night sky.
　　"Hello, Sophie," a voice said from close beside her. "How nice to see you again. It was such good fun we had at college. Do you remember me?"
　　"Yes," she said, recognising the scar on his left ear. "Where's Sean?"
　　"Good," Donal said, latent anger in his voice. "Our dear brother Sean has left us. In fact you should be pleased to know that he left all because of you."
　　"But what happened? I thought that he was your leader."
　　"No, my dear. He was too much influenced by father and

you, our dear half-sister, to be a real leader of the brotherhood. Now I represent the Brotherhood. I am the Brotherhood." There was a chorus of approval from around the small square where the rest of the Clone Council sat on the circle of ancient stone seats that had now become illuminated by a ring of lanterns.

"But where is Sean? What happened to him?"

"How you must have loved him," Donal rejoined, smiling at her. He was now standing in front of her, holding the point of her chin by the tips of his long fine fingers, so that she had to look him in the eyes. "Sean's all right. He's working in Southport where he can cause us little harm. He had a slight illness and is now glad to be away from the centre of things."

Donal motioned to the guards who suddenly took Sophie by the arms and forced her lie down flatly on the stone dais. A guard held her firmly by the shoulders. She struggled for an instant, but then all resistance vanished. The silk gowns of the clonemen reflected the light of the lamps and they droned an ancient lament as they approached step by step hands now linked, until they were clustered around the dais. Then they stretched out their arms, touching her. Sophie was transfixed and only felt the churning of her mind as they probed deeper and deeper. It did not hurt, but one part of her brain felt revolted at what the other part was doing. She feared that all the secrets and aims of the Omega Corps and all her friends and loved ones were being stripped from her, but she could do nothing as her memories seemed to leak away like data flashing on a computer screen, she felt a growing emptiness. A great void filled her head as though her mind had been stolen. The void spread downwards, her heart dissolved and her limbs felt like jelly. The hands were supporting her, lifting her off the stone dais and carrying her above their heads. She recalled mythical stories from her childhood about the ancient sacrificial pit that was believed to descend to the centre of the world and that occasionally belched fumes when the Gods were angry.

Chapter Forty Two

Frank Tooley sat on a rocky ledge high up on a crag just west of Dunfooey Pass. Below him, scattered across the snow that still lay in patches on the broken ground that bordered the road, were the Omega forces. He was in radio contact with the unit commanders and guided each heavily armed group into safe strategic positions, behind rocks and in sheltered gullies, ready to attack the crowd approaching the Pass from the South.
    Frank watched through his strong field glasses the clone forces at the head of the valley. He could see in the distance the great central plain that stretched away to the horizon and far beyond. The snow had melted in the valley and the crisp clear spring air allowed a good view of the encampments that grew in size daily. The fresh green grass of the valley was turning white with the pitched tents following the arrival of each convoy of clonemen and their trained warrior gypsies.
    "There they go again," Frank sighed, handing the strong binoculars to his companion who had climbed the steep ridge to their vantage point. "I just can't believe that they will use the clone girls to fight for them," he added.
    "It looks as though each cloneman has a squadron of under its control and that they'll send wave after wave against us. They must be hypnotised. They'll tear apart anyone who isn't a clonie."
    "Isn't it strange," Frank murmured, recalling to himself his favourite Little Greta. "They were so petite and fragile when they were young and we said they were simple, but now the one part of their brain that functions properly is their fighting and hunting instincts. They are ultimately ruthless, as they don't know when to stop. Once their anger is up, they'll never leave go or stop until their prey is dead. They have no understanding of fear or death."
    The dull drone of the heavy lorry engines drifted up the mountain side in the still morning air and below on the Pass the defending Omega soldiers shuffled their feet and kept an anxious eye on the ridge, anticipating their first contact with the enemy would be very soon.
    From his vantage point high up on the crag Frank saw the first of the convoy nose its way around the last hairpin bend and

slowly, with painstaking effort, creep over the ridge into full view of the Omega forces stationed at the top of the Pass.

The armoured coaches drove into the large parking area at the top of the ridge and the clonemen spilt out, all instantly looking up at the Pass through dark glasses.

Throughout the afternoon, coach after coach arrived at the parking area. Gypsy girls poured out laughing and giggling and ran to their masters for a sweet and an occasional cuddle. Then to a shrill whistle they ran into a tight formation behind the clonemen as though they were gun dogs coming to heel at their masters' bidding.

Frank watched them intently as the clonemen started up the long walk to the Pass. Compared to the small dot-like figures he had seen in the valley below, at this relatively short range the high-powered lenses brought the figures close enough to see the individual faces. Frank picked out one of the clone leaders and steadied his aim and smiled.

"I could hit him from here," he said, fondling his rifle. "But look at his face. He's sweating already and panting heavily. His eyes were streaming, his face roaring red. He's obviously got the disease. They must be desperate to put men like that out to fight."

"They're not going to fight," his companion said, taking the binoculars and focusing on the approaching army. "They're putting their gypsies into the front line. The clonies are only there to guide them and get them started. Look," he said, after a short pause as he concentrated on what was happening below at the mouth of the steep gorge leading up to the Pass. "The gypsies are now in front and the clonemen are just standing in a line across the road. They're just beyond our range. They're running, trotting. They've been given knives and short spears. There'll be a slaughter if they keep going like that."

"God help us!" Frank said sadly. "They'll fight by primitive instinct. In this terrain they'll wreak havoc on our men." He spoke into the transmitter to his commanders below and warned them of what was happening.

"Some of the gypsies have left the road and are in the shrub and among the rocks on either side. There's plenty of cover for them there. They can hide behind a rock half the size that we'd need for protection. Within a few minutes your guns will be useless. It will be hand to hand combat. They are already approaching you through the grass. They are spreading out, hunting like a pack. From now shoot on sight! Open fire! Shoot to kill!"

Suddenly a cry went up filling the narrow Pass, echoing from the surrounding cliff, piercing Frank's ears and making him scream. "Fank, Fank!" The gypsies bounced up among the rocks, laughing, their camouflaged kits helping to merge them with the mountainside. Within seconds they vanished from sight. "Fank, Fank," they called, rushing from cover to cover. Shots rang out. The gypsies appeared, laughing, from behind other rocks, but always coming closer and closer to the armed Omega guards. "Fank, Fank." Now the cries of delight and excitement were mingled with wails of pain and death, but closer and closer the little moving, jumping, darting figures came. Now they were on all sides of the well placed Omega men with their long barrelled guns, who became surrounded and were powerless.

"Fank, Fank!" A gypsy jumped on the back of a man and he collapsed, the bright silver of the blade stained with blood as she withdrew it. A shot rang out and she tumbled down on top of her prey, and for a second all was still and silent.

The little women were strong and agile. The Omega guards had not been prepared for the ruthlessness of their attack and had to abandoned their guns and fight hand to hand. But for every successful punch by the guards, the gypsies would inflict a dozen fatal strikes with their deadly knives and spears.

From the safety of his perch high up on the crag, Frank watched, transfixed by the carnage that he was unable to stop. He could see in the distance that the clone soldiers were straddled across the valley, row after row, standing silent, watching. He could feel them, inside his head, weakening his resolve. He could see that many of his men had been killed, or were confused, struggling in a half-hearted attempt to repulse the gypsy warriors, who continued to fling themselves forward. Frank watched with dismay the collapse of the Omega resistance, many retreating down the valley, others finding themselves surrounded by the gypsies now chanting, "Fank, Fank, Fank!" Then they went in for the final onslaught.


Chapter Forty Three


Sophie opened her eyes. She was in darkness, absolute blackness and silence. She felt her body and found it naked under a light silky sheet. Her head rested on a soft pillow. There was a pleasant aromatic smell of herbs. She wondered if she'd been buried alive in some ancient tomb in the depths of the Palace. The fading memory of a nightmare was just leaving her and she struggled to clear her mind and fix herself in reality. She was on a couch or bed but how far below was the floor? Her hand and arm stole out from under the sheet and stretched down the side of the bed. She felt a soft fibre carpet. She stretched her arm upwards, expecting to find the top of a coffin, but it stretched forever and she sat up in the bed.

Her mind had cleared now and she remembered what had happened. Had Cara been captured as well? How much had she told the clonies about the Omega plan? Where was she now? Could she escape? She stretched her bare legs over the side of the bed and gently reached for the floor and stood up. Suddenly the room was flooded with light, a door opened and three clonemen entered.

Sophie spontaneously grabbed the white sheet from the bed that she now realised was one of the long gowns that the clonemen used. She hastily wrapped it around her shoulders, turning away from the clonemen.

"You might have waited a second," she snapped at them.

"You must come to the Master. He has been waiting for you for hours. You should be well rested by now," one of the clone guards said, coming forward into the room and taking hold of Sophie's arm.

"Leave me alone! I can walk myself," she responded, shrugging off the clonie's hand, but finding her legs weak and her head giddy.

The corridor led into the main entrance hall and they started up the grand staircase towards the presidential suite. Sophie heard giggling voices above and looked up to see laughing faces of clone women looking through the balustrade and there was a flurry of movement as the guards shooed them away out of sight.

"Come in, my dear," Donal said as her escort left her at the door of his palatial room. "You are looking much better. How well our traditional gowns suits you. You look like a princess, if not a Queen." He came across to the doorway where she stood, resisting the invitation to enter the lion's lair. He reached for her hands and held them gently, encouraging her to enter. "Look, my dear, relax, the bad part is over. You are safe now. We can be friends. We know the truth. You were very co-operative and everything is now clear. After all, you are our half-sister. You are part of the family."

"I see the rumours are true that you keep the clonegirls here."

"Indeed. You will see a lot of them. They are very happy here. Much better than when they were in the Home. So long as they are on the correct drugs they love the freedom of the Palace. My pet is very special to me. She's always collecting things. You'll see her at dinner."

He had eased her further into the room and the door was closed. Sophie glanced around and saw the large bed and the luxurious settees and chairs. His hand had slipped around her waist and was holding her firmly, but there was a slight tremble in his fingers as they pressed into her back, through the single layer of silk.

"Come Sophie," he urged, "I want to be friends. I've loved you since we were at college. Look at the photo of you I've kept all these years." He motioned across the room to his bedside table where there was a photograph of her in her orange dress.

Sophie felt the warmth of his breath and his lips brushed her cheek as he held her tightly. She looked into his eyes and noticed that they were bloodshot and his face covered with red blotches.

"You can't!" she shouted at him, trying to resist. "I'm your sister. It's wrong!" Her mind was whirling and she realised that he was taking over again.

"No my dear Sophie, the laws of your society no longer apply in our new world. Think of me as Sean." She felt her resistance vanish as she sank under his control, her body, but not her mind, yielding to the movements of the man she hated.

Their eyes were transfixed on each other.

Donal's mind was flooded with the vision of Sophie in the shower. The rich suds streaming between the cleft of her breasts and down her long slender legs. Every night he had dreamt that she would eventually come to him. With the gypsy girls he would roll and toss and fondle, but always it had been the vision of Sophie in the orange dress that would stir him to the ultimate heights.

She held his gaze, their eyes challenging the way ahead.

Would she yield willingly or would he have to control her? He was tempted to take the easy way and subvert her mind completely, but he wanted more. He wanted to know that she was his, not forced, but really his, won by the sheer strength of his passion and love.

She felt him close as they moved slowly across the room

towards the bed. Suddenly his eyes were streaming and tears poured down his cheeks and she tasted salt on her lips. She felt him wither and he drew back, releasing her, and he sneezed violently. He lost his grip on her and she pushed him away. He turned away, sneezing again, his eyes streaming red and his nostrils clogged with green mucus. Donal sat on the edge of the bed, his face red and sweating and blew his nose repeatedly on the hastily grabbed sheet.

Sophie had retreated to the other side of the room and had lifted a large ornament as a potential weapon.

"Damn," he said, through his nose, "we all got a chill last night on the Terrace. It's too early in the year to be outside so late. You'll probably catch this as well," he added, going to a washbasin and rinsing his flushed face. "You know, I think I have a temperature." He looked in the mirror and examined his bloodshot eyes. "My God, this has come on really bad. I've got spots too!" He took a tablet from a small bottle that the Palace doctor had prescribed earlier in the day. "These help," he said, swallowing it with a glass of water. "Perhaps you should take one," he said, offering Sophie the bottle. "These attacks come on very quickly. But they don't last long." He had fixed his open gown and approached Sophie, gently taking the ornament from her. "Don't break that," he said smiling. "That's very ancient."

"Donal, you must leave me alone. You must not try that again," Sophie demanded, more confident now than she had been since wakening a short while ago. Her mind was free and she realised that the disease had broken the control that Donal had over her. Also the fact that Donal believed that it was just a chill caught during their late night in the open air meant that they had not completely stripped her mind of all the secrets about the Omega attack. Perhaps she had more resistance to them than she'd thought due to being only their half-sister. In fact only a few of the key Omega agents knew the full facts of what was being released. Most had been told that the canisters contained poison gas so that they would release false information if they were caught. Perhaps the clonies had got the wrong message and had not probed any further.

"Perhaps I should take one of the tablets," she said, humouring him. She moved to the sink and swallowed the small white pill that she felt sure could not do her any harm.

"Yes, that's a good idea. Look, Sophie, we can talk about things later, but now I want to take you down to dinner and meet someone who is very special to us both."

He led the way out of the room and down the corridor to the dining room where the members of the Clone Council had already gathered. There was a babble of conversation, mixed with a few sneezes from around the table. Sophie froze when she saw the old man in a wheelchair sitting at the end. He was grey-haired and had a wizened complexion and his hands were moving slightly with a permanent tremble. But his eyes were alert and looked younger than his face or body and he recognised her as soon as she entered.

"Your father has not been well," Donal said as they moved across to take their seats on either side of him at the end of the table. "But he still likes to come to dinner for special occasions. I know he'll be delighted to see you."

The old man took Sophie's hand and held it in his cold trembling fingers. For a long moment his eyes held hers. "You're so beautiful," he said quietly. "Just like your mother. I remember the hair." He touched the long red strand that curled over her shoulder as she pulled her hand away and shrank back.

"What have they done to you?

"They are good boys. They will look after you, my dear. It was good of you to come. I should have brought you long ago. I'm sorry. I should have brought you and Karen back long ago."

"But my mother is Tessa. Don't you remember?"

"Yes, Yes, Tessa. Lovely Tessa." He smiled and his head slumped back on the chair.

"He can only stay awake for a short time," Donal said. "But he will wake greatly refreshed. Now, do eat some supper. You must be hungry," Donal added, reaching her a plate of salad.

For a while she ate in silence, watching the clonemen around her. They were silent too, except for the occasional cough and sneeze and most of them had developed a rash on their cheeks and necks. The disease was taking, if only she could hold on.

Towards the end of the meal, Donal rang a small gold bell and called clearly to the attendants: "Bring them in."

A door opened and a number of the gypsies ran in. They were dressed in colourful attractive mini-tunics and they seemed happy. Each ran to their master and one appeared beside Donal and jumped on his knee. She kissed him, her small bare arms clasped tightly around his neck. Suddenly looking over Donal's shoulder she saw Sophie and recognising her, cried, "Fank, Fank." She slipped from Donal's knee and rushed into Sophie's arms.

"It's Little Greta! We had her in Dunfooey when she was a child," Sophie cried, delighted to see her little sister again. "Are you all right?"

"Of course she is," Donal answered. "You know they can't speak. But they're happy here. With the proper treatment they've grown and matured, at least physically, and it seemed to us wrong that they were shut up in an institution because they were supposed to be sick."

"But she was happy in Dunfooey. They took her away from us."

"Be sensible, Sophie. The natives out there could not give her the proper treatment. The gypsy girls became far too aggressive when they reached their teens to be left free."

"They were only aggressive when they got into groups. Little Greta was always happy when she was with us," They hugged, Greta trying to kiss her

"Come on, you little vixen," Donal shouted, reaching over and pulling her off Sophie." You're on the wrong knee," he laughed. "You've had too much saxa."

At that moment the door at the end of the room opened and a clone youth rushed in carrying a printed message which be brought over to Donal. There was suddenly a hushed silence as Donal read it. He stood up, allowing Little Greta to slip to the floor and hide under the long folds of his gown. Her face peeked out, grinning with delight at Sophie.

"Brothers," he said, his voice taking on an air of authority and seriousness, "we've just heard from Southport that our guards there have arrested one of the senior Omega terrorists and have discovered the real truth about these attacks and canisters."

"But what is it? I thought you'd probed Sophie completely," Michael said. He had wakened up and his eyes were bright and alert.

"She must have had more resistance than we had thought," Donal continued. "The truth is that the canisters contained a biological agent, some type of genetically engineered virus that will only attack us. They've made it specific for us. First it will give us a bad cold and then within a few days it will develop into a neurological illness."

"My God," Michael leaned forward in his wheel chair. "Only Karen could have done that. Only she among the Omega Corps could know how to do such experiments. Sophie, am I infected? Are you infected?"

Sophie stood up facing the ring of clonemen, who were clearly now frightened and angry at the same time.

"You've no chance," she said quietly as a hush descended around the table. "It's measles. Most of you have spots already. It's a neurotropic mutant and you have no chance. It will attach the parts of your brains that gives you your damn gift!"

"No!" Michael said, his weak voice carrying down the length of the table, silencing the murmurs of anxiety and fear that were erupting from his sons. "No!" he repeated, demanding silence as his mind worked on the complex avenues of thought that haunted him. "Sophie," he said sternly, as though he was speaking to his daughter, reprimanding her for a misdemeanour. "You must tell me the truth. Otherwise they will probe you again, so deeply that you will never recover. Like they did to me. Are you immune?"

She knew exactly what Michael meant. The clonemen had been gentle with her the previous night probably because Donal had such a passion for her. But now the others would be merciless and she would never resist their probing and they would cast her aside in a mental void forever.

"Yes," she said quietly. "I am immune. We made a vaccine especially for me. But if you let me go free I promise that you'll get some vaccine once the clone council gives up power and allows normal breeding to start again. You all know that Fex-2 is a complete cure of the infertility. You should never have stopped us from using it."

"It is a way," a cloneman said from across the table, more disturbed than the others by the severity of his sickness.

"No!" snapped Donal, before his brother could continue. "I don't trust her or any native. If they use Fex-2 and start breeding like animals they will dispense with us. If we depend on them giving us vaccine they will reduce our numbers until we have no power. They will control our production units and our future. No, I say that if they have made a vaccine then surely we can make one as well. Anyway we must get the vaccine before the virus reaches our brains and we lose our special powers."

"Wait," Michael said, still leaning hard on the edge of the table. "There is another way." He spoke slowly, his mind still working out the principles, going back years to the time when he was an active scientist involved in developing the most advanced biology that Emanon had ever known. He had cloned Emanons, saved the nation's inhabitants from extinction. "Sophie is immune," he said, grasping her hand again. "She carries the antibodies that will protect you and me. She is your half-sister. A sample of her blood will save you."

"But have we time?" Donal queried.

"You have a few weeks before the second phase reaches a crisis point," she said lamely, knowing that to resist now was useless. "The virus will remain latent for a while and if you can immunise before the final spread starts, the symptoms can be greatly reduced, if not completely avoided." Her words came out freely and she felt her mind under their spell.

Sophie sat down, her hand still in Michael's firm grip. She was shaking from head to toe and had broken out in a cold sweat and the damp silk robe clung to her skin. She wondered if somehow her immunity had failed and she was also infected. She prayed that that would be the case. She hoped that the vaccine hadn't worked. It had been made especially for her. But the thought that she would be used, her body, her blood, sickened her to the pit of her being. She realised that she was clinging on to Michael's arm with both hands, her head leaning on his stooped shoulder.

"Good luck, my dear," he whispered in her ear, while the clonemen were beginning to leave the table and general excited conversation was dominating the room again. "Good luck, my dear, you're safe now. You're too precious for them to harm you now. Just hold on."

She heard a deep rustle in his chest. He coughed coarsely and she wiped the beads of sweat from his brow. Green mucous oozed from his nose and lips, the spots on his forehead had merged into an intense redness. There was no doubt that he had caught the disease as well. What a life he had led. Had he been trapped by the clonemen all these years, his selfish possessive streak dominating the clone's basic character, twisting and controlling his life? Now he was of no use to them and they would destroy him. They would destroy them both. But worse, they would keep her as a pet like the gypsy girls. They would control her mind so she could not resist. They would take her blood and overcome the illness and defeat the Omega Corps. Had Harry and the others been captured as well? Was she the only one left?

Suddenly Donal was behind her, his hands pressing into her shoulders. "You will be a good girl, Sophie. You have come to save us," he spoke nasally and his voice was thick with phlegm. "But when we are better, you will be our Queen. Like long ago. You were always meant to be our Queen."

## Chapter Forty Four

Harry and Jose were taken to the clonemen's headquarters and roughly put into a cell in the basement. The image of his father lying on the floor, bleeding would not leave him. He cursed the clonemen. A little later, Harry was taken to the interrogation room and he was seated in the centre of a ring of clonemen. They did not speak, just looked at him with penetrating eyes, their hands clasped, completing a ring of mind-power around him. Harry knew that his thoughts and secrets had spilt out before them. The probing left him exhausted and afterwards when he was flung back into his cell he crawled onto his hard bunk, without saying a word to Jose who tried to get him to drink a little water from a cracked mug.

When Harry eventually woke, it was pitch black, and he felt a cool shaft of air that must have roused him. Suddenly from the darkness in the depth of the cell a strange voice said quietly:

"Don't make a noise. I'm here to help you."

"Who are you?" Jose said from the bunk above in a coarse whisper.

"Don't talk now," the stranger said. "Just do as I say. The guards are asleep. I'll guide you out of here. Can you walk?"

"Yes," Harry said, struggling to his feet as the stranger opened the cell door and allowed the faint stream of early dawn light enter the cell.

"Come on," he encouraged from the corridor, "we've no time to waste." The stranger moved on down the gloomy passage and through a grilled door into the guardroom. A single light bulb hanging unprotected from the ceiling blinded them for a moment but Harry could see against the glare that three clone guards were lying sprawled on the stone floor sound asleep and one was snoring and breathing heavily, his chest thick with catarrh.

The stranger knew his way and followed a number of dimly lit narrow passages and stairways until they reached a heavy studded door. He looked back and listened. There was silence behind them. The door opened into a narrow side street and the grey dawn was creeping over the city.

As they emerged into the light, Harry realised that the stranger was a cloneman, and his heart thumped with apprehension and disappointment. But the cloneman had gone on down the street, waving to them, and they followed him to the corner where he was waiting.

"It's all clear," the stranger said confidently, looking around the edge of the stone wall. "Come on. Quickly. Get into the car. Harry, you go in the front."

Harry got into the front luxury seat and closed the door with a gentle thud. There was plenty of room for his long legs and he glanced around the leather headrest to see Jose safely in the back beside another man who wore dark glasses and had a thick black beard. For a fraction of a second Harry thought he recognised him, but the cloneman slid into the driver's seat and the engine simultaneously purred into life. Without a word he moved the car out into the main street and crept a few hundred yards to the next cross roads. Then turning into the main highway, the driver accelerated and the car sped away, humming like a bird, on the empty highway out of the city, heading north.

Harry recognised the car as the top of the range, a Galaxy. The cloneman beside him was dressed in a dark uniform and had now put on a peaked cap. Harry realised that he was a chauffeur and probably was responsible for the car of one of the members of the Clone Council that governed Southport. No one spoke until they had left the city far behind and had begun to climb up the gorge through the mountains and on northwards into the central plain. Frequently along the roadside, cloneguards stood to attention and saluted as the big car with its Emanon emblem flickering in the breeze, cruised past.

"Who are you? And where are we going?" Harry eventually asked, still uncertain as to whether they had been rescued or merely being transferred to the Capital, the man in the back being an additional guard.

"You may remember me," the cloneman said, looking briefly at Harry. "We met once at the Garden Party when my father was made President. He introduced me to Karen and your daughter, Sophie. I'm Sean."

"Yes, I remember. Sophie talked a lot about you while she was at college. I thought you were Michael's favourite. What on earth are you doing here?"

"I was. But the brotherhood didn't like that and they drove me out."

"Why?"

"It's a complex story. Basically a few of us led by me and with Michael's support wanted to have the Brotherhood accept the discovery of Fex-2. There was a mind-coup and we lost. Michael was crippled and the purists have taken over. I was sent to Southport to work as a driver for the Head of the Council."

"But why are you helping us now?"

"You better explain, Mel," he glanced back to the stranger in the rear.

Harry looked around as the man took of his glasses. "My God! You're Mel Higgins. We all thought you were dead."

"Hi, Harry," Mel moved forward, touching Harry on the shoulders with restrained emotion. "It's a long story."

As they sped northwards, Mel quietly related what had happened. "The last I remembered of that night at College was jumping from the window into the Shanna. My mind went completely blank. I must have been washed down the river towards the Falls, but got caught up in a fishing net that had been strung across the river by poachers. I somehow managed to struggle ashore and hide. I was terrified and was sure that everyone was trying to kill me. I stole food and wandered for days not remembering who I was or why I was there, only just believing that I must get as far away from Tanark as possible. Gradually my memories came back and I realised what had happened. I was afraid that if the Clonemen learnt that I was still alive that they would come after me again and I decided to stay underground. By then I had reached Southport and made contact with the Omega Corps, but didn't tell them whom I really was. They got me a job working in a garage washing cars. That was when I met Sean. He recognised me immediately one day when he brought this car in for a wash and polish. I thought I was a goner. But I soon realised that he was on our side. He told me about Sophie being the clone's half-sister. He explained what had happened at the Palace and how the clone had become dominated by Donal and his cronies. His own supporters had all been sent away from the Palace to different parts of Emanon and opposition to Donal had been completely fragmented. But we kept in contact, giving me information that would be useful for our cause. Then last night he called me urgently when he realised that the Omega attack had started and that you have been arrested."

"By chance I was able to infiltrate the group that mind-probed you yesterday." Sean took up the story. "I learnt all about what the Omega Corps have planned. Then late last night the news came through from Konburg that Sophie has been arrested and that she is immune from the disease. They have announced that they intend to use her blood to give the clonemen protection and that they will hold her hostage until the Omega Corps give them vaccine.

"Great God!" Jose said excitedly from the back. "If they recover, they'll eliminate all of us."

"Exactly, but we must stop them," Sean continued. "The clone has become ultimately selfish. It will sacrifice the whole of Emanon for its own preservation. I realise now that most of us did not fight hard enough against our baser instincts and we allowed the extremists to take over. You see," tears were running down his cheeks and his voice was suddenly hoarse, "I loved Sophie. I didn't realise that she was my half sister, but our relationship was real, for both of us. She taught me to respect my mother, our mother. She's spent her life searching for a cure. She sacrificed her love for us in an attempt to preserve the great diversity of species that has taken millions of years to evolve. Now the clonemen will sacrifice all of that for the sake of perpetuating their genes. I know that is not what Karen and Michael made us for. But there were two Michaels. One taught me and the other Donal. But, now, I must fight along with you. It may not yet be too late."

Sean sneezed heavily and drew the car onto the hard shoulder. "Harry," he said, nasally, "you will have to drive for a while." He removed a small bottle of tablets from his pocket and swallowed one. "The Palace doctors have recommended that we take one of these every few hours to stop the fever."

They all got out and stretched their legs. Harry went back to the driver's door and waited a moment as a large truck passed. He noticed that it was a Seal Meat Company truck and waved casually to the unseen driver and smiled to himself as he got in and settled behind the steering wheel. He had never driven a Galaxy and this one could really move along.

"I need some sleep," Sean said as Harry drove off, "if we are stopped by guards wake me. I'll have to try and talk my way through. But when my boss reports that I've disappeared with the car they'll be looking for us."

Sean slumped down into the big seat and was soon sound asleep. For some miles Harry tailed the large refrigerated truck belonging to the Seal Meat Company and felt at ease as he thought of the new world that was being constructed out on the barren rock in the distant ocean. Soon he had got the feel of the big car and sped past the truck, spontaneously flashing his lights at the driver as the Galaxy roared ahead on the fast lane.

"There's Mount Croagh erupting again," he said softly, not wishing to waken Sean, but noticing the great pall of smoke that hung over the distant mountain range to the north.

"I've never seen them so active before," Jose said

"There's a lot of activity all along the western range," Harry said, recalling his recent voyage. "And, my God, there's a lot of activity in front of us, too," Harry said, concern creeping into his voice as the car crested a hill and they could see the long stretch of road leading into the heart Konburg from the east. "Sean, wake up!" he shouted, nudging the cloneman with his elbow. "Sean, there's a road block ahead. You'd better get ready to do some talking. You better take over." He drew the car onto the hard shoulder and they swapped seats, Sean rubbing his eyes and sneezing heavily.

A few miles further on they saw the barrier again. A truck had just gone through but there were no other vehicles in sight. Sean slowed down to a crawl along the level road for the fifty yards from the checkpoint. They were in an isolated part of the countryside. A wood of pine trees and rough shrubs provided shelter from the strong winds that swept across the high plain. "Pretend you're asleep. Look as though you're drugged. Leave all the talking to me," Sean ordered as the car stopped, its bonnet close to the red and white banded barrier. The door to the guard hut was open, but no one was lounging outside as was normal for these check points.

Sean pressed a button in the door control panel and the side smoked-glass window slid open. He held his peaked cap in his hand leaning out of the window.

"Any of you men awake?" he shouted at the open door of the hut, his voice carrying a strong mark of authority and confidence. "Come on, open the barrier. We have an appointment at the Palace."

A face appeared at the door, the cloneman's eyes straining against the strong sunlight. "What's the hurry? Don't you know there's an emergency?" he added, walking deliberately slowly around the car, looking at the number plates. "Have you a pass?" he said, coming up from the rear of the car to Sean.

"Of course," Sean said confidently, reaching the guard his identity card. "I am taking these natives to the Palace. I have to get them there as soon as possible."

"Is that so?" the guard said, not impressed by Sean's statement. "Why haven't we been told? We always are if anything is urgent. Are they drugged?"

"Of course. How else could I travel with three of them alone? They'll not stir until I get them into Konburg when I can hand them over to the Palace Guards."

"Exactly what I was asking myself," the young clone guard said, blowing his nose noisily on a large handkerchief and moving round the car to look at Harry through the smoked glass window. He opened the door and shook Harry roughly by the shoulder. Harry opened his eyes, pretending that he'd just awakened and looked up at the cloneman, whose eyes held him in a fixed stare. Harry knew the game was up. His muscles froze and he felt his thoughts flow out to the guard like metal filings to a magnet.

"Men!" the guard called towards the hut. "We've got them." Suddenly three more clone guards appeared surrounding the car and all the passengers were pulled out and made to stand spread-eagled, their arms stretched on the car roof.

The guards were searching them for weapons and all hope of escape now seemed to have vanished when Harry recognised the rough rumble of the heavy refrigerated truck bearing down on the checkpoint at speed. Spontaneously he looked up at the cab window and knew his earlier suspicions had been correct. The driver was Ron, an old friend from his sealing days out on the Rock, who had now taken a land-based job with the Company and was a secret and active member of Omega. Grabbing Sean and kicking out viciously at the nearest clone guard Harry threw himself away from the Galaxy just as the huge truck crashed into the back of the car with a great roar of screeching brakes, splintering glass and twisting metal.

Before the dust had settled and the remaining guards recovered their senses, the cab driver and his mate were on top of them, their sharp, ever ready seal knives completing their nasty work. Harry was still struggling on the ground trying to regain his feet that were stiff from the long drive, but Sean was on his feet, petrified at what had happened and seeing his brothers lying, gutted like fish in a pool of blood. Harry, turning from his prey, and seeing another cloneman, sprang at him, pinning Sean against the truck's huge front wheel.

"No!" shouted Harry from his knees. "He's a friend. Don't

harm him."

Harry drew his knife back from within an inch of Sean's throat and looked back at Harry.

"Are you sure? No clonie's worth saving."

Harry quickly explained how they had escaped from Southport by Sean's help.

Harry and Harry grasped each other around their strong shoulders, laughing at having met again under such surprising circumstances.

"How did you know it was me?" Harry asked.

"I passed you miles back this morning when you were parked. Then you followed me for a long while and I could see you clearly in the rear mirror. Never forget a face, not one like yours, Harry, even when your beard's turned grey," his old friend roared and slapped him again on the shoulder. "I know this route well," he added, smiling. "Just had a feeling that you might have some trouble at this checkpoint and dropped behind you in case you needed help. Come on, we'd better get this mess cleared up before more trouble arrives."

Harry and Jose carried the bodies of the clonemen into the wood behind the hut. Harry used the truck to push the crumpled wreck of the Galaxy off the road and down a steep escarpment out of sight. Fortunately at this time of the late evening intercity traffic had practically stopped and they were on their way again before any other vehicle came along.

The truck thundered along the freeway into Konburg, unquestioned by the clone guards that patrolled the city streets. Harry took them to a safe house in the southern suburbs. They would still have to get across the Long Bridge, into the centre of Konburg, but would await information and the latest news about the revolt. They hoped that the bridge would not be blocked.

Chapter Forty Five

Harry moved quickly ahead down the steep dark forest track towards the rear wall of the Palace estate, leading the small Omega Task Force that he had brought together from the remnants of the agents that had remained free in Konburg. The news of Sophie's capture had demoralised the Omega movement in Konburg, but Harry and Mel Higgin's appearance had given them new hope and vigour. Sean's fever had not abated and for days he lay in a wheezing stupor, sweating and shivering and staring into the distance, unable to speak or think. All they could do was to keep him sedated until they could get him back to Dunfooey where perhaps there might just be time to vaccinate him.

In the meantime Harry had planned the attack on the Palace in an attempt to rescue Sophie. For a few days after the release of the virus the streets of Konburg had been relatively free of clonemen and most that were seen were suffering from heavy colds and were flushed and feverish. Only a skeleton guard had been maintained at the Long Bridge and even at the gates of the Palace those on duty were lounging around, disgruntled and disinterested.

Harry had hoped to penetrate the Palace while the clonemen were at the height of the first phase of the disease but by the time he had co-ordinated a Task Force, it was clear that the clonies were recovering from their initial sickness. In fact, Sean too was eating again and was well enough to accompany them.

Late one evening, Harry, Mel, and Sean and a small group of Omega agents made their way through the forest behind the Palace grounds. The rear fences had been neglected and it had been easy to get undetected right up to the old servants entrance at the back. Sean tricked the guard at the door with a mind-call and Mel silenced the clonemen with a heavy blow on the head.

Harry stepped cautiously into the corridor, after checking that no one was around. The ten other armed agents followed and Sean now led the way down a number of narrow corridors and through the silent kitchens. If their luck held they would complete their mission and be safely beyond the walls again before dawn.

The Palace was asleep. Sean led them up a small staircase at the rear of the building and along a number of corridors lit only dimly with the lamp. He knew the way as after his collapse he had had to attend the medical unit for treatment a number of times before they'd sent him to Southport. The smell of disinfectant increased greatly and they held their breath as Sean edged round the corner and the tenseness of his raised hand held them in suspense.

He saw two clone guards were sitting outside the entrance to the Clinic. One was asleep and the other reading a book, holding it at an angle towards a small light on the wall. That was a good sign. It meant that Sophie was most likely in the ward, as they had suspected. If she wasn't there, they would have to search further and the second choice would be the President's suite as Sean predicted that if at all possible Donal would have forced Sophie to be with him. If that was the case then they could expect to have a full-scale fight as the clone guards would be more readily available there. On the other hand if Sophie could be rescued from the clinic they might be able to get out of the Palace before the alarm was raised.

Sean moved out into the corridor and approached the two clone guards. The one that was awake dropped his book and looked up, surprised at the intrusion.

"I need some tablets," Sean said as he came close. "I'm still having attacks of this damn bug."

"Don't we all," the young guard said, lifting his book from the floor and standing up, recognising that Sean was one of the senior brothers. Briefly their eyes met and the young clonie gasped. Sean's hand was in his jacket pocket and moved slightly. There was a slight thud and the youth collapsed on the floor. The second guard moved in his chair, disturbed by the noise, but before he was fully awake Sean had put a second bullet through his head.

Silently the agents spread up the corridor, taking defensive positions around corners and behind pillars and melted into the shadows. Harry and Mel followed Sean who had opened the door into the ward.

The dim light showed a single bed attached to numerous tubes and drips with flickering lights on instruments showing that the patient was under constant medical surveillance. Was it Sophie? The figure lying in the bed could be anyone. If they raised the alarm unnecessarily they would never get the chance of finding her.

Mel gently went forward. He sensed that the person was sound asleep and breathing deeply, the face was half buried by the blanket. He shone his torch at an angle to try and see better. His heart thumped as he saw the strands of long red hair that he knew so well, now tangled and untended, on the pillow. His hand was shaking as he pulled away the blanket and touched the brow and brushed back the strand of hair from Sophie's forehead. Moaning gently, she turned onto her back, still asleep, but then opened her eyes, blinking against the strong light of the torch. Mel's hand quickly covered her mouth to suppress her scream and he switched off the torch.

"It's me, Mel," he said, holding her by the shoulders.

"Oh Mel! It's not true. I'm dreaming. You're dead!"

"No, you're not dreaming. It's true. I'm alive. Harry's here too. You're OK."

Sophie was fully awake now and sat up in the bed. A number of tubes were attached to her arms and legs. Sensors and wires led from many parts of her body to the instruments at the bedside.

Nonetheless they kissed, the wire and tubes forgotten in their moment of reunion.

Harry was now on the other side of the bed and kissed her on the forehead and held her hand tightly for a moment, relaxing after the tension of the last few minutes. "We have a nurse with us. He'll take out the tubes. But will this machine raise the alarm?"

"No," Sophie said, smiling. "At the start I stripped them off myself. But the young clone doctors just loved having the excuse to put them back on me so I gave up. I think they're just playing games. Wanting to make me think they care." She tore away the sensor pads on her chest and thighs and began to dislodge the needles that entered the veins on her arms.

"I'll do that," the nurse came forward and completed the removal of the tubes.

"We needn't keep that," Sophie said, reaching for the half-filled bottle that was collecting under the bed. She tore off the stopper and spilt the fluid over the empty bed, saturating the mattress with a red pool of blood.

"Can you walk?" Harry asked, as she stood up and started dressing in the warm tracksuit that they'd brought for her.

"I'll need help. They've taken too much." She looked at the red gore now starting to clot on the mattress. "They're taking as much blood as possible without actually killing me."

"We'll have to go." Harry said, glancing at the clock on the wall. "It's getting late. We'll carry you if you can't manage. We'll have to get to the main gate. Help will come when we signal."

"But father!" Sophie suddenly called, "Harry. We can't go without Little Greta. She'll be with Donal in the presidential suite. She's your own real Little Greta. I've seen her. She knew me. She's taught the other clone girls to say 'Fank, Fank'. But she's our own Little Greta. We can't leave without her."

"You're sure? She's really my Little Greta."

"Yes. Donal told me. He'd checked her registration number. Even showed it to me at dinner on her bare bottom, the bastard."

Harry's eyes flared and hatred pulsed through his body at the thought of his Little Greta being abused by these fiends. He looked at Sean.

"Come on," Sean offered, without hesitation. "I know the way. The rest of you get to the main gate. Shoot on sight. Don't let them get near you."

"No, you stay with Sophie," Harry ordered Mel who wanted to help rescue Greta. "Get to the main door and signal for the others. Don't wait for us if the clonies attack."

Sean led the way along the corridors and into the main wing, coming into the presidential living quarters by the rear stairway. The Palace was still silent, but the slight touch of grey had lightened the black sky, beckoning the approach of dawn

As Sean had expected the guards were more alert than before and two were standing at the far end of the landing leading onto the main staircase. They had not anticipated any hazards from the rear, which was the way up from the kitchens. Simultaneously both Sean and Harry took aim with their handguns and the two clone guards collapsed with a single gentle thud. Ignoring the possibility that other guards might be around the corner on the grand staircase, Sean dashed down to the door of the president's room and flung it open. Harry was beside him. The heavy curtains were drawn and it was black inside. Harry flashed the torch across the room and saw the large bed at the far end. There was a stirring under the blanket. Both men crossed the room in a few strides and flung themselves on top of the figure. Tearing off the sheet and grabbing Donal by the hair and throat, they smothered his shout for help. There was a child-like cry, "Fank, Fank" and Little Greta crawled out from under the sheet between Harry and Sean.

The three men struggled on the bed. Little Greta giggled with delight and her agile body sprang into motion and she jumped on Harry's back and started pulling his beard, just like she used to do as a child, but now her arms were strong and muscular and her sharp nails clawed at his cheeks. "Fank, Fank," she cried, bellowing from the depths of her lungs, her legs wrapped around Harry's chest and her fingers seeking the sockets of his eyes.

For a moment Harry lost his grip on Donal's throat as he spontaneously tried to protect his eyes from Little Greta's scratches. Donal broke free and roared at the top of his voice, but Sean hit him on the side of the head with the butt of his gun and he collapsed back onto the pillow.

"Don't Greta!" Harry shouted at his daughter and pulled her round into his arms. "It's me, Daddy."

She recognised him and instantly flung her arms around his neck and covered him with kisses. "Come on, Sean. Let's get out of here."

Sean hesitated a moment. Donal was sprawled on the bed, blood oozing from his temple, the pillow a wet bright red. He was his brother, could he kill him in cold blood, his hand was shaking, he pointed the gun at his head and pulled the trigger and dashed out after Harry to the door and down the landing towards the grand staircase.

Harry carried Little Greta under one arm and around the waist, her arms and legs waving in the air, giggling and laughing and "Fank, Fanking" all the way. In the other hand he held his automatic pistol and started firing as he reached the top of the stairs.

The others had already reached the main entrance hall by another route and were fighting their way to the great door. Clonemen, most in their white robes were coming from all directions. They had been awakened by the screeching of the fire alarms and, assuming it was another emergency, rushed to get out of the Palace. There was a complete state of chaos, the clone guards in their neat black uniforms milling with the mass of white-robed clonemen.

It was only Harry's sheer weight and size that took him through the crowd of clonemen that now blocked his way across the entrance hall. He cast them aside at every turn and blazed away with his automatic, painting a red avenue on the white silk in front of him. Sean followed closely firing to the right and left and behind him, seeing his defenceless brothers wilt before the power of his metal shield.

At last they were through the great door and onto the top of the steps above the Square. The others had nearly reached the foot of the steps and the roar of a heavy armoured coach that had been hijacked by other Omega agents broke across the dawn as it ploughed through the Main Gate, guns blazing on either side, and raced up to the foot of the steps just as Sophie and her rescuers reached the Square.

A few Omega marksmen had taken advantage of the huge pillars that edged the large steps and were now firing at the main doorway, giving Harry and Sean cover as they hurtled down the steps to the waiting bus. Little Greta was still laughing and giggling as Harry bounced down the final steps, two at a time, and flung himself in through the door of the bus.

Working their way down from pillar to pillar, three of the Omega men managed to reach the coach but the last one was hit by a bullet from a group of clone guards that had opened fire from one of the high windows.

The driver roared the engine and the coach moved off as the clonemen flooded out onto the top of the steps.

Harry saw a figure with white hair in a wheel chair being pushed to the top step. He recognised Michael, the man he hated more than anyone else, the man he believed was possessed by the ultimate evil of the universe, the man who had brought anarchy to Emanon.

The coach had to make a great sweep around the square to get back to the Main Gate. As it roared back past the foot of the steps Harry looked up at the top of the steps again.

"That's Donal with Michael!" Sophie cried, seeing what was about to happen.

A cloneman in a white flowing robe, his head bound with a blood saturated bandage, was holding the wheelchair and had a gypsy girl under his arm. As the heavy coach approached, Donal pushed the chair violently so that it tumbled onto the steep marble steps. The chair and Michael's fragile body, strapped together, hurtled down towards the oncoming bus. Harry and Sophie shouted. The driver looked sideways and swerved. But it was too late. The chair shot off the bottom step and collided with the front of the bus. There was a slight bump and the momentary scraping of metal against metal.

Chapter Forty Six

Harry was relieved to see the mountains loom ahead and felt a surge of excitement as the packed bus sped along the winding road up the valley leading to Dunfooey Pass. A great pall of smoke that hung above the mountain ridges showed that the volcanoes around Errigal were active again. Three of the five armoured buses that had set out from Konburg a few days earlier carrying the remnants of the Omega Corps had been lost by sporadic attacks made by the clone forces during the journey. But now there was only one more obstacle to overcome and if the Omega Corps still held Dunfooey Pass they'd be home and safe. At the top of the valley, they passed the earlier encampment of the clone army. It was deserted now and smouldering fires were the only indication the rampage and the sickness had also spread among the clonemen who had not been in the cities.

"I hope Frank Tooley and his men have been able to defend the Pass. If that crowd has reached Dunfooey they'll have wiped it out by now," Harry said anxiously to Mel as the bus driver selected a lower gear and the engine revved up as they began to climb the steep hill.

As had been obvious from the events at the Palace, the second phase of the disease had commenced much sooner than Karen had predicted. Also, it took on a much more severe and violent form. The plan had been to incapacitate the clonemen and allow the normals to re-establish their authority. Contrary to expectations, the onset of the disease had released the most primitive and violent passions and within a few days the clonemen throughout Emanon had lost their self control, they roamed the cities and the countryside in packs, looting, burning, raping, fighting, killing. Their 'gift' had become an evil tool and they drove men and women mad across the land.

Chaos reigned in Konburg. The remnants of the armed Omega agents had managed to hijack a number of coaches and taking as many refugees as they could, Harry and his group set off in convoy heading north towards Dunfooey. The roaming bands of clonemen that were now scattered across the countryside were little problem to the well armed Omega Corps as they sped along the clear roads towards the distant mountains of the northern range.

Sean had become violent the night after their escape from the Palace. Sophie had insisted that he was given an injection of her blood as it was his only hope until they reached Dunfooey. Now he had been on a sedative and was sitting, dream-like in the back of the bus. Sophie hoped that when they reached Dunfooey Karen's vaccine might cure him.

"Do you think they used the clone women in the attack?" Sophie asked.

"It looks like it," Harry replied, as they crested the ridge and saw the large parking area strewn with burnt out buses and the remains bodies that had been left where they had fallen.

"They must have broken through our defences," Mel shouted from the front of the coach, "otherwise they'd have regrouped here. We'll have to fight our way into Dunfooey."

Harry had felt confident that the Omega Corps, fighting under the leadership of Frank Tooley, would have held the Pass. It was really so easy to defend and the clone soldiers had no experience of mountainous terrain. But his heart sank as the bus reached the top of the long hill and the road flattened out through the narrow gorge. Ahead they could see dimly through the haze. There was a barrier across the road and the surrounding land was obscured by the drifting smoke and mist belching down from the volcano. The road was covered by a layer of grey ash.

The driver slowed the coach down and stopped just before the barrier. "We'd better not risk driving through. It may be a booby trap."

Suddenly out of the surrounding mist and smoke, figures appeared with guns pointing at the bus. It took Harry and his friends a moment to realise what was happening but then it became clear as a cloneman pulled open the coach door and jumped in, and an automatic gun aimed down the length of the bus.

"So you thought we were finished?" the cloneman said with a sneer. "But you've misjudged us."

"You're Donal!" Sophie roared, shocked beyond belief that she could ever see him again.

"Yes, indeed, my dear. Only you could ever tell us apart. It was always a great mystery just how you knew our brother Sean and ignored the rest of us. But of course now we know. You're really one of us."

"How did you get here?" Harry snapped.

"It's all your fault, my dear," Donal sneered again, continuing to address Sophie. "When your friend here, stole you from us, we guessed that they would bring you here. You see, our dear late father was right. You are very precious to the brotherhood. Your blood extract did cure me. What a pity it is too late for most of the brother hood. Then Sean's bullet only grazed my scalp."

Everyone in the bus was silent, straining forward to hear what was happening, horrified at the sudden, unexpected turn of events.

"We also want the vaccine. You told us about that. You even bargained your life for it," Donal continued at the front of the bus, still holding his gun at the ready.

"Have you already taken Dunfooey?" Harry asked, anxious to know the situation.

"No," Donal answered. "We have too small a force now. If we attack they might destroy the vaccine. We need Sophie and you as hostages. The situation has changed. We know that the clone society is finished. We want now to talk. We must all work together for the future of Emanon. We need Karen's vaccine. Once we are fully cured, we will talk."

In the back of the bus, Sean stirred from his semiconscious stupor. The voice of his brothers at the front of the bus brought him to his senses there was a sudden rush of blood to his head. He heard the tension in Sophie's voice as she leaned forward, challenging his brother. She looked so beautiful and yet fragile. He felt the lust that lingered in Donal's mind and the smell of fear from the passengers excited him beyond anything he'd ever experienced. The intensity of Sean's feelings and flux of his thoughts focused on Donal, and for a fraction of eternity their minds clashed in mortal combat.

Shocked by the realisation that his hated brother Sean was hurtling down the aisle of the bus towards him held Donal momentarily in a trance. Sean sprang the length of the coach with an unknown reserve of strength and grabbed Donal by the throat. They tumbled through the door and rolled in a tangle of legs and arms on the ground. The sudden release of the sickness, built up during the days of sedation, burst out in an orgy of indescribable violence. They rolled on the ground. Sean's legs were wrapped around his brother. He was foaming at the mouth and his teeth bit into Donal's neck.

The other clonemen hearing the disturbance and seeing the men struggling on the ground came running to help their Master, but it was too late. Suddenly from high above the road among the broken rock and shrub that bordered the narrow Pass, but was now blanketed in misty smoke, cries of 'Fank, Fank' could be heard. The excited cries on either side became shrill and suddenly out of the mist hordes of gypsies surged and attacked the last of the clonemen as they struggled to separate Sean and Donal.

Little Greta, who had been sitting beside Sophie throughout the journey, being happy and content, suddenly grew agitated and cried at the top of her voice, 'Fank, Fank'. Climbing over Sophie, she dashed down the aisle and shot out through the open door of the coach before anyone could stop her.

They watched horrified as she disappeared into the mist with her clone sisters.

Seeing his chance of escape the coach driver accelerated through the barrier, praying that they would not be blown to smithereens and was soon descending the twisting road down towards Dunfooey. They only could guess what carnage would take place up in the mist, hidden from all but the Gods.

But the Gods were angry. On the seaward side of the ridge the volcanic ash had built up into drifts and great flows of lava were burning up acres of mountain side as they flowed down gullies and river-beds making the mountains steam and burn. It was nearly impossible to see the road and as they got further and further down the mountain side the fall of ash became thicker and thicker. Great falls of rock from roadside cliffs left the road strewn with boulders that made the coach slow down to a crawl. The roar of falling cliffs and explosions above increased and a great fracture appeared across the road causing the driver to break hard to avoid crashing into the chasm that opened before them.

Harry's party abandoned the coach and started down the mountain on foot. Due to the mist they could not see behind to know what had happened to the other coaches but between gaps in the noise of the explosions and falling rock they could hear screams and shouts of others in pursuit.

They were now struggling to keep their feet. Fresh molten lava oozed out of fissures beside and in front of them. The gorse was burning along the side of the road. Sophie needed help at every step and Mel and Harry half carried her along. Sometimes they had to leave the uneven road and climb into the ash-covered mountain side to avoid cracks and large fissures. The land seemed to be turning and twisting in front of them as they ran down the hill. Their throats were dry and burning with the hot ash that now smothered everything and the fumes and smoke made them cough and tears poured down their cheeks.

Eventually they reached the coast road leading into Dunfooey. They could see across the bay. There was a spontaneous cheer as they spied the Tall Ships were still in the harbour, just visible through the mist, and prepared to sail.

Now on the level road along by the sea they were running as fast as they could, but still Sophie had to be carried. Harry flung her across his broad shoulders and plodded on toward the harbour, the others guarding his rear as the remnants of the clonemen and gypsies were rapidly catching up now they were on level ground.

The town ahead was burning and Harry heard the noise of falling walls and roofs as he approached the outskirts. As they passed the old Inn where Sophie had been conceived and Karen had converted the hayloft into her laboratory, a crack opened down the length of the old gable and the wall fell out, making Harry dash sideways to avoid the falling rafters. Tables and chairs and dishes from the restaurant spilt out onto the street as the floors collapsed and tilted sideways.

From the noise behind, Harry realised that the clonemen must have regained control of the gypsies and they were both now in hot pursuit. They had caught up with the slower of the Omega group and there was still some way to go before they reached the safety of the harbour.

Suddenly a volcanic explosion just above the town ripped half the mountain apart and shook the town like a leaf. Harry stumbled and fell, throwing Sophie in a pile against the fallen rubble.

In an instant, before he could regain his feet the pursuing clonemen were on his back, pinning him to the ground. Their rage and anger were intense and beyond anything Harry had ever experienced. His head was wedged between two sharp rocks and a cloneman was thrusting at his throat with a blood stained knife.

Sophie had been slightly concussed by her rough fall and recovered to realise that a cloneman was on top of her. He was smothering her face with kisses. She struggled to throw him off. Was it to be her fate to be eventually overcome by the clone, even at this late hour? But her body was weak and she had no strength to resist. Her mind drifted, as the man clung to her, confused and uncertain.

Was it Donal? Was it Sean? She saw them both and she screeched as she tasted the sour foam of madness and then suddenly the body on top of her went limp and rolled off into the gutter.

She opened her eyes to see Mel. He still held a large stone in his hand that he had used to kill her attacker. But now he knelt down to help Sophie to her feet.

"Who was he?"

"It doesn't matter," Mel said quietly. "Come on. Quickly."

Harry had managed to get free and had broken the jaw of his assailant with one devastating blow to the cloneman's chin.

The gypsy clonies were still coming behind them and getting closer every second. They were on the harbour now. But Frank Tooley was there ready and waiting and the surviving Omega Corps members tumbled into the boat and Frank prepared to cast off.

Above them on the pier the remaining gypsies appeared screeching at the escaping boat. Suddenly one broke away and dashing down the slippery stone steps leapt aboard the small boat just as the engine started and it roared off across the bay, her arms clinging around Frank Tooley's neck crying, "Fank, Fank."

By evening the little fleet of Tall Ships was far out to sea, the warm breeze from the stricken Emanon blowing them westwards towards the Rock. They watched from the deck as the land disappeared below the horizon, leaving only a pall of smoke to mark the tragedy of their beloved Emanon. Mel held Sophie, tears were streaming down her cheeks, held back so long since his return from the dead, and their final dash for freedom. The others watched and smiled.

"How long will it take?" Sophie asked, holding Mel around the waist and crying into his chest.

"A year may be more." Karen answered. "The disease will have to burn itself out. It was more severe than I thought. There was always the chance that it would be fatal. Only a few will survive. The production units will collapse. They are finished. But it will take time. Until then we will be safe on the Rock. The clonemen can't sail the Tall Ships."

"But we will return. We will return," Harry said sternly, looking east at the distant pale of smoke over the horizon, glowing red in the sunset. "We will return. When the madness is gone. We will return! We cannot forsake Emanon. She was our gift from the Gods."